# UP UP IN A WAY

## BLAIR MCLEAN

MoonCrawler Press

# YOUR FREE BOOK IS WAITING

SUPERPOWERED MAYAN WARRIORS.
DISGUSTING SKYCRAWLERS. A RUTHLESS
MOTHER-TO-BE. GO TO BLAIRMCLEAN.COM

Issued in print and electronic formats.
ISBN 978-1-9992269-2-3 (hardcover)
ISBN 978-1-9992269-0-9 (paperback)
ISBN 978-1-9992269-1-6 (EPUB)

Original cover art and design by Dzikawa © 2019
https://www.instagram.com/dzikawa

Published by MoonCrawler Press
blairmclean.com

*For my family.*
*My parents Ann and Doug, my sister Alison, and my wife Lorilee.*
*You gave me everything but the cape.*

# UP UP IN A WAY

*a novel*

*by*

BLAIR McLEAN

❧ I ❧

# HOME OF THE GOLDEN BOY

Ever since he was a boy, Nigel Nakagawa knew that he was meant to become a crime-fighting superhero. This fact was written in each rock, in each leaf on each tree, and in each face surrounding him in the cult where he lived, deep in the mountains of Nagano, Japan. Or so his mother said.

Nigel had never seen any evidence of his destiny engraved in the landscape and although he wanted to make his mother and father proud, wanted to serve his community, and wanted justice for all people, he had no wish to become a superhero. That was his secret.

As a man, costumed and masked, Nigel would stand over the lifeless body of the mayor of New York City and long to be rid of the crushing responsibility and endless frustrations of being the lone super-powered vigilante in a world in which, it seemed, he would receive neither pity nor gratitude for his sacrifices.

Yet, from a young age, Nigel knew that there in the old smokehouse, behind the massive woodshed, hung the blackened skeleton of the cult's previous Champion, the last drop of power-giving *Resident* oozing pitch black and viscous, about to drip from the skeleton's charred heel bone. Soon, probably by autumn 1983, that last drop would drip into the chrome vat that had stood collecting the tar-like substance for the last one hundred years and the *Resident* would be prepared for a new host: Nigel himself. And, once the two were bonded, there would be no going back. Or so his mother said.

Nigel Nakagawa's childhood home was a traditional Japanese alpine village with thatched roof A-frame dwellings in the *Gassho* style, where he lived from his birth until he left at the age of fourteen for Tokyo, en route to New York, with a mountain on his shoulders. It was also the seat of the cult's power.

Most villages of its kind had been abandoned by that time in Japan's history, with waves of new generations making for nearby towns and cities to embrace each new iteration of modernity. Across the country, many of the old rural ways were dying out; it was not so here.

The inhabitants had named the village '*Ryūiki*,' which means 'watershed' or 'drainage basin,' literally meaning 'flow area.' The town's name was not particularly original or poetic, but was simply taken from a geographic term describing the collection of precipitation and ground water into a common outlet.

The outlet was, for good or ill, the village. Here there was always enough fresh water for drinking and for growing things but sometimes there was far too much to be contained. At the outset of the rainy season in late Spring, the river, located on the doorstep of the village, would become a raging torrent as it filled steadily with rain. At that time, the river would burst its banks and sandbags were required to protect the village structures from water damage. In these circumstances, every able-bodied man, woman and child would help to place the sandbags. It was hurried, back-breaking work, especially for Nigel and his mother and father, which was how his mother liked it.

Nigel's muscles were aching as he lifted his smaller sand-filled burlap bag and placed it next to his father's larger one. Most of his body was uncomfortably hot but his feet were freezing, stinging-numb, as he waded around in the frigid spill-over water from the river. It was an odd sensation, the cruel sun beating down on his brown bare back and the ferocious cold of the river lapping at his feet, feeling now like two small blocks of ice.

Nearby, his father was trudging and sloshing around, working doggedly to finish their portion of the wall, at the edge of the slope down to the river, now fully submerged after three days of heavy rain. It wasn't raining now though, Nigel noticed, and the river was probably due to fall back again soon. *Why are we out here then?*

"Because more rain is coming," his father said in English, opening another burlap bag and handing it to Nigel. Embarrassed, Nigel realized he had been thinking aloud. He spread open the mouth of the bag and held it out, his head down. His father, a hulk of a man, crouched and began filling the sack with sand purchased from the nearby quarry. Each scoop tugged on Nigel's sore arms and he winced.

"Like this, like this," his father said and, gently gripping Nigel's wrists in his meaty hands, he guided his son's arms down so the bag rested on the ground and was partly submerged in the river. He resumed filling.

"Won't the sand get wet?" Nigel asked, though he saw that some of it already was.

Nigel's father emitted a deep rumbling chuckle. "The wetter the better. Water holds the grains tightly together. The damper they are, the better they keep the river water away." He tied off the bag and watched as Nigel struggled to lift it over his head to place it on the top of the wall. "The water makes it heavier though," he said and, one handed, scooped the bag from Nigel's hands and tossed it halfway up the base with a muted thud.

Nigel's mother trudged up to them, a grin plastered on her face, despite the difficult work she had been doing with a group of villagers, part way down the line of sandbags.

"It looks like we have beaten the river again this year," she said, also in English, surveying their handiwork.

Nigel's father swivelled his head to look down the line. "I didn't know it could be beaten," he said mildly, "but the bulk of the work is done, certainly. At least until we have to take the wall down again in a few weeks."

The village would soon require access to the river again, so the sand would be emptied onto the slope and the bags carefully stored for the following year. Nigel's father produced a handkerchief and offered it to his wife who shook her head. He carefully wiped his brow clear of sweat, then handed it to Nigel who did the same.

Nigel's mother, a flinty-eyed former Tokyo executive, named Fuyuko, joined 'Hitsujikai' or 'Shepherd,' after working for Japan's largest bank for the better part of a decade. Frustrated by the lack of true leadership opportunities at the bank, Fuyuko had abandoned her post, unthinkable for a woman so high up the corporate ladder and had travelled about the country in search of people to lead. In her wanderings, she had discovered the cult and had immediately begun to work her way into a position of influence.

She stared at Nigel's father, as if weighing the qualities of the Japanese-American street tough who called himself Frank Nakagawa. Although Nigel's mother claimed that she had selected his father because of his street smarts and physical prowess, Nigel always hoped there was something more to their relationship, something like love. It was his father whom she had sought in New York in the three years between joining the cult and moving to Ryūiki, and he who had agreed to come with her even though he was a third generation American and had never even been to Japan. Nigel's father stared back, strong and sure, but docile before her gaze.

Nigel watched as the other villagers placed their final sandbags and began to make their way home. He had been aware and somewhat envious of the fact that his mother had been helping Aika's family, who were the Grandmaster's kin and central to the community. His fondest wish was to spend more time with Aika.

"Maybe next time I could help some of the others like you did?" he suggested.

Nigel's mother turned her gaze on him. "And what is behind that noble suggestion?"

Even at the age of seven, he knew a rhetorical question when he heard one, though for the life of him he could not think what she meant. Growing up in the village as he had, he learned early that assisting people helped them to accept him. Where normally he was set apart, due to the unique role he was to assume in the cult, he found that he felt almost normal, working side by side with the other villagers.

Aika was by far the friendliest, addressing Nigel warmly and informally, as she did the other children who flocked around her. That was why he wanted to help her family, but he did not believe this was the reason his mother was driving at.

She narrowed her eyes, perhaps disappointed by his apparent lack of comprehension and impatiently flicked aside a loose strand of hair that had blown into her face. "I have been meaning to talk to you about this anyway and I suppose now is as good a time as any."

She squatted down so her face was level with his, the seat of her pants brushing the water and becoming wet, but she didn't seem to notice. "Aika is the prettiest little girl in the village. She is clever and funny and treats you sincerely, I think, but you cannot allow yourself to become used to her company. Your duty does not allow for close relationships," she said, raising her eyebrows at him.

"I wish we could just speak in Japanese, like everyone else," Nigel muttered, blushing furiously and looking down at his feet, which were white in the water. He could not properly express the pain of having his secret crush revealed in such a casual way, though even if he had, it probably wouldn't have done any good. His mother was ruthless with his emotions.

"You're tired and sore," said his mother, heedless of his shame, "so I'll choose to ignore that comment. I'm pleased you worked hard; it is important that the others see you doing that." And with that, Nigel's mother straightened, touching a hand to the seat of her pants, her mouth twisting with displeasure as her fingers found the damp patch there, and then tramped back toward the village, splashing water. After a moment, Nigel's father followed his wife, brushing his fingers ever so slightly on the boy's shoulder as he sloshed by. The touch was so light that Nigel wondered if he had imagined it.

AT SEVEN, NIGEL HAD A MURKY UNDERSTANDING OF WHAT SORT OF superhero he was supposed to be. He came to that awareness one day, playing guiltily and unbeknownst to his mother, with Aika in the grove of cedars surrounding the Shinto shrine at the outskirts of the village.

The shrine was old, older than the cult Nigel thought, and it served to remind him of the existence of the outside world. In his imagination, the shrine was a portal, and if one crossed the threshold, bowed low and clapped loudly, one could be transported, if not bodily, then in spirit to another shrine of one's choosing. He was describing this to Aika, who was listening with rapt attention.

"It makes sense," she agreed, nodding thoughtfully. "Do you think it's the deity that carries your spirit or are you bestowed with special powers?"

"I'm not sure," he conceded, "but I don't think it matters. The powers probably fade away after you step foot outside the *torii* gates again."

She looked at him then as if she had just remembered she was playing with a boy alien from outer space. She hesitated. "What powers do you think *you* will have?" she asked in a breathy rush.

Nigel felt himself blushing and he looked at the ground. It was not a topic with which he felt comfortable. His future rarely came up in conversation and when it did, he felt secretly afraid. To Aika, it was probably a mere curiosity, however.

"I don't know," he said.

Aika perked up. "Do you think you will be like Gambit from the X-Men," she asked, "with the power to charge objects with kinetic energy?" She was a great lover of American comic books. Through her, Nigel had developed somewhat of an interest himself and he enjoyed translating the English captions for her. "Or maybe Mr. Fantastic of the Fantastic Four? What could you do with a stretchy body I wonder? Oh, look," she exclaimed, pointing at two trees close together. "You could stretch between those and I could lie on you and go to sleep. How peaceful!"

*Oh, for that eventuality!* Nigel was warming to the discussion now. "Maybe I'll grow claws like Wolverine and I'll battle the Yakuza and put a stop to crime in Japan!" he said, with enthusiasm. They had been recently reading a riveting miniseries with roughly that story.

"Not without Kitty Pryde you won't! Look, I can walk through trees." She dodged quickly around the trunk of a nearby tree and peeked at him from the other side.

He laughed and then roared, pretending to slash at the trunk with imaginary metal claws protruding from the backs of his hands. "Now I've cut down the tree and there's nowhere for you to hide!" He grabbed her around the waist and they toppled to the ground, laughing. Their laughter gradually subsided and they stared up at the forest canopy, thinking their separate thoughts.

"I guess you probably won't have a sidekick, will you?" she asked, glancing over at him.

He sighed. "I doubt it, but anything is possible."

"What will you do as a superhero?" She wrinkled her brow and then answered her own question, "I guess you'll fight crime. What kind of crime will you fight?"

"I'm supposed to be a sort of protector, I think. So, I'll fight any crime that hurts people, probably."

"Doesn't most crime hurt people?"

He said he supposed it did.

"Who will you protect?"

"Maybe I will protect the village from thieves."

"We've never had thieves here that I know of," she said thoughtfully, "and we are quite safe in the village. Maybe you'll go where people don't feel safe and protect them?"

"Maybe." He was realizing he had some significant knowledge gaps about his future career, which made him feel vaguely nauseous.

"Do you think your powers will fade away eventually, like at the shrine?"

"No." He was sure on that score. "My mother says it will be a permanent change, bonding with the *Resident*. She says its threads will travel through every channel of my body and enter every cell, millions of meters of it."

"I guess it would be hard to pull all that stuff out." She sighed and closed her eyes.

Nigel imagined that it would indeed be difficult. He gazed out and saw through the trees that a dark cloud had appeared and was billowing on the horizon. He pictured the cloud moving through his own body, too slow for the eye to detect, while at the same time rapidly expanding.

"Maybe you'll have powers like Spider-Man," said Aika, eyes still closed, a smile playing on her lips.

Silence stretched for a few moments. "Yes," he said, "I hope so." And he smiled too.

THE SEASONS PASSED WITH A STEADY INEVITABILITY AND, IN WHAT seemed like no time at all, the last midnight drop of the *Resident* fell into the chrome vat. It happened overnight and by morning the village was buzzing with the news. Nigel was awakened at dawn, shaken by his father out of a dream in which he had been using all his strength to pry himself free from the grasp of a snake that had wrapped its body around him and had been pressing and pressing. Nigel gasped as he came awake.

"It's time," his father said.

"The last drop fell?" Nigel asked, the constricting feeling from his dream persisting into wakefulness as the realization closed in on him.

"Yes, today is the day."

The morning was a blur. In a daze, he ate a simple breakfast of steamed vegetables and mushrooms while sitting on the edge of his futon, his father seated on the mat nearby. Then, Nigel was fitted in a skin-tight suit like a diver's but made of a heavy mesh that glinted metallically in the morning sunlight and sporting a heavy black iron spigot in front. The suit covered every inch of his body except his face, which felt pinched by the surrounding material. Over top, his father cast a plain white robe, emblazoned on the front with the character that meant 'Golden.' His father never left his side, which might have been a comfort, except for the grim expression on his face, *like a funeral speaker*, Nigel thought.

His mother was all smiles when she entered his bedroom. "This moment has been coming for over one hundred years," she said, tugging his robe straighter, "and by the grace of destiny we are the ones who will participate. Go my heart, and meet yourself for the first time."

Nigel realized that it was almost time for the ceremony and a sudden panic welled inside him. The panic had been there all along he realized, simmering almost undetectably, but now his body physically rebelled. His knees grew weak and his vision blurry. He slumped to the floor and toppled sideways. His father caught him and Nigel vomited his breakfast down his father's beautiful kimono worn only on special occasions. His mother knelt next to him and he understood she knew that it was all but impossible for him to voluntarily participate in the ceremony.

She tried her best to convince him anyway. "Come on, stand up, and let's get you clean. There are people waiting to receive you before we begin. The Grandmaster is here and his family." Nigel remained motionless in his father's arms, his eyes tightly closed. His mother strode to a cupboard and removed a cloth, which she dampened in the wash basin. She crouched and began to remove the vomit from Nigel's face. "Remember what we talked about. Today will be difficult and will require bravery, but tomorrow it will all be over and a new day will dawn." She crooked her fingers under his chin and turned his face toward her. "You must gather yourself and then we will go."

"Please," he said in a hoarse whisper, "I can't." His mother hesitated. Looking into her eyes, he saw a spark of compassion flickering in their dark depths but there was resolve too, so much resolve. The spark seemed to go out as she made her decision.

"You can," she said and stood up. "Carry him."

His father transported him bodily, barely conscious, past the waiting attendants. He was vaguely aware of their concerned faces and murmuring voices, and, before he was whisked outside, he caught a glimpse of Aika, stretching out her arm to him, calling his name anxiously as her mother ushered her away. *Nigel.*

In the courtyard, the villagers had gathered in a semicircle, the ancient cobblestones covered by a carpet of red, yellow and golden leaves beneath their feet. Nigel saw through bleary eyes that there were no children, apart from himself. A keening wail went up from one, then a dozen voices, then all the villagers were screeching like animals; in lament or celebration, it was difficult for Nigel to tell, for he had never heard such a thing before. The sound of it ripped through the still mountain air and seemed to reverberate from the very clouds above, which had closed in, silent and brooding, hanging low, their dark fleshy mass blotting out most of the thin light from the late-autumn sun.

Nigel's father placed him gently down on a rough-hewn slab of grey granite, polished on top and he stepped back, melting into the onlookers. His mother remained, a sentinel in her midnight blue kimono. She stood beside the Grandmaster, who was turned to face the crowd, resplendent in his robes of silk and gold, which hid his wizened, grub-like form. Nigel expected there to be oratory but there was none. The importance of the moment was self-evident.

The Grandmaster nodded to six men who struggled to bring the chrome vat, which Nigel had seen many times throughout his life. The contents were not what Nigel remembered, however; the dark *Resident*, which before had been an almost solid substance, was now shifting and moving like mercury in the vessel, its hue changing from deep black to silvery blue to gold, like an oil slick on water, and a chemical steam rose, causing the bearers to gag. The vat, Nigel realized, was melting. He sat bolt upright and looked around him wildly, wanting to run but there was nowhere to go. At another gesture from the Grandmaster, two men sprang forward and quickly and methodically bound Nigel to the slab with thick leather straps. Nigel's father stepped forward but was halted by a hand from his wife.

"For safety's sake," the Grandmaster said.

*His safety or mine?* Nigel thought, a flash of anger mingling with his fear, bringing him viscerally into the moment. *Is this really happening?* He struggled at his bonds and watched as the six men set the vat down beside him. The chrome was bubbling now and rivulets of the metal commingled with the material of the *Resident*. One of the men put on great thick gloves, like a smithy's and began to fit a silvery hose to an iron housing at the end of the tub. A second man attached the other end of the hose to the iron spigot beneath Nigel's robe and then snapped something like a visor on Nigel, covering the rest of his face.

The visor was opaque, the same material as his diver's suit, and Nigel gasped for air, but there was none. He could hear, muffled by the hood over his ears, the rising wail from the crowd beginning again, and then another sound, a gurgling, like the drain in a bath and, as he gasped for breath, the *Resident* flooded the inside of the suit, covering his skin and eyes and rushing into his ears, his nose and his open mouth.

The agony was so great that he immediately dissociated, his spirit leaving him and floating high above, riding the eddying wind from the heat of his now-smoking body. He surveyed the scene from a detached perspective.

There was the watching crowd, silent now, struck dumb by the awful spectacle of the convulsing boy's body, which was producing as much smoke as a bonfire. There was his father on his knees weeping silently, head down. There was his mother, triumph and horror mingling in her face as one. Now his white robe had burst into flames and scraps of the smoldering material were falling, setting alight the autumn leaves scattered beneath, which formed a burning ring around the granite slab. Now his body lay motionless, still smoking and, as the smoke became a haze and the haze began to dissipate, Nigel's spirit drifted down and he returned to himself. There was a heavy silence.

Suddenly, Nigel burst the scorched leather bonds with a sound like a dozen whips cracking and split the stone in two with a great kick of his heels. He toppled to the ground and lay there, dazed. Shakily, he removed the visor and looked at his hands and arms and down at the rest of his body. A shimmering dark grey material crawled and shifted there, like folds of liquid chainmail, with hints of gold. He stood up, chest heaving and felt the pain recede as if it had never been. He stared around him at the speechless throng and darkness closed in. He collapsed in a heap, unconscious amid the embers of the leaves scattered around him. The only sound was the coughing of those whose lungs had been affected by the smoke.

## 2

# LIKE FATHER, LIKE DAUGHTER

Ever since she was a little girl, Karissa Lacey had wanted to become a crime-fighting superhero. She knew it was never going to happen though, because that's what her father said, and she always listened to her father.

She was a tough-as-nails eleven-year-old in high-tops, who would sooner whip the other girls in her class with the nylon cord than jump rope. From her first day of elementary school, she, with her wild blond hair and challenging green eyes, was labelled by her classmates as 'weird,' and by her teachers as 'problematic,' and though she wore these labels as badges of honor, the fact remained that she would never count herself as one of the group.

Years later, standing over the prone body of the New York City mayor, alongside the gutless superhero, Kintarō the Golden Boy, she would wish again, hands clenched painfully tight around the 21-inch ASP telescopic baton, for the power to lift the bastard politician and throw him through one of the beautiful floor to ceiling windows of his office, and then abscond through it herself, bounding up, up and away, while he fell down, down and splat. That would be justice.

In her youth, Karissa spent a lot of her time pawing through washing machines, looking for lost change at the Chinese laundry near the third-floor apartment she shared with her father on the Bowery. With the money, she bought comic books – lots and lots of comic books. The year was 1974 and Marvel had just introduced its Giant-Sized series, which Karissa felt at least partially made up for the publisher raising its price the same year from twenty to twenty-five cents for a thirty-six-page magazine.

She liked the military superheroes like Captain America, and Sgt. Fury and his Howling Commandos, and avidly detested the evil hordes they fought, like the terrorist group Hydra. She adored the X-men, a super-powered circus of sideshow freaks, with whom she always felt at home while she read. She particularly admired Jean Grey, a powerful telepath and Storm, a Kenyan woman who could call down the lightning of the gods. To Karissa, these women were symbolic of swift and righteous justice.

That year too, the Punisher made his first appearance, in Amazing Spider-man #129. Later, as she was exposed to the city's grimy underbelly and to more and more of her father's cynicism about the criminal justice system, she began to identify with this fictional vigilante, who had appointed himself judge, jury and executioner. She wasn't the only one. New York City was a mess and the Punisher, fast becoming a hit, was a response.

Karissa's father, whose name was Callahan Lacey and who went by Sergeant Cal or simply Sergeant, depending on who you were, hated comic books.

"They're a waste of money," he would say and called them "the fire-starter funnies."

"They're not funny," Karissa had retorted once and he had wordlessly shown her just how flammable her comics were, using three of her favorites to kindle a roaring fire in the hearth that evening.

It always seemed odd to Karissa that her father should be so against superhero comics, when he was so passionate about the ongoing tension between right and wrong. To his mind, wrongdoers were to be duly punished, and those who managed to do things right merited an approving nod, which Karissa coveted above all else.

Night after night, her father would come home from the precinct, ranting about the impotent NYPD and the useless court system, describing in painful detail the wrongdoings for which there had been no justice. For Karissa, who was deeply affected by her father's anger and frustration, reading about comic superheroes assuaged her own pent-up vicarious desire for justice. It was only when her father began slipping out at night on clandestine errands, that his rants became less frequent, leaving Karissa to wonder what had changed.

Karissa's father brooked no backtalk, especially when it came to the topic of Karissa's mother, whom Karissa had only met a handful of times. Irena Ponomaryova, or 'Irene' as Karissa's father called her, hailed from a clan of local Ruska Roma, Russian Gypsies who had been living in New York for more than a decade, having immigrated together in the early sixties after escaping from under the Iron Curtain. The circumstances of her parents' first meeting were unclear, but Karissa supposed they might have met on the streets of the Bowery, when her father had been a lowly beat cop. All she knew was the approximate time of her conception and that, at some point, a mutual hatred had developed between her parents.

It was a particularly frigid and inhospitable December day, as far as New York standards went, with a gusting wind that whistled through the streets and alleys of the Bowery, rattling gutters, shaking chain-link fences, and causing fire escapes to groan and clank. Karissa was playing in her room with a battalion of her father's old army men when she heard raised voices coming from elsewhere in the apartment. She crept around the corner and saw her mother and father, each standing on opposite sides of the front doorway, rocketing toward a shouting match.

"What are you doing here?" her father was demanding.

"What do you think? I am here to see my daughter," said her mother, trying unsuccessfully to duck under his arm, which barred her way.

"Have you forgotten our agreement?" he asked, shouldering her back beyond the threshold.

"I don't care anymore," she spat, moving to push past him again, but again he moved to block her path, pushing her back into the hallway.

"First you sign away your custody rights," he bellowed, "and now you show up unannounced, after all this time? Go back to your family." There was venom in his voice as he said the last.

"You know damn well why I signed those papers!" she shrieked.

"You signed them because you didn't want the burden," he said maliciously.

"Lies!" she shouted. "How dare you accuse me of—"

Karissa heard a door open and the muffled voice of one of the neighbors from down the hall.

"No," her father said, addressing the unseen neighbor, "she's just leaving."

"I am not. I'm—"

"Go back inside Tom, I'm handling it," her father said firmly, and the door closed.

"Listen you crazy bitch," Karissa's father said in a deadly whisper, "if I ever see you again, there are going to be consequences. You know what I'm talking about." And he slammed the door in her face.

It took five or ten minutes for Karissa to find the courage to approach her father, who had moved to stand in the kitchen, his head down, hands gripping the metal sides of the sink.

"Dad?" she said in a quiet voice.

Her father spun around, regarding her with narrowed eyes and she proffered the bottle she was holding, a quart of whisky she had taken from the liquor cabinet in the hall with the hope that it would make her father feel better.

"Put that back," he said, pointing in the direction of the liquor cabinet.

Without moving to comply, she asked, "Why was mom here?"

A muscle twitched near her father's eye. "Your mother is a very selfish woman."

"I know that," she said, looking down at her feet.

"She's selfish and she's a liar," he said forcefully.

Clutching the whisky bottle to her chest, Karissa asked, "What does she lie about?"

His eyebrows went up. "She pretends to want to see you," he said, snatching the whisky bottle from her and slamming it down on the countertop, "but all she wants is to hurt me."

Karissa thought about this. "It really did seem like she wanted to see me," she said, remembering the way her mother had tried to push past him to get to her, but then she realized that she'd gone too far.

"What did you say?" her father asked in a soft, deadly voice.

"I just thought that maybe she did want to see me," she mumbled, looking down again at her feet, shifting them uncomfortably.

His eyes bulged. "Let me tell you something," he said, "your mother has never wanted to see you in your entire life. How often has she come around here?"

"Almost never."

"That's right, almost never. And does that mean that she wants to see you, yes or no?"

"Probably not," she said, "no."

"*Absolutely* not!" her father bellowed. And although a part of her questioned this logic, she was so eager to agree with him that she shoved that part away. "You will not question me like that again, ever. Do you understand me?"

"Yes sir," she said, kicking herself for having angered him. No wonder he was always disappointed in her; she could never seem to do anything right. As she turned the corner and walked down the hall, she heard the soft *thwop* of the cork coming free from the bottle and the sound of liquid being poured into a glass.

UNFORTUNATELY FOR KARISSA, HER FATHER REMAINED ANGRY WITH her for days following her mother's unexpected visit. Though she tried everything, including making them dinner, cleaning the toilet, and leaving him alone to brood and drink, he wouldn't speak to her or acknowledge her presence. It was like she wasn't there.

One night, he left the apartment, as usual without saying anything about where he was going, and for some reason, though she knew she shouldn't, she slipped on her boots, her mitts and her winter coat, and went out the door after him.

She followed him at a distance for three blocks in the dark and the cold, the sound of her crunching boots breaking the crusty surface of the snow causing her to wince. Once or twice, she was forced to duck into the shadows to avoid his roving gaze as he turned around, checking to see if there was anyone following him, but he didn't catch sight of her.

Eventually, he rounded a corner into an alley and was lost in a cloud of steam issuing from a vent. Karissa paused, waiting before entering the alley herself, hardly daring to breathe. She listened for any sound, but none came. She peeked around the corner and saw her father about fifty paces away. He was standing with his back to a door and was fumbling for something in his jacket pocket – a mask. She watched as he pulled the black balaclava over his head and slowly slid a solid-looking metal pipe from his sleeve, about the length of his forearm.

Just then, the door opened and out strode a man with a woman in tow. The man wore a double-breasted wool overcoat and matching fedora and the woman with him had on a leopard print fur trim coat, fishnet stockings and a miniskirt, which seemed to shorten her steps. Soundlessly, her father raised the pipe and was about to bring it crashing down on the man's head when Karissa let out an involuntary scream.

"Dad, no!"

Her father whirled around and saw her. The man let out a cry of surprise and the woman an ear-splitting shriek. Her father was just turning back to the pair when the man pulled a revolver from his coat pocket and then the two were wrestling for the gun. Karissa, who couldn't bear to witness any more of the nightmare scene, covered her face with her hands and ran from the alley.

When she arrived home, panting and sobbing, Karissa went straight to her room and, pulling the banker's box containing her comic collection from under her bed, she emptied the magazines on the floor and began ripping them to shreds.

She was in the process of tearing the pieces into smaller ones, when her father came through the front door. She froze, listening to him bang around in the other room and then heard his heavy footsteps in the hall. She climbed to her feet, hurriedly wiping away the tears as he entered her room, a grim expression on his face. He opened his mouth to say something and then stopped, taking in his eleven-year-old daughter with her dirty, tear-stained cheeks, standing over a pile of destroyed comics. Instead of speaking, he sat on the bed and picked up one of the colorful fragments of paper. He gazed at it for a time, then patted the bed beside him.

"Come and sit down," he said. She did as she was told, flinching a little as he shifted on the mattress next to her. "I've been quiet lately," he said. She shrugged, wanting to wipe her nose but didn't. "I bet you've been wondering where I've been going at night." She shrugged again. He bent over and dropped the scrap of paper with its fellows on the floor. "I've been beating up bad guys," he said, watching her carefully. "I know it might not have seemed like it a few minutes ago, but your Dad is like a superhero, not a criminal. There was no need to rip all those."

She realized he thought she destroyed her comic collection because she had become disillusioned with him after witnessing the events in the alley, when the opposite was true; she had destroyed the comics because she had been punishing herself.

"I'm sick and tired of it," he said, angrily. "Lotta times the police can't do a damn thing. Most are back on the streets again the next day, doing the same shit. You know how many are back on the street after I get through with 'em?" he asked, pointing at his chest with his thumb, "Zero."

"What kind of bad guys?" she asked, looking up at him.

"All kinds," he replied, quirking a tiny half smile, "drug dealers, racketeers, money launderers, mobsters, and thugs. The man in the alley was a pimp with his whore."

"Were you going to hit her with the pipe too?" Karissa asked.

"Of course not," he said, running his fingers over the stubble on his chin. "I would never hurt one of them."

Karissa nodded, digesting this. "Did you hit the pimp with the pipe?"

He chuckled, an odd grating sound she had rarely heard before. "Used my mitts instead," he said, spreading his thick hands before him.

"He deserved it," she said with such ferocity that her father's eyebrows rose in surprise.

"Yes," he agreed, "he did."

He stood up and scratched the back of his head. "Sit tight, I'm going to show you something." He left the room and returned a few moments later with a large metal box, which he had exhumed from someplace in his bedroom.

"Fighting is not about strength or speed," he declared, "It's about having an edge. You plan it ahead of time, so you always have surprise on your side and you always use a little something extra to guarantee you have the upper hand."

Sitting back down on Karissa's bed, he placed the box between them, popped the latches and opened the lid, motioning for her to have a look. Inside lay an array of unfamiliar objects. She selected a row of metal loops fused together by a short pommel, on which an inscription read: "NEW YORK – 1864 – METROPOLITAN POLICE"

"These were your grandfather's. God knows where he got them – probably a hand-me-down. They're called brass knuckles." He reached out. "Like this." And he slid the loops over her fingers, closed her fist for her, and took ahold of her wrist, raising her hand to his jaw. He jerked her arm forward, startling her, and her fist collided hard with the side of his face. She felt guilty, seeing the bright red marks appear on his stubbly chin, but he only grinned.

"You can have 'em if you like," he offered.

Feeling delighted, she pocketed the brass knuckles and he plucked another object from the box. It was a long tubular bag made of a fine wire mesh. He upended it onto the bed and several hundred pennies poured out.

"Back in the day I used tube socks," he chuckled, "but they kept breaking." He swept the coins back into the bag and swung it in an arc, smashing it down on Karissa's night table with a sound like a piggy-bank exploding, though the bag didn't break. He rubbed at the dent on the table with his hand and shrugged.

Karissa reached into the box and her fingers closed around a solid wooden cylinder, about two and a half feet long, with a leather strap fixed to the base, at the end of a carved wooden grip. She lifted out the police baton, whose polished mahogany surface shone dully in the light from the lamp in the corner.

"That was your grandfather's too. He used it in more than a few riots in his day, let me tell you. They don't make 'em like that anymore." Karissa ran her fingers along the smooth surface of the baton reverently, thinking about the generations of police that had come before.

"Want to learn how to use it?" her father asked.

Karissa's brows knit together and, after an momentary pause, she nodded her head, taking a firm grip of the baton's handle. It felt solid, dangerous, like she could knock down any bad guy she chose.

"Alright," said her father, "but we have to make an agreement, you and I."

Karissa nodded again, wondering what he could mean.

"We need to agree that people who hurt others have to be hurt back. It's that simple," he said gravely. "Say it."

"People who hurt others have to be hurt back," she intoned. She must have sounded convincing, because her father gave her one of this rare nods of approval.

"Good girl," he said.

## 3

# A FROG IN A WELL

Nigel Nakagawa would always appreciate that his mother let him choose his own superhero name. When he was old enough to understand the words, and even before, she had taken the time to read him stories of *Kintarō*, the 'Golden Boy,' who was a hero of legend, and who, even as a toddler, was reputed to have the power of incredible physical strength. In one story, which Nigel asked to hear again and again, Kintarō, clad only in a bib and baby fat, wrestled a giant carp and won, while in others, he broke boulders with his hands, helped woodcutters fell trees and snapped the trunks for them like matchsticks.

The Golden Boy had used his great strength as protector and helper, and Nigel had admired him for it. That was why, when his mother assigned him the task of selecting a name for himself, he did not hesitate. He called himself, fully, 'Kintarō, the Golden Boy,' which was part-Japanese and part-English, and carried with it a sense wonderment from his childhood.

The name was somewhat redundant, as his mother had pointed out, but she had let him keep it intact. It was an identity that he would later try his very best to shed, but the memories of the experiences with his mother, sharing stories and real affection, remained as some of the happiest of his life. And, as their relationship changed over the years and his feelings toward her grew complicated, those experiences became for him, her one saving grace. Unbeknownst to Nigel, however, they were also the bars of an invisible prison cell, which he would make and remake for himself as time went by, for his loyalty to his mother was fundamentally unshakable.

THE SEVEN YEARS SINCE NIGEL'S TRANSFORMATION HAD PASSED relatively uneventfully. This seemed strange to Nigel because, on the one hand, it still felt as if something had been taken from him that day in the square, but, as he looked around at the people of Ryūiki, all going about their business as usual, and at his parents, who seemed more content than ever, it was difficult for him to believe that there had ever been any harm done to him.

He was fourteen years old and had plenty of work to do, especially now that he possessed enhanced physical strength. He toted lumber, dug boulders from the earth and helped to stack loaded crates on high shelves in the storehouse, which otherwise required a forklift. There were frequent ceremonies to attend, where he received the adulation of the other cult followers, who joined in ritual acknowledgement of both his status as Champion and of his shimmering liquid metal suit. But outside these ceremonies, the people of Ryūiki dealt with him as they always had, by keeping a wary distance; perhaps even more so now. All except one.

"We shouldn't be alone like this. Someone might see," said Nigel, during a clandestine meeting one night with Aika, out behind the old smokehouse.

"Come on," said Aika, "your mother won't find us back here, and even if she does, what could possibly come of it? I know she likes me."

"She does," agreed Nigel, "but that's not the point, is it? The rules are just different for me, that's all."

"That's what I wanted to talk to you about," she said, chewing her lip. "Lately I've been seeing you less and less."

"I know," said Nigel looking at the muddy ground, "I'm sorry about that."

"It's okay. I know you're busy with official business as Champion and all that," she said, quirking a smile, "but we have been friends for a long time and I want to continue being friends in the future. It's important to me."

He looked up at her. "It's important to me too." She had no idea just how important.

"So it's settled then," she said cheerily, "we stay friends."

"Yes," he agreed.

"Great, but what about this problem of ours?"

"You mean the problem of spending time together?" She nodded and Nigel considered for a moment before shaking his head. "I don't know," he said.

"You don't know?" she asked, incredulously.

"I don't see a solution." He gazed at her steadily.

Her face fell. "You're Champion," she said, "and you can't even choose who to see?"

"That's the way it has always been," he replied.

She made a noise of exasperation and half turned to leave, but Nigel reached out and gently gripped her forearm.

"Wait," he said, a sinking feeling forming in the pit of his stomach, "I can talk to my mother. Maybe we can work something out."

She looked at him appraisingly and her shoulders seemed to relax. "That would be great. I don't want to lose you Nigel-chan," she said and smiled.

He smiled back, reassuringly he hoped, though his heart wasn't in it.

Slowly, Nigel made his way back to the main part of the village, following the pinprick of lamplight emanating from the front window of the tall, angular structure that was his home. He was thinking about Aika, about asking her to run away with him of all things, and was immediately ashamed of the thought. The village was Aika's home, the same as it was his, and she had a bright future ahead of her in the cult, over which her uncle presided as Grandmaster. Nigel had a still more significant role to play, and a sacred duty, one that he couldn't imagine so selfishly abandoning.

Crossing the threshold, he guided the heavy wooden front door silently closed. Somehow, though, his mother detected his entry, as she always did.

"You're late," came her voice from the next room. "Come and join me. Your father will be back soon, and I have prepared us supper."

Removing his shoes and arranging them neatly on the tiled *genkan* floor, Nigel stepped into the kitchen and, seeing that his mother was laying out side dishes on the table, he moved to help her.

"That's a good boy," she said in English. "Pour us some tea. If you had arrived earlier, you could have helped more," she added, raising her eyebrows at him. "Where were you?"

"I was speaking with Aika," he reluctantly replied.

"Oh," said his mother, kneeling on the tatami floor next to the low dining table, "yes, I had asked you to take that paperwork to the Grandmaster's house. Was there any message in return?"

"No," he replied, squatting down and pouring them tea from the cast iron teapot, "there was no message." His mother sipped her tea with thin lips and he cleared his throat, deciding that it would be better to come to the point. "Aika and I talked about spending more time together."

"What is keeping your father?" his mother asked, her eyes flicking in the direction of the front door. "He is the chattiest man alive."

Nigel held the opposite opinion of his father, who was the very personification of silence, as far as Nigel was concerned, and he couldn't fail to notice how his mother had ignored his statement. He had known, going into the conversation, that it would be little use trying to convince her to let him see Aika more often, considering the years his parents had spent tightly controlling his schedule. But, despite this, he chose to soldier on.

"It would make us both very happy if we could be allowed see each other, even once a month. I ask for your approval, for yours and father's both."

His mother set down her teacup and he expected her to launch into a tirade, but instead, she asked, "Do you know why I joined Hitsujikai?"

He thought for a moment, tapping his finger lightly on the rim of his own cup. "Tell me Mother," he replied quietly.

"My life before I came here hardly seemed real," she began. "There was nothing to work toward, except to increase profits and minimize losses and maintain the bank's reputation. I left because I wanted to lead people; to really lead them," she said, her eyes shining, "and to protect them, not only from the evils of the world, but from the drudgery I had known, to give them a life safe from harm and filled with meaning."

"Selfishly," she added, almost as an afterthought, "I wanted to do something great. But I think you know all this already. What you might not know," she said, folding her hands in her lap, "is that I joined the cult, not only to enact my vision for humanity, but to submit myself to it. I am an offering, my Golden Boy. I am prepared to dedicate my life to this cause, and I ask that you only trust enough to do the same."

Nigel was still, kneeling there on the tatami, thinking about what his mother was asking him to do. He believed her when she said that their cause was an essential one, and he wanted to do his part, he knew he did, but why must it be as Champion? Couldn't he have contributed in some other way that better suited his personality? Recently, Nigel had come to the realization that he might have been more useful as a missionary, connecting on a personal level with potential converts and persuading them to open their eyes to the possibilities of the cult, rather than defending it with his fists. Why couldn't she see that?

As if she knew his thoughts she said, "It is the highest honor to serve as Champion. Without the living embodiment of the *Resident*, we cannot hope to make a difference in the rest of the world. And if the world burns," she said, "we will burn with it." Nigel almost thought he could see those flames, flickering in the dark depths of her eyes.

"All are the sheep of Hitsujikai," he intoned.

His mother nodded gravely.

Nigel shifted his legs on the floor beneath him. He understood what she was saying, though it did not ease his mind. "I will do as you ask," he said at last, and bowed his head, and that was all.

"Good," she said and stood up, as if concluding a business meeting. "Now, help me serve the rest of the dinner."

Nigel was distributing the remaining side dishes around the table when the front door creaked open and, a moment later, his father stepped into the room.

"You're late," said Nigel's mother, bustling between the stove and the table.

"The food smells delicious," Nigel's father said, sitting down, cross-legged on one of the cushions fringing the table. He plucked up a cup of steaming tea with thick fingers and took a long, quiet swallow.

Nigel sat next to him and served himself a helping of steamed fiddleheads and, passing the dish to his father, he reached for the bowl of thinly-sliced beef, mingling with rivulets of oil in a rich broth that his mother had prepared early that morning.

"How was your afternoon Father?" Nigel asked politely, sipping broth from his bowl.

"Successful," his father replied, laying several young smelt fish on his plate with his chopsticks, their pale underbellies charred in places from the grill. "The pine has been felled, sectioned and readied for chopping tomorrow." He wiggled his eyebrows at Nigel, perhaps remembering that chopping wood was one of Nigel's favorite tasks. He enjoyed the way the wood splintered and flew with his mighty strokes and the repetitive rising and falling of the axe helped him to empty his mind of all worries.

"Nigel will be going to town tomorrow to choose new clothes," his mother said evenly.

"I will?" Nigel asked excitedly. Seldom was Nigel allowed to pick his own clothes and was used to wearing hand-me-downs under his leather outerwear.

"Yes," she replied, sharing a conspiratorial look with his father.

"You haven't told him yet," said his father, suddenly intent on his fish.

"I thought you should be the one," replied his mother. She raised her bowl of beef broth to her mouth and sipped softly, her eyes closed.

"Tell me what?" asked Nigel, suddenly worried.

His father laid a thick hand on his shoulder. "It's time for you to begin your training," he said, a hint of unsteadiness in his voice. "You will go to Tokyo to study with one steeped in our history and practices."

"How long will I be gone?" asked Nigel, suddenly feeling as though the bit of fern he had just swallowed had become lodged in his throat.

"For at least three years," replied his father, releasing Nigel's shoulder and going back to eating his meal. For a time, the only sound in the tiny room was the clicking of chopsticks.

"Three years?" breathed Nigel, trying but failing to conceal his dismay.

"At least," his father repeated.

"But I'll miss so much!" Nigel exclaimed. "And who will help move the boulder in Yamata-san's field?"

"We have a tractor for that," said his mother, setting down her bowl and giving his father a meaningful look. His father nodded slowly.

"There's more," he said to Nigel, clearing his throat and taking a swallow of tea. "From there you will go to New York City."

"New York City?" exclaimed Nigel.

"Nigel-san," said his mother sharply, "lower your voice."

"New York City?" he asked again in a husky whisper, his throat dry.

"That's right," said his mother definitively. "We have spoken with the Grandmaster and the council and we all agree that New York is the place you will go."

"But why New York?" he asked.

"Because you're needed there," said his father firmly. "Because, at this moment in history, humanity's greatest threats – drugs, crime, civil unrest, are all thriving there and are on the verge of being exported to the world."

"Your destiny is to stem the tide," his mother intoned, gazing at him with hard eyes.

Nigel looked between his parents, who sat silently before him, waiting for his reply. He swallowed hard. "When do I leave?"

They glanced at each other. "At the end of the week," his father said, looking at him with a mixture of anxiety and compassion. "Don't worry son, I know you must feel like the frog in the well, who can't imagine the ocean, but soon," and again he laid a strong hand on Nigel's shoulder, gripping it tightly, "soon all that will change."

· · ·

AIKA SEEMED HURT, ANGRY EVEN, AS THE PROCESSION MOVED PAST her. Nigel was dressed in resplendent golden robes draped over the gleaming living metal of the *Resident*, which crawled sickeningly over his skin as he marched solemnly alongside his mother and father, the Grandmaster at their head. He tried to catch Aika's eye as he walked by, but she looked away from him. He tried to call her name, imploring her to look at him, to see the pain in his eyes from leaving her, but the words were drowned in the keening wail of the villagers, congregated to see off their Champion.

There were others too, other followers who had come from the cult's many communes spread across Japan. They formed a massive throng that stretched beyond the village square, filling the spaces between the thatched roof dwellings, and spilling onto the fields, where they trampled the soil flat, pressing the newly sown seeds deeper into the ground.

It would be the last image he had of Aika – arms crossed, brows drawn together, her face turned pointedly away, before she was lost in the seething mass of people, all intent on howling him out of the village.

## ✻ 4 ✻

# A HOP, A SKIP AND A STUMBLE

arissa's face felt hot and itchy under her sky-blue balaclava. She slid a slender finger under the bottom of the mask and scratched the irritated patch of skin on the point of her jaw, thinking back to the preparation that had gone into tonight.

Going on information from her father's top informant who, for some reason, went by the name 'Admiral Rat,' she and her father were to carry out a meticulously planned ambush of a loan shark, whom they had been watching for some time. The shark had broken the legs of a local Chinese grocer, an elderly man whom Karissa knew and liked, and they had vowed to teach the shark a lesson he wouldn't soon forget. They had learned his habits, noting where he spent his time and who his business partners were. And tonight, predicting that the shark would be alone, working late in his seedy shop off Delancey Street, she and her father had laid their trap.

After the incident in the alley, her father had asked her to come with him the next time he went on a "night run," to act as lookout. She had been instructed to warn him if the cops were coming, or if there were any witnesses nearby and, after she had capably performed this task, he had asked her to come out with him a second time, then a third.

As they went out together more and more at night, her father began to teach her things. He showed her the proper way to throw a punch, by putting her weight behind it and twisting her hips, and how to use her knees and elbows in a fight. He put her in martial arts classes and gymnastics and took her to work where she sparred with some of the cops at the precinct. They had suggested she take boxing, so she had. And above all, she practiced with the baton; that hard, dark cylinder that could bring a man to his knees.

Over the past six years, her father's attitude had slowly changed toward his only child. Although he was still gruff and strict as ever, rarely permitting her to see her classmates outside school hours, he had taken her on as a kind of sidekick, and a fondness had grown between them, fueled by time spent together in dangerous circum-stances. The fact was that Karissa had become useful to the degree that he now relied on her and, for her part, she enjoyed her father's company, though if she was honest with herself, hurting people always made her feel more than a little bit sick.

However, despite harboring secret misgivings, here she was in the darkened lot behind the loan shark's shop, her back pressed to the wall on one side of the rear door, breath coming hot from the opening in the front of her mask. She glanced at her father, positioned on the other side of the door, his expression indecipherable beneath his own woolen mask. She looked up at the sky, the last light having bled from it minutes before, and then back at him. He nodded to her, motioning with his head toward the caged window, behind which a light could be seen.

She took a deep breath and stepped up to the window, lifting her baton and shoving it through one of the gaps in the bars. The end of the baton crashed against the glass, creating a spider web crack, radi-ating outward from its epicentre. There came a shout from within and Karissa slipped the baton out of the cage and quickly rejoined her father at the door. A moment later, the door banged open and two men burst out, carrying baseball bats, closely followed by the loan shark. Her breath caught; he was supposed to be alone.

"Teach you kids a lesson," the shark was saying and then stopped when he saw Karissa's father, masked and holding his pipe. "Jesus," he said, "Who the fuck are y—"

Silently cursing Admiral Rat for having neglected to inform them of the two goons, Karissa knocked the loan shark's feet from under him with the baton, sliding sideways as the shark toppled onto his back, writhing on the cement. The heads of the two other men snapped around and her father was on them. He smashed the nearest of them across the shoulders with his length of pipe and Karissa scooted forward, striking the second man's hands with her baton. He dropped his bat and let out a wail, cut short as her father clubbed him with the pipe.

Grimacing at the blood that ran in a narrow stream from a gash in the man's head, Karissa carefully stowed the baton in the loop at her belt. Her father kicked aside a baseball bat as he swung a leg over the loan shark, standing astride the man's prone body.

Wait!" gasped the shark, "Just wait! Time out!" He made the shape of a lowercase 't' with his fingers, as though attempting to ward off a vampire.

"I think it's this," said her father, wedging the pipe in one of his armpits and making the shape of a capital 'T' with the full length of his hands.

Karissa thought about how the grocer had been forced to close his store while he struggled to recover from his injuries; he probably never would recover and maybe he would lose his livelihood, she thought.

The man whimpered as her father took a fresh grip on his pipe, raising it above his head.

Karissa, whose anxiety had been mounting, found that for some reason, she couldn't stomach watching her father beat the defenseless man.

"Maybe that's enough," she said, reaching a hand toward her father.

He paused, lowering the pipe and tapped his lips through his mask, as though considering what she'd said, then he gave a mirthless, grating laugh. "Out of the way," he told her.

"You," she said sternly, addressing the loan shark. "You'll pay Mr. Chu for his medical bills and replace the things you broke in his shop."

The loan shark nodded avidly, "O-of course, whatever you say."

The man winced as she tapped his knee with the toe of her shoe. "And you'll leave the Bowery and never come back."

"Uh huh, sure sweetie. I'll be on the next train to Chicago."

"After you pay Mr. Chu."

"Right, after I pay him, I'll be on my way an' you'll never see me again," said the loan shark with a watery grin.

"It's not enough," said her father, and Karissa looked up at him.

"Why not?" she asked.

"You know why not," he said. "This scum will do the same thing to someone else the moment he gets off the train in Chicago."

"Maybe he won't," Karissa said, chewing her lip. "You won't will you?" she demanded of the loan shark, who adamantly shook his head.

Her father gave her a stern look, a note of impatience creeping into his voice. "Do you remember our agreement?" he asked, fingering the pipe.

"Yes," she said reluctantly, a sinking feeling forming in the pit of her stomach.

"What is it?" he demanded sharply.

"People who hurt others have to be hurt back," she recited, "but—"

"But!" he roared. "You know how I feel about the word *but*. Here," he said, yanking the police baton free of the loop at her hip. He grabbed her hand and pressed the wooden club into it, closing her fingers tightly around the grip. "You do it."

"B—"

"No buts!" he yelled, his voice echoing over the lot.

A tear leaked from Karissa's eye, dampening a small patch of her mask as she moved to stand astride the loan shark. He cowered away from her as she brandished the baton and she closed her eyes.

"No," he begged, "No!"


IN JUNE 1982, KARISSA WAS NEARING THE END OF HER SENIOR YEAR of high school and prom was only a week away. Having never been to a dance before, she had no idea what to expect, but was surprised to discover that she was looking forward to the event, which by all rights she should see as laughably juvenile. She was doubly chagrined when she found herself accepting an invitation from Ted Weissenberg, a shy Jewish kid in her class, with a curly mop of dark hair and freckles. Ted had never been on Karissa's radar, but he seemed to have had his eye on her for some time, and she was baffled by how good she felt when he asked her. She had agreed to be his date and it wasn't until the ride home on the subway that Karissa began to think about what her father would say when she told him.

It was with anxiety that Karissa greeted him that evening as he hung his policeman's hat on the hook by the door and shrugged off his blue shirt with its three stripes on the upper arm. He sat heavily into one of the wooden chairs at the table, slouching in his sleeveless white undershirt, waiting for dinner. She had prepared the meal for them, as was their agreement on weekdays and, since the casserole needed to bake for ten more minutes, she sat down with her father at the table, placing an open beer next to his hairy arm.

"Thanks," he grunted.

"How was your day?" she asked, sitting up unusually straight in her chair.

"Terrible," he replied and then, taking a sip of his beer he asked, "how was yours?"

"Not bad," she said cautiously, playing with the hem of her t-shirt. "What happened at work to make it terrible?"

Her father made a noise of disgust. "The usual bullshit. The captain won't let us go after a drug dealer because he's the son of some rich asshole. Not much older than you," he added, taking a swig of the beer, "but damn prolific. Luckily," he said, his thin smile failing to touch his eyes, "I know where he lives. We'll make a night run on Friday, see if we can catch him alone."

"Friday?" Karissa asked, looking up.

"Yeah," he said, rising and moving to wash his hands at the kitchen sink, "best time I think."

"Prom's on Friday," she said looking down at the table.

"Just tell anyone who asks you're going out of town," he said, sitting back down and plucking up his beer. "It's as good an excuse as any." He looked at her, still staring at the tabletop. "What's wrong?" he asked, then, "You don't want to *go*, do you?"

"I thought—"

"We've talked about this Karissa," he said reprovingly, "a party like that means drugs. Why did you ever think that you could—"

"It's stupid anyway," she said, giving in quickly.

He said nothing in reply, drinking the last of his beer in silence.

"I saw mom the other day," Karissa said suddenly.

She didn't know why she said it, especially since it wasn't even true, but something inside her had chosen that moment to dig at her father, knowing the topic would make him upset. She immediately regretted doing so however.

"What?!" he roared, standing up from the table, his eyes blazing. "Where?"

She quailed, but again, that part of her that wanted to dig, to get back at him somehow, decided to double down on the lie. "I saw her on Grand Street, walking toward Greenwich Village," she said, staring into her father's crimson face. "She waved at me."

"She—waved," her father whispered, staring out the kitchen window into the gathering gloom outside. "Well that's fucking it then, isn't it?" He pushed away his chair and grabbed his windbreaker from its hook by the door and made to leave the apartment.

"No," squeaked Karissa, "Dad, stop!"

"I told her there would be consequences!" he shouted and then, in a quieter voice, "It has to be done."

He opened the door and was halfway out when Karissa flung herself at him, wrapping her arms around his middle and her legs around his right thigh, weighing him down.

"You can't," she cried, almost hysterical.

"Get. Off." he said through gritted teeth, trying to shake her clear of his leg, but she held on tightly. "Karissa if you don't let go by the count of three – One! Two!"

"I lied!" she shrieked, weeping now in earnest, "I lied."

Her father went still and she collapsed to her knees on the floor just inside the front door. He closed it with a bang, looming over her.

"Explain," he barked.

Between sobs, a string of words came bubbling out of her: "You never let me do anything. I can't see my classmates outside school. I can't make friends. I can't do anything a normal teenager does. I can't even see my mom."

"Your mother is a deadbeat!" he shouted. "A good for nothing Gypsy deadbeat who's never done an honest day of work in her life. I'm *protecting* you from her, just like I'm protecting you from those troublemakers at your school. She's a bad influence and so are they!" He paused, shaking his head. "I thought we saw eye to eye. I thought you wanted to make the neighborhood a better place, that all that kid stuff was stupid."

"I do. It is." said Karissa in a tiny voice.

"Which is it then?" he asked, his lip curling in disgust.

"I don't know," she replied, staring hard at the floor.

"Your mother doesn't want to see you anyway," he sneered.

"Yes," she said meekly, though, for the first time in a while, she suddenly remembered that this might not be true. She had witnessed her mother fighting to see her that time in the doorway of the apartment, but the woman had stopped coming around after her father had threatened her. But what had he threatened? Karissa suddenly felt the need to find out.

"Go to your room," he ordered, "and think long and hard about what you want, because in the end," and his voice carried an ominous tone, "it might come down to them or me."

Black smoke began issuing from the oven and her father swore. Dashing to the kitchen, he snatched the casserole from the oven, its top charred black; the dish was ruined.

# SHIMOKITAZAWA

I t was in the dusty branch office of Shimokitazawa, a bohemian neighbourhood in Tokyo's labyrinthine Setagaya ward, that Nigel was confronted directly regarding his feelings about becoming the Champion of Hitsujikai.

A bell tinkled faintly as the door shut behind him and he crossed the threshold into the cramped office. Placing his bags on the floor, he stood and waited for the proprietor. From a dimly lit back office, hobbled a small balding man of indeterminate age. At first glance, and because of his gait, he gave the impression of a man in later life, though, as he bowed and the golden light from the window fell across his smooth, fleshy features, Nigel was not so sure.

"Nigel-san" the man said, his dark eyes glinting, "I am Hiroji."

Nigel bowed deeply. "Sensei."

Hiroji gave the hint of smile, running a rough hand over the bald part of his head with a hiss, minute flakes of skin coming loose and joining the dust that perpetually swirled in the atmosphere of that place.

"Welcome," he said. "Please, sit down." He seated himself behind an ample desk, littered with all manner of papers and writing implements. Nigel sat in a low wooden chair before the desk, his eyes respectfully averted from Hiroji's penetrating gaze.

"I should say up front that I am primarily a bureaucrat," Hiroji announced, "and my ability to train you may be limited by a single-minded focus on detail."

Nigel paused, slightly taken aback by the declaration, then spoke haltingly, not wanting to offend the man. "But you must be more than equipped to teach me Sensei, otherwise why would my parents send me here?"

"What do you know about the purpose of Hitsujikai?" Hiroji asked unexpectedly, peering quizzically at Nigel as though he hadn't heard him.

Nigel thought for a moment. "Our purpose is to guide and protect people," he said, remembering what his mother had taught him. "Human civilization depends on proper protection."

"Exactly," said Hiroji, scribbling a line in a notebook, "but you are missing some details."

"I am?" said Nigel, blinking.

"Yes," Hiroji replied. "For example, from what do people require protection?"

Nigel considered the question. "From others?" he suggested. "People require protection from those who wish them harm. Criminals perhaps."

"Right again," Hiroji said, leaning back in his chair. "People require protection from a wide range of dangers: from governments, from corporate entities, from gangs and thugs, from terrorists, from the police, from militaries, from liars and cheats, from exclusion, from rape, from murder, from disease and from death. This is not an exhaustive list," he pointed out, raising a finger in the air, "it is only a sample of some of the details you must learn in-depth to be effective in your role."

Nigel nodded, feeling slightly queasy. The details were all well and good, he thought; it was the *how* that worried him. "If I may, Sensei?" he asked, and Hiroji spread his hands in a gesture of encouragement. "Of course, I intend to learn all the details that pertain to being a competent Champion. But what of skills? Will I learn how to deal with those threats, using martial arts perhaps?"

Hiroji made a waving gesture with his hand as though dismissing a small dog from the room. "I cannot teach you those skills. You must have faith in the power of the *Resident*. Your speed, strength, hardiness and agility, these are all foregone conclusions. You will discover how to use them on your own."

Nigel sincerely doubted his own ability to discover these hidden talents. The superheroes he knew hopped and leaped about, performing death-defying gymnastic feats as they sailed across the city skyline. How would he manage to learn that?

"Tell me Nigel-san," asked Hiroji suddenly, "do you truly wish to be Champion of Hitsujikai?"

"Sensei?" asked Nigel, perplexed.

"It's a simple question," his teacher said mildly. "Put a different way then: if you had your choice, would you continue on this path?"

"Of course," said Nigel, thinking it was the only answer he could possibly give.

"Come now," Hiroji said, not unkindly, "if I were you, a boy of fourteen, born into this world with a mountain of responsibility on my shoulders, I would be reluctant to submit myself."

Nigel remained silent, his fingers anxiously playing with themselves in his lap, as if they had a will of their own.

"I encourage you to speak your mind," Hiroji insisted, his eyes shining darkly in the shaft of golden light from the window. "If I am to be your teacher and you my pupil, we must be honest with each other."

"If I could choose," said Nigel, continuing uncertainly after a nod of encouragement from Hiroji. "If I could choose, I would be a missionary rather than Champion, because I believe the former would suit me better."

Hiroji sat back in his chair, nodding as though confirming something, then he began to write in his notebook. "You realize of course," he said, still scribbling, "that your becoming a missionary is impossible. You are bonded with the *Resident* and there is no going back. The sooner you accept that the better."

"Yes Sensei," Nigel replied quietly, with the vague impression that he had been duped.

"And yet a part of you is resistant." Hiroji scratched the crown of his bald head, sending more skin flakes spinning into the half-light of the tiny room. "Your mother was headstrong at first too. She also wanted to do everything her own way."

Nigel looked up, feeling the heat rising in his cheeks. "I do not believe myself to be headstrong, Sensei," he said defensively, "only that I am unsure of my suitability. Maybe if I learn more about becoming Champion, then perhaps my reluctance will fade."

"You know Nigel-san, a cult is an organization that, by its very definition, uses its followers." Nigel nodded. "So you must become accustomed to being used," Hiroji said simply.

"Yes Sensei," said Nigel, and the little man made another addition to his notebook.

"If you don't mind me asking," said Nigel, feeling suddenly irritated by the older man's incessant notetaking, "what is it that you are writing?"

Hiroji gazed at him for several moments before replying. "The reason you are here," he said at last, neglecting to answer Nigel's question, "is first, to learn significant details pertaining to becoming the protector of New York City and second, to learn to submit yourself fully to our cause." He regarded Nigel appraisingly. "As I mentioned a few moments ago, I can help you with the first task, but the second one will be up to you."

He held up the notebook. "I will use this to record the details of your progress, so that, at the end of our time together, the leadership may evaluate your readiness to leave this place and go out into the field. If they deem you ready, it's off to New York at the end of three years, and if not, remedial training will be necessary and you will be required to stay with me in this place."

Hiroji closed the notebook with a snap, stood, and wordlessly directed Nigel toward a flight of stairs with an outstretched arm, sporting a reptilian smile.

. . .

THE YEARS PASSED SLOWLY, EACH DAY SEEMING MORE OR LESS THE same as the one before it. Nigel would waken after six hours of sleep, light the lamp in his spartan bedroom and begin his readings, which he was supposed to know intimately by the time Hiroji emerged from his own bedroom at sunrise. Soon after, Nigel would be given his first lesson of the day, during which he and Hiroji would discuss the details of that morning's readings.

The topic was most often history, pertaining to the cult and its interventions abroad over the last 800 years. Nigel also read about the American legal system and was instructed to memorize New York crime statistics going back to the turn of the century. Hiroji would inject the lesson with a series of tedious details and Nigel would make precise notes containing names, dates, places, facts, figures, and all the information that his teacher insisted was relevant, though Nigel could hardly see how.

He noticed that Hiroji said little in these lessons about the *Resident* and assumed that there must be very few written accounts of the mysterious substance if the balding man, a champion record-keeper and paper-pusher, had no information to share with him about it.

Nigel's lessons were uninteresting to the point of becoming painful, but he worked doggedly at learning the material. His determination to digest those bland details was mostly for fear of the shame of having to face failure and remediation, and out of a burning desire to get clear of that place as soon as humanly possible.

However, the main problem with the branch office in Shimoki-tazawa was not the boring lessons, nor the feeling of always being hemmed in, whether he was indoors or out. It was not the lumpy bed or the repetitive cuisine. It was the oppressive silence that seemed to permeate the very foundations of the place. The silence was especially difficult for Nigel because it meant that he was left alone with his feel-ings of inadequacy and his shame. Perhaps this was what Hiroji intended because, more than anything, it was the dead spaces of empty time that finally drove Nigel to address his fear of becoming a superhero.

It was late afternoon on a spring day in Nigel's third year of train-ing. As usual, he was lost in thought, ambling down a narrow winding street, paying little attention to the intricate shopfronts and distinctive vintage clothing stores, wandering past restaurant workers as they prepared lively little eateries and off-beat hole-in-the-wall bars for the arrival of customers.

At some point, he stopped, staring up at a cluster of the slim, densely-packed three-story buildings that were typical of Shimokitazawa, having the sudden urge to view the sunset.

*I should be up on that roof*, he thought and his shoulders slumped a little. He was supposed to have explored his superpowers by now but had been too cowardly to attempt any death-defying acts. He was about to turn and leave when something caught his eye.

In the narrow alley between two of the buildings, where the space was wide enough for only a single car to fit through, he spotted a flimsy-looking aluminum fire escape, approximately eight feet from the ground and, across from it, he saw a concrete utilities box, about three feet high, built against the adjacent wall.

He imagined taking a run at the box and using it as a launch point, pushing off with his feet, spinning around in mid-air, reaching behind him and grabbing hold of the lowest metal rung of the ladder. Usually, he would never have considered such a manoeuver, wishing to avoid the inevitable failure, but picturing Hiroji's forensic gaze over dinner that night and remembering the silence that would descend on him in his lonely room at the end of the day, stopped him from dismissing the idea outright.

He looked around, checking to see that nobody was nearby, and slowly he made his way over to the alley. He stopped, looking up at the ladder, then down at the box next to the wall. He walked a little way down the alley, turned and surveyed the scene again. Calculating the distance and estimating the force required to make it to the ladder from the box, he took a deep breath and broke into a sprint. Coming at the wall on a diagonal, he jumped onto the box, felt firm concrete beneath his shoe, and pushed off in the opposite direction, letting out a whoop as he sailed into the air.

He was so surprised at the height he gained with the jump that he nearly missed the rungs of the ladder, which he frantically grabbed near the top. With one push, he had made it almost three stories above the ground. He easily climbed the remaining six feet of ladder, hand over hand and, reaching the roof, he stood, gazing over the series of low rooftops that stretched before him like the boxcars of a train. The orange sun hung stretched over the horizon, bathing his body in its warm glow.

Squinting, he took a few steps forward and peered over the edge of the roof. Every few building clusters there was another alley and then, after five or so of these, there was a wider street, where he could see vehicles moving. An outlandish thought struck him: *I'm going to jump between those buildings.*

He knew from his days in the village that he was strong, strong enough to move boulders and chop hard, knotted wood with ease. He had once lifted the back end of a tractor, which had run over one of the other villagers, and his legs had just shown that they could propel him through space with enough force to leap up most of the height of a three-story building. And so, with all this in mind, he screwed up his courage and hurled himself into space.

Back at the branch office, Hiroji was nowhere to be found, though Nigel didn't mind. The elation remained with him as he prepared them a simple dinner of pan-fried tofu and *yaki-wakame* in the confines of the grimy kitchen they shared. Taking in the salty odors of the seaweed as it sizzled, he breathed deeply, feeling the rush of the wind again, and hearing his own laugh from a few hours before. Hiroji would want to hear of his breakthrough. Perhaps even Hiroji would be proud, Nigel thought as he served the hot food and sat down to wait for his teacher.

The food was cold when Hiroji pushed his way through the back door of the office. He shook his coat, which was covered in droplets of the rain that had begun to fall over the last few hours. Wiping the bald part of his head clear of moisture, he scooped up a plate of the cold food and gave it a sniff, wrinkling his nose. Nigel watched him, opening his mouth to tell him what he had accomplished that afternoon, but his teacher forestalled him.

"The Grandmaster is ill," said Hiroji, tasting a small bite of the food using a pair of chopsticks.

"Oh," said Nigel, who didn't much care for the grub-like specimen of a leader, "is it serious?"

"No one can say for sure," replied Hiroji. "The cause of the illness is a mystery." He set the bowl on the counter next to the sink, rinsing the tips of the chopsticks and letting them fall onto the drain board with a clatter.

"You must be concerned about him Sensei," Nigel commented politely.

"What concerns me," said Hiroji, "is the prospect of succession. One thing we handle poorly as an organization is the filling of leadership positions. For such a high position as his, there would certainly be a power struggle."

Nigel opened his mouth to ask more about this, but Hiroji spoke first. "All this reminds me that I must teach you details about the Grandmasters who have shaped Hitsujikai over the centuries." He disappeared through the sliding door between the kitchen and the front room of the office, reappearing a moment later with a thick volume. "Here," he said, thrusting the leather-bound book at Nigel, "take this to bed with you."

The next several weeks were characterized by more readings, daily lectures, which had become longer lately, and Nigel enthusiastically probing the limits of his powers. Soon, he had explored all the rooftops of Shimokitazawa, and had been practicing watching the people below, his eyes scanning for potential dangers.

Once, he had called out to a young cyclist who was at risk of being wiped out by a flatbed truck, and the boy had skidded out of the way, narrowly avoiding serious bodily harm. Nigel thought that next time he might leap straight off the roof and knock the cyclist out of the way instead, such was the brazenness that was building inside him.

He had also begun to experiment with his suit, made of metal *Resident*, which he rehearsed forming around his body, perfecting the inner process that forced the material out his pores and allowed him to release it at will, the metallic liquid dissolving and draining away from his skin.

In a nearby construction site, he found an old ruin of a concrete wall and practiced kicking and punching it with *Resident*-protected

45

hands and feet, making great holes in the surface. He laughed as he did this, all the while enjoying the increased confidence that came with the feeling of making progress. *I can do this,* he thought, *I'm ready*.

One night, Nigel decided to enter through his bedroom window on the second story of the building that housed the branch office and, as he was shedding the *Resident* down the little drain in the floor of the bathroom that he shared with Hiroji, he heard voices emanating from downstairs. Wrapping a towel around his waist, he silently made his way onto the landing and sat there, listening intently.

"I wish I could say my visit was under happier circumstances, Hiroji-san," said a male voice Nigel didn't recognize.

"I also wish that were so, Watanabe-san" said Hiroji formally. "What news from Ryūiki?"

"The funeral rites have been observed and the family is in mourning," Watanabe said.

The Grandmaster was dead then, thought Nigel, and Aika and her family would be grieving his loss.

"The succession struggle you feared failed to materialize," said Watanabe. "It seems Fuyuko Natsume was ready for this eventuality and, with the help of her husband, she has almost completely united the leadership in support of her, and will become the new Grandmaster of Hitsujikai."

The breath caught in Nigel's throat. His mother had made herself Grandmaster? The role suited her, certainly, and she would be happy, yet he felt a strange sense of foreboding deep in the pit of his stomach.

"What of the boy?" asked Watanabe.

"What of him?" asked Hiroji, with a hint of bad-temperedness.

"It has been almost three years since his training began," Watanabe suggested.

"Three years this morning," Hiroji said, with a sigh.

"And?"

"And he's far from ready."

Nigel covered his mouth with his hand, staring wide-eyed into space.

"Ah, but the Grandmaster-to-be has said that the boy is to be sent to New York City, immediately."

There was a silence and then came Hiroji's voice, flat and cold, "We will leave tomorrow then."

"Very good," Watanabe said and Nigel could hear the tinkle of the bell above the front door as the man exited the office.

New York. Tomorrow. The idea of it both thrilled and terrified Nigel. He looked down at his fists, which were tightly clenched and forced his hands to relax. Hiroji was wrong. He was ready. And he would prove it when he got to New York. Kintarō, the Golden Boy would be the best superhero the city had ever seen. He wrinkled his brow; he would just have to sort out one or two more details.

## ※ 6 ※

## THE SOVIET THREAT

The day after the failed prom request, Karissa took a detour on the way home from school. It was surprising that she remembered where her mother lived, considering how closely her father guarded any information about the woman, but somehow she knew Irena lived in the basement of a tenement building on the corner of Rivington and Essex, in the Lower East Side. She wasn't sure which building it was exactly, but she thought she could probably ask around. In such a small enclave of Roma, any of the people there should be able to point her in the direction of the apartment where her mother lived with her parents and brothers.

Karissa thought back to the previous night. After the incident with her father, she had sat on the floor of her bedroom thinking about her mother and justice for the better part of an hour. The more she thought about it, the more she felt that there was something wrong about the way her father intimidated her mother, something bad, and that maybe she should be the one to get to the bottom of it. Her father might be angry, *but screw it*, she thought. She was beginning to care less and less about keeping him happy, and more and more about her mother's feelings, even though she had spent almost no time with the woman.

48

Rounding the corner at Rivington and Essex, she walked past a deli with tables on the sidewalk. Three men were seated at one of them, presiding over a large platter of cutlets and boiled eggs. Two of the men wore ponytails and one a flat cap. The one with the cap treated her to a gap-toothed grin and said something in Russian. Karissa stopped and the other two men joined the first in leering crookedly at her.

"Irena," she blurted.

"Your name is Irena?" said the man with the hat, chuckling hoarsely.

"No," she replied, embarrassed, "I'm looking for Irena. Irena Ponomaryova."

The man stopped laughing. "Why do you look for her?" he asked suspiciously.

"I'm her daughter, Karissa," she said, shifting her feet uncomfortably.

"I don't know no Karissa," said the man, laboriously working his mouth around the name and staring at her intently, "and I would know."

"How would you?" Karissa asked, feeling annoyed.

"Because I am Irena's brother," said the man, treating her to another glimpse of his remaining teeth.

"You must be my uncle then," said Karissa, surmising that the man was one of her mother's three older brothers, whom her father had mentioned during one of his tirades.

The man paused, scratching his chin thoughtfully. "She did have a child, but a long time ago."

"Yes, seventeen years ago," said Karissa impatiently. "Where does she live?"

After appearing to consider for a few moments, the man stood up. "I will show you," he said.

He led her across the street and around the back of the red brick tenement building on the corner. Unlatching and tugging open a section of chain-link fence across the entrance to a side alley, he motioned for her to go ahead of him with an exaggerated wave of his arm, grinning wryly. He led her down some crumbling concrete steps and, fumbling with a set of keys, let them into a stuffy basement flat.

The living room was crammed full of threadbare furniture, including more than a dozen upholstered chairs and three couches. Religious paintings and framed posters of pastoral vistas hung on the walls, and there were several mismatched standing lamps, casting a warm glow over the faded red carpet. Two women, one older and one younger, sat folded into the cushions of the plush couch nearest the door. They blinked up at Karissa in surprise.

"This girl," her uncle said, addressing the younger of the two women and pointing at Karissa, "says she's your daughter."

The woman narrowed her eyes and sat very still, peering up at Karissa, then she stood and walked over to her. The two were almost exactly the same height.

"My daughter!" she exclaimed suddenly and hugged Karissa fiercely. Karissa, startled by the abrupt display of affection, stood limply in her mother's embrace. "It is you," said her mother, breaking away to look at her. "How you've grown!"

The older woman said something sharply from the couch and Karissa's mother turned and snapped something back.

Karissa's uncle partly translated: "She says you can't be here."

"Who says?" asked Karissa, turning to him.

"Your grandmother," he replied.

Karissa's mother said something in Russian and her grandmother replied shrilly from the couch, making emphatic shooing gestures toward the door with both hands. Irena looked anxiously between Karissa and her own mother, chewing her lower lip.

"She says it's too dangerous and you have to go," said Karissa's uncle.

"Is that true?" Karissa asked Irena and the woman hesitated, finally nodding, a pained look in her eyes. "I don't want to put you in danger," said Karissa, bewildered and crestfallen. She turned to leave.

"Wait," her mother said, "let me walk you for a couple of blocks."

THE TRAFFIC WENT SWISHING BY AS THE PAIR WALKED DOWN ESSEX

toward Delancey. For a while, neither of them spoke, each with her own gloomy thoughts, and then Karissa voiced the question that had been on her mind.

"Why is it dangerous for you to be around me?"

"It is a long story," replied her mother in her soft Russian accent, watching her daughter out of the corner of her eye. "I met your father when I was the age you are now. Cal arrested my friend for a crime, for, how do you say it, for a fraud, and I went to the police station and requested to meet with the officer who had made the arrest. He seemed to like me from the beginning and asked me to go out with him. I refused, but then he offered to talk to the police captain about my friend and I agreed to meet him for dinner. She was released from jail soon after."

"Was your friend innocent?" asked Karissa, having difficulty imagining her father allowing a guilty person to go free.

Irena shook her head, "I do not know. Cal said there wasn't enough evidence and I believed him."

Karissa thought for a moment. "Where did you go for dinner?" she asked, trying to picture the two of them sitting at a table, attempting to make conversation.

"Some diner on the Bowery," said Irena, waving a dismissive hand. "I thought it would be the last I saw of him, but he had other plans."

"What plans?"

"He pursued me relentlessly," said her mother with contempt. "He was always at the deli across from our home, approaching me when I walked past, asking me to spend time with him. He even had his police route changed to my neighborhood, so he could protect me and my family, he said." She scoffed. "Really, he wanted to watch me."

"That's awful," said Karissa, clenching her jaw as she imagined how it would feel to have her father as a stalker. "But how did you two," she faltered. "You know, how was I born?"

Her mother sniffed. "My family hated Cal," she said, "especially my father. After a while, he had had enough and went to the police to complain. We thought that might be the end of it, but Cal stopped him on the street the next day and demanded he withdraw his complaint." Her mother made a little growling noise deep in her throat. "He told my father that he had done some digging and learned that, while my father was here in America legally, my mother was not and neither were my brothers; neither was I." She shrugged her shoulders helplessly. "After that, I was forced to agree to do whatever he asked. We had no family in Russia, no prospects, and the situation was very dangerous for Roma people; what could I do?"

Karissa looked at her mother in horror, thinking of the terrible circumstances under which she must have been conceived.

Sighing heavily, her mother went on. "Cal tried his best to win over my family, helping around our home, drinking with my brothers, sitting with my father at the deli," she recalled, chuckling dryly. "He was persistent, I will give him that, and I think he truly wanted to be a part of our family, but he could never gain our trust. Eventually, he had had enough of our contempt and gave me an ultimatum: either we married and I came to live with him or he took you away from me. By that time, I was pregnant," she added, brushing the sleeve of Karissa's sweater with the tips of her fingers. "I couldn't believe that he would follow through on his threat to take you, so I said no."

Karissa looked over in time to see twin tears leak from the corners of Irena's eyes. "I told him I would rather have a mangy jackal for a husband. I am truly sorry," she said, looking at Karissa with a miserable expression. "I should have gone to live with him as he demanded, but some things," and she stopped, gazing steadily at her daughter, "some things cannot be unsaid."

Karissa reached out and grasped her mother's hands. "I'll come and visit you in secret," she said. "He doesn't need to know." Her mother looked at her sadly and shook her head. "But mom, I—"

"Your name should not be Karissa, you know," she said, suppressing any further protests from her daughter with a palliative squeeze of her fingers. "I wanted to call you by another name."

"What should my name have been?" asked Karissa, sadly.

"I wanted to call you—

"Irene!"

Karissa's blood froze. It was her father's voice, coming from the other side of the street. And there he was, sprinting across the road, dodging around a moving taxi, which honked, the driver yelling obscenities before speeding off. He was snorting with rage, his bullish eyes darting back and forth between the two women. Irena took several paces backward, her hands going to her mouth in fear and surprise.

He roared at her, "I told you that if I ever saw you again I would have you and your whole family deported! And I am nothing," he hissed, rapidly clenching and unclenching his hands, "if not a man of my word."

"It was an accident," squeaked Karissa, her words all coming in a rush. "We met on the street and I stopped her and forced her to talk to me."

He rounded on her. "Go home," he said, pointing down the block.

"It's not her fault!"

"Go home NOW!"

They were attracting some attention. Two concerned passersby stopped and looked as though they wanted say something, but Karissa's father forestalled them, flashing his badge and they scuttled away down the sidewalk. Another man crossed the street to avoid the altercation.

Irena was backing away down the sidewalk, a stricken look on her face. "I'm sorry," she said.

"Take me with you!" cried Karissa.

"I'm sorry," her mother said again and rushed off down the sidewalk, the heels of her shoes clicking away into the dusk.

"Come with me," her father said, grabbing her arm, his face a thunderhead.

"Where are we going?"

"Home, so you can pack your things."

"Where am I going?"

"I don't care where you go. You're not living with me anymore, that's all I know."

"Fine!" she screamed, ripping her arm free of his grasp. "I don't want to live with you anyway. I'll go and live with mom instead!"

He stopped short. "If you do that, I'll see that she's on the next plane back to the USSR and we'll let the Soviets have her."

"You couldn't," she said, pleadingly. "You wouldn't."

"Wouldn't I?" he asked, his eyes sparkling with malice. "Try me."


AFTER THAT DAY, IT WOULD BE YEARS BEFORE KARISSA SAW HER father again, and things would never be the same between them. Over time, she blamed herself for that. She hoped to see him when she graduated from the police academy, in 1985, or when she was inducted as a federal agent of the Immigration and Naturalization Service, the INS, in the spring of 1990, but he was at neither event.

Over the next decade, she never once saw her mother, being too afraid that visiting the woman would result in her deportation, along with Karissa's other relatives, whom she barely knew. And although her father's threat hung around like a spectre, and despite everything he had done, she found that she still craved his approval, such was the hold that he had over her. Such was the hold he would always have.

She gave up going on night runs for, unlike her father, she preferred to deliver justice solely from within the law. Sometimes, while she was on duty, she would run across her father's handiwork: a drug dealer beaten down and left in the gutter, an arsonist admitted to hospital after having been forced to swallow several of his own plastic lighters; these encounters elicited painful memories of when she had participated in similar acts of cruelty. And though on these occasions, she let her father's brutal acts of vigilantism go, perhaps out of a latent love for him, Karissa never forgot that one day her father would have to be brought down, because for her, their old agreement still stood: people who hurt others had to be hurt back. It was that simple.

II

## ❀ 7 ❀

## STRAY

From his perch atop the New York County Supreme Courthouse, Nigel Nakagawa peered out over the Five Points and into Chinatown beyond. He cut a vague silhouette, a compact, stocky figure against the iron sky, the twinkle of reflected light from the street catching a glint from the living metal covering his body. A stickiness clung to him, despite the cooling effect of the *Resident* and the moisture that ran from its surface like oil across a hot pan. He sighed, releasing the congealed air from his lungs. Clouds of mist rose silently from grates and vents on the shadowy pavement below. The June night was a black dog, panting steam into the muggy pre-dawn twilight.

In the three weeks since he had arrived in the city, Nigel had been frantically trying to find his bearings, while simultaneously attempting to watch over his new neighbourhood as Kintarō, the Golden Boy. His surroundings were at once familiar and intensely alien. New York City had transformed from the depictions he remembered from the panels of Aika's comic books into a brick and mortar leviathan, an urban Mecca on the eve of a new century and although he had lived in Tokyo for three years before arriving in New York, he felt completely overwhelmed by the place.

How was he supposed to protect these people if he didn't know them, couldn't understand their actions and, least of all, comprehend what motivated them to commit their crimes. Reading the paper, he was staggered by the sheer randomness of some of the brutal violence in the city and, with ubiquitous firearms, unfiltered mental illness and more than a little crack cocaine, Nigel never knew what was going to happen next. Maybe this was what his mother had meant about a civilization teetering on the brink.

Despite all of this, Nigel had yet to encounter any violence or crime, or at least he hadn't witnessed any crimes in progress, though there had been plenty of police sirens screaming in the night. Dressed as Kintarō, he had arrived late to scenes that police and other first responders were already addressing. In those situations, he had difficulty identifying what had happened: was it a carjacking gone wrong or merely a traffic accident? A heart attack or a fatal stabbing? He found that he could never say for sure.

He knew that he had been sent here for a reason. At this point, especially in Chinatown and in the surrounding area of Lower Manhattan, drug activity and gang violence had reached a crescendo. Nigel was shocked to learn that three years before, in 1990, 2245 people were murdered in the city, which constituted a murder rate more than seventy times that of Tokyo. Over the following two years, 1991 and 1992, the Crown Heights riots had happened, there was a double homicide shooting at Thomas Jefferson High School, a Cuban-born journalist was killed in a diner by the Cali drug cartel and a school principal in Brooklyn was caught in the crossfire of a drug-related incident and shot dead, while attempting to locate a wayward student. Meanwhile, a serial killer stalking victims based on their Zodiac signs was at large after a three-year killing and maiming spree, and a shocking and deadly terrorist attack had recently threatened the structural integrity of the North tower of the World Trade Centre when 1,500 pounds of explosives planted in a Ryder transport truck exploded, killing six people and injuring over a thousand others.

Nigel had been forced to memorize the facts and figures of those crimes in the latter days of his training in Japan. Now it was his duty to protect the innocent people of New York and turn the tide of wrongdoing so the city might enter the new millennium cleansed, as the cradle for future human civilization, or something like that. Nigel remembered the difficulty he'd had following his mother during one of her passionate lectures about the importance of keeping people safe. Basically, crime was bad and he was supposed to give it a righteous punch to the face, though Nigel, who had been flooded with reluctance and anxiety since his arrival, felt very little desire to do this.

The truth was that he was afraid, afraid because he had been told that the lives of others depended on him, afraid because of the pressure to succeed and of the possibility of failing his parents and community, and afraid for himself, because although he was fairly certain that he was invulnerable to most forms of burning, cutting, piercing, falling and crushing, he wasn't sure how well his suit, made of extruded *Resident*, really would protect him in the event of a major trauma to his person. In fact, he wasn't sure just how much it was protecting, rather than harming him already, for recently he had begun to experience intense headaches, like miniature firestorms in his head and a sensation of dizziness, both new to him. He had at first written these episodes off to stress but now wasn't so sure. He remembered the blackened bones of the previous host to the *Resident,* hanging in the old smokehouse in his village and shivered, despite the heat.

Nigel caught sight of the Jacob K. Javits Federal Building looming off to the right. He knew the forty-one-story giant well already. It housed the INS, whose gruff agents he had encountered at his port of entry. He had been to its offices twice already to complete the paperwork required for his student visa application, which was proving surprisingly difficult to obtain.

The night was quiet and the dawn had almost come. Another night without so much as a vandal crossing his path. Glancing down, he saw a small flicker of movement as a stray neighborhood cat slunk behind a garbage can at the edge of Columbus Park. Nigel sympathized with the creature, feeling far from home himself. He sighed and hopped down from his perch onto the ledge below, which ran uninterrupted along the entire rooftop perimeter of the hexagonal courthouse structure. Breaking into a jog, he turned the corner and loped along the ledge away from his perch. Dressed as he was, he wished to avoid prying eyes. To return to his apartment in Chinatown via the rooftops, he was required to avoid the park, which presented a barrier between the courthouse and the tenement buildings beyond.

As he came to the point on the ledge closest to Worth Street, he carefully gauged the distance across to the building opposite. With three powerful strides, he launched himself out over the street, the night air blowing hot in his face as he sailed over two lanes of traffic and the tree-lined sidewalk beyond. He landed with an almighty *CRUNCH*, peeling back several layers of heat-treated tar paper from the roof's surface, exposing the rubber membrane beneath. There were several other skid marks around where he had landed on previous nights. Wrinkling his forehead, he wondered if he should change his route, feeling guilty about the damage he'd caused.

Pushing down the guilt, he was up again, running with ground-eating strides. He catapulted himself over the forty-foot gap where the building's inner courtyard lay, then rolled in a summersault as he landed on the other side. He ended in a crouch and paused, listening. Only the whirring of the rooftop fans was audible. Looking cautiously around him and then up at the cluster of enormous buildings ahead, he glanced down at the street sign on the corner: 'Baxter St. and Hogan Pl.' Ahead was the office block that housed the New York County District Attorney.

He swallowed, choosing a point approximately ten stories from the ground, on the side of the nearest building in the cluster. He knew that the purchase there would be scant but there were ledges beneath the windows, about six inches deep and made of solid granite, which he could grasp. The last time he had attempted the jump, he had torn off not one but two air conditioning units. He silently vowed to do better tonight.

Like a bullfrog, he leaped upward from his squatting position across Hogan Place, the pavement a grey blur beneath him and collided with the building, banging his face against one of the windows. Dazed, he almost fell backward but caught himself with his fingers on stone. He paused, shook his head and began to toss himself up the building, ledge to ledge, using the strength of his arms.

He reached the top and, with a soft groan, hoisted himself up into a crouch on the building's lower tier, about a hundred and thirty feet from the ground. He paused for a moment to catch his breath. It really wasn't much effort for him, he reflected, about the same energy he imagined a normal person might expend jogging up a few flights of stairs.

On he went, hopping to a higher rooftop and, running a few steps, he performed one handspring then another and then, using his momentum, he flipped up and onto a tier still higher, transitioning into a dead sprint.

Leaping into space, he landed on the rooftop below with a *thump*, immediately jumping across the alley to the adjacent building. The top was caged in chain-link and the metal shrieked as he landed. He turned ninety degrees, ran thirty more feet and sprang off the cage as if from a trampoline, diving headlong toward the nearest Chinatown tenement with the form of an Olympic diver.

It was an eighty foot drop and, he remembered, the trick would be stopping himself before he careened off the side of the building below *and, please, oh please, without destroying anything.* He turned his body in the air so his feet faced the ground, which rushed up to meet him, and he tucked his knees into his chest and spread his arms wide like a falcon swooping in for a landing.

Wheeling his arms in the air, semi-uselessly, he struck the roof with a *crack* that jarred his teeth and then he was tumbling over and over, limbs flailing, tearing off first one television antenna then another, now becoming tangled with a set of lawn furniture, which he carried with him as he spun helplessly, suddenly approaching the edge of the building, having to lunge for the drain gutter and ripping it almost fully off, the lawn furniture clattering onto the empty sidewalk below.

Hanging precariously, Nigel was forced to climb the mangled length of corrugated metal, further detaching it from the building. After his feet were on the solid ground of the roof, he spent a few frantic moments attempting to manipulate the gutter back into its original shape but it sagged miserably, clearly broken, noticeable even from the street.

Nigel froze. Half way down the block, on the corner of Bayard and Mulberry, stood three people; two men and a woman, who didn't seem to have noticed him, despite the commotion he had caused. The reason for this appeared to be the argument they were having. Nigel hopped somewhat stealthily to the next rooftop on Bayard and belly-crawled over to the edge, overlooking the trio's corner so he could hear and see better.

"I told you, we're closed," spat the woman, dressed in leather pants and an unseasonable fur coat, "and I don't do two-fers."

"Baby, we're not here for the sex, we're here for the drugs," said the man nearest. He looked about twenty-five but then again, Nigel could never guess the age of white people with any accuracy.

"Do I look like a fucking drug dealer?" the woman asked reproachfully.

The man muttered something to his compatriot, who was holding a whisky bottle and grinning.

The woman interrupted them, "If you're not gone in five seconds, I'm going to call Lin Little."

"Chicken little? Look princess, you're not making any sense, just give us the rocks and there won't be any trouble."

This was his chance, Nigel realized. He tensed all the muscles in his legs, feeling the considerable strength there, his sinew reverberating with pent-up energy. He was about to leap from the roof but was halted by a lung-shredding screech from the woman.

"Little!!"

A moment later, an enormous Chinese man burst through the cage door of the entrance to the closed and shuttered Chinese restaurant behind her.

"I WAS ASLEEP!" He bellowed, waking, Nigel imagined, every sleeping person within a five-block radius.

Lin Little stood taller than seven feet and had to stoop to pass under the lintel. He was carrying two double barreled shotguns, one in each hand, propped under the crooks of his elbows and he pointed them at the men.

After a moment of hesitation, Nigel was off, sailing over the last rooftop and landing in a tangle on the pavement about a hundred strides from the little circle of people. Nobody heard him over the sustained bellowing of the man with the guns and Nigel was forced to sprint over to them, yelling at the top of his voice.

"Stop!" he shouted. "Stop!"

He closed the distance rapidly and the group fell silent, regarding him in his metallic outfit made of shifting otherworldly material. He felt a bit self-conscious at the contrast between his magnificent suit and the black Zorro mask he wore, which he had purchased from a costume shop to disguise his identity. For some reason, the *Resident* didn't cover his face, for which he was normally more than grateful, but in that moment, he wondered, absurdly, if he looked comical to these people.

"Nice outfit," the woman said without much enthusiasm.

"Real nice," said the man with the bottle.

There was a silence.

Nigel cleared his throat. "I am Kintarō the Golden— Ooof!" he said, as Lin Little took a great stride toward him and struck him with the butt of one of the shotguns in the solar plexus. Nigel recovered almost instantly and thrust up his hands to grip the barrels of the guns, sharply bending them at right angles. Lin Little stared at the mangled shotguns and retreated a few paces toward the door he had come through. "As I was saying, I am—"

"YAAAAAAA," Lin Little screamed.

He had produced a machine pistol from somewhere and everything seemed to happen at once. Lin Little began firing the pistol, which was extremely noisy, point blank at Nigel's center mass. Nigel doubled up in pain and bullets ricocheted off his suit, hitting parked cars and building walls, smashing windows, pinging off lamp standards and, unfortunately, passing through the bodies of several of those present. One caught the man Nigel had heard speak first in the thigh, his scream drowned in the bedlam, one struck the woman in the upper chest near her shoulder and she fell backward. And the last stray bullet passed through the other man's bottle, shattering it and, ricocheting off the pavement, it entered Lin Little's forehead. He was dead before he hit the ground, landing with a massive thump that seemed to echo in the relative silence after the pistol had stopped firing.

Nigel was horror-struck. He had just made a colossal mess of his first attempt at protecting someone. Not only had he failed to prevent the crazy giant from shooting people, he had made the situation far worse with his suit. Now everyone was down, except the man with the bottle. He gaped at Nigel, terrified, then sprinted off, still tightly gripping the broken bottle neck in his fist.

"Help me," begged the woman on the pavement and the man who'd been shot in the leg moaned softly.

Instead of helping them, Nigel turned and ran in the opposite direction. Sirens keened on the still air, which seemed almost too thick to breathe as he ran. He sprinted up Bayard street and took the first left on Mott in the direction of his nearby apartment. He cringed and let out a whimper as the sound of more sirens and the distinctive *whop, whop, whop* of a police chopper filled the air.

Hurling himself up the fire escape, he yanked open his apartment window, which was ajar, and threw himself inside, tumbling onto the sofa. He lay there sobbing, the tears running down his chin and bouncing off the metal of his suit. Ripping off his mask, he tossed it into the corner and, as if on cue, his suit began to disintegrate, becoming liquid and sliding away like body paint under a hose. The liquid became a dark stain on the tan upholstery of the brand-new couch but he hardly noticed, descending into a spiral of rumination that would keep him awake until the bright, uneasy dawn came.

## 8

# FLOOD TIDE

T he feeling of melancholy stayed with Nigel throughout the sunny, breezy day after, like a bad smell. He tossed and turned on the *Resident*-stained couch in his still unfamiliar apartment, trying in vain to doze, while the hubbub of Chinatown filtered in through the blinds. It was too noisy to sleep and too hot to close the window. Shifting fitfully, he was plagued by thoughts of the previous night, and although the memory of the shooting was by far the most distressing, he found himself fretting about the property he had damaged on the rooftops too. Today there would be no escape from the thoughts of self-recrimination that thundered in his head.

In the late afternoon, the weather changed. The wind picked up and cool gusts rattled the metal blinds and froze Nigel where he lay. He found a blanket and slid the window closed with a soft squeal. Lying back on the couch, he attempted to make himself comfortable, which proved impossible. He checked the clock: 3:30 p.m. He was famished, having neglected to eat since the previous afternoon but the last thing he felt like doing was eating, especially from the greasy takeaway places dotting the surrounding streets like carbuncles. He realized that he hated this couch and this room and understood he couldn't stay there any longer that day.

Nigel found himself on the subway with the vague desire to be near the ocean. He had travelled to the sea on the northwest coast of Japan with his parents as a boy, one of the few getaways they had taken from the village, and he had made trips to the beaches of Tokyo Bay on the metro during the three years he had lived and trained in Tokyo, before coming to New York. Something about the ocean's dark depths calmed his mind and he liked to imagine his worries flowing into it, being folded away beneath the waves.

He took the subway from Canal Street station to Fulton Street station, changed trains and sat restlessly through fourteen stops as he crossed Brooklyn in the direction of JFK Airport. He changed a third and final time at Broad Channel, located on a sliver of an island south of the airport, and got off at 'Rockaway Park - Beach 116 St.'

Once outside, he could see the shoreline at the end of the block, the sand only a short walk away, but he hesitated, uncertain if this was the place where he truly wanted to be. He had heard Brighton Beach and Coney Island were more popular but, for him, one beach was probably as good as another, and besides, the presence of fewer people fit his mood. The smell of the sea tickled his nostrils as he began to walk.

Wind buffeted Nigel as he made his way southwest along the seaside boardwalk, following the beach at Rockaway Park. He stopped to read a brass plaque, embedded in a cairn of mortar and stone, informing the passing reader about the area.

*Rockaway Peninsula has long been a haven for local and migratory shore-birds. In spring, Canadian and Brant Geese nest in the dunes west of 169$^{th}$ Street and compete for food and shelter with other species of waterfowl, which migrate from the Southern United States.*

Accompanying the text was an artistic rendering of each bird, with its Latin name. The plaque continued:

*The name 'Rockaway' is from the Canarsie word 'Reckouwacky,' meaning 'place of our own people.' Canarsie was one of 10,000 local Indian dialects that predated the arrival of the first American settlers.*

*During the War of 1812, Rockaway Peninsula housed battlements with canons, erected to defend the people of New York from British attack, though no such force ever made landing here.*

Nigel stared out at the Atlantic, a thin, seemingly infinite strip of water on the horizon and he imagined the soldiers posted at their fortifications, straining their eyes, looking out to sea for any sign of the enemy. *They watched in vain*, he thought.

He ambled down the boardwalk, his hands thrust in his pockets, away from the biting wind. Perhaps there is no enemy, he thought. Perhaps there are only people who, thinking they are right, step on the toes of others, or perhaps on more than their toes. And because they overstep they must be stopped, but not because they are evil, he decided, only because they have done wrong and an example must be made. The question was, stopped by whom? *The burden falls on me*, he reminded himself. But he was less and less certain that this was true and, even if it was true, he still longed for an alternative. Today especially, he would rather have been anyone else.

Ahead of him the sun was sinking on the horizon but he shuffled on, heedless of the gathering dark. He stopped briefly at a hotdog stand on the end of the boardwalk at 126th Street, buying the last hotdog of the day and, after he paid, the vendor closed, chaining his cart to a nearby railing for the night. Nigel chewed the American fare methodically, in the lee of a low concrete wall, sitting on a small mound of sand that had collected there. It tasted good but he barely registered the effect of the food on his body.

After a little while and without giving much thought to the time, Nigel headed onto the deserted beach, taking off his shoes and feeling his feet sink into the cool sand as he went. The wind began to die as the sun sank lower but considerable six-foot breakers continued to crash upon the shore. The sound beat at the core of him, like the noise of a great door knocker. *Let us in. Let us in.*

He passed the residential neighborhood of Belle Harbour, which he had seen on a map, and the flat expanse of Jacob Riis Park and the Marine Parkway Bridge beyond. He passed the golf course and the baseball fields at Fort Tilden and, as he wandered by, he gazed at the brown dunes that fringed the military base there, covered with scrub grass and low wind-weathered bushes. Finally, when he had made it beyond the Silver Gull Beach Club, he settled himself in the curve of a sand dune at the suburban foot of Breezy Point. There he lay, looking up at the stars as they appeared one by one in the sky. And, though he was somewhat chilly, he nevertheless felt comfortable and continued to lie and stare upward. As full darkness descended, his eyes fluttered closed and he fell asleep, truly a long way from home.

Nigel dreamed he was adrift on a lake surrounded by a sandy desert. The water around his rickety boat was evaporating in the harsh sun and the lake shrank in volume until it was no larger than a duck pond. In the dream, Nigel frantically pawed at the water, trying to scoop it into his mouth, for he was terribly thirsty but he couldn't seem to swallow fast enough before the water was gone and then it was sand he was shovelling into his mouth. He retched and spat, trying to expel the sand, which was drying up his insides.

Then he was awake and grabbing fistfuls of the frigid sand around him on the beach. He dropped the sand and, his hands shaking slightly, he checked the illuminated display of his digital watch. It was almost a quarter to two in the morning. He looked around him, disoriented.

Fog had materialized, muting the yellow light from the houses and street lamps of Breezy Point. Nigel swivelled his head around and looked out to sea where he saw a foggy blackness, and something else. A single point of green light bobbed in the gloom. At first, he thought it was a beacon far out at sea, but then he realized the light was much closer to shore. His eyes widened as he discerned the faint silhouette of a ship, which looked to have run aground and was precariously listing, several hundred yards from the beach. Huge breakers were crashing around it, causing the ship to shift and tilt. Nigel heard voices coming from behind him and he whipped his head around, suddenly staring into the blinding light of a flashlight. There was a young police officer at the other end of the beam, standing next to another officer, whose legs and shoes were also visible.

"Sir, the beach is closed," the young officer said firmly. "I'm going to need you to get up and move along."

Nigel stared at him for a moment, then wordlessly pointed out at the shadow-cloaked ship, looming off to his left.

"What's he pointing at?" the other officer asked, shining his own light out to sea.

It was then that they heard the first screams, panicked voices amid the sound of the pounding surf. The police officer's flashlight illuminated four heads bobbing together, caught in the swells just off shore. Nigel leapt to his feet and, both emitting wordless cries, the officers took off running toward the water. After a few moments, they ran back again, past Nigel, leaping up the dunes toward their vehicle, yelling about a life-preserver and a radio.

Nigel paused. The sea was dark again without the presence of the flashlight, but he could still hear the desperate wailing of the people in the water. Here was his chance, he realized, to save lives. But, to his dismay, he discovered that his urge was to run away from the water, rather than toward it, for though he liked the sea, he harbored an acute fear of animals of the deep, including sharks. He fought to suppress his fear and considered his chances of survival. These people were in very real danger, there was no doubt, and so might he be if he swam out to them. There was the *Resident* inside him of course, and he was reasonably sure that it would protect him from the cold of the sea and give him the strength to swim against the waves, even with people in tow.

He considered pushing the *Resident* material out the pores of his skin to form the suit but he dismissed the idea. Doing so would reveal his identity to the officers who were now bounding back down the sandy slope and he would lose precious moments. The men ran by him again and, without hesitation, both charged into the ocean, fully clothed. Nigel closed his eyes, hearing the shouting and splashing and, with a hiss of breath, he took off running.

The water was cold, about ten degrees Celsius, or fifty degrees Fahrenheit; he easily converted the units in his head as he swam, which was a good thing. It meant he wasn't panicking. He felt the cold but it wasn't as biting as it would be for the others in the water. He reached the cluster of people in a few strong strokes, having passed the police who were in up to their chests and tossing the life ring, which kept falling short.

The people in the water were men. One was clothed in what looked like a full business suit and the rest were shirtless. They were slapping at the surface, flailing wildly with their arms and calling out in what sounded like a Chinese dialect. Nigel knew the sound of the language from Chinatown but did not know how to communicate with the men.

"Hold on to me," Nigel called, hoping they spoke some English.

Regardless, two of the men paddled over to him, scrabbling at his arms, chest and neck, weighing him down. He managed to keep his head above water with the men attached to him but was nevertheless gripped by a claustrophobic feeling that caused him to gasp.

"Over here!"

He could hear one of the officers calling over the sound of the waves and the desperate grunting of the Chinese men. He focused on the sound and kicked his legs powerfully. A moment later he heard a splash. The life ring had landed next to his face. He pried the fingers of one of the men from his arm and guided the man's hands over to it. Once the man had a hold of the ring, he was yanked away by the officer at the other end. Eventually the ring was tossed back and Nigel guided another man to it and then another.

When the last man was safely on the beach, they all took a moment to catch their breath, Nigel feeling proud of the part he had played in the rescue.

"You're quite the swimmer," said the officer who had first approached him with the flashlight.

His partner grinned as he helped one of the men wrap an emergency blanket around his shoulders. "You can say that again. But next time stay out of the water, okay? It's too dangerous and there might be more of these guys."

As if to prove his point, more gut-wrenching screams issued from out to sea.

"Jesus Christ," the officer said, "see what I mean?"

The other policeman grabbed the radio he'd left in the sand and shouted into it: "We've got a large number of people in the water. Alert the coast guard in addition to backup request."

"Already done," came the crackling reply. "There's a ship run aground right?"

"Affirmative."

"Coast guard is en route."

The officer stood holding the radio for a moment, chewing his lip.

"And notify immigration," he said. "These folks don't look like Americans."

For Nigel, the next forty-five minutes was like something out of a nightmare, as dozens of people, in various states of distress and disarray, washed ashore with the incoming tide. Some of these were either lucky, having caught the right current, or were stronger swimmers than the first four men. Some hit the beach running, dodging this way and that to evade capture. Three more police officers and a coast guard apprentice had arrived and were busy tackling the livelier of the new arrivals to the sand.

Nigel, disturbed by the contrast between the effort to save some people from drowning and violently subduing others, decided his talents could be put to better use at sea and resumed towing in the people who were jumping from the ship in droves.

Many of the ship's passengers were not strong swimmers and were in desperate need of rescue – men, and now women and children. Several times Nigel swam toward the sound of cries in the foamy water, only to find that the people who had made the noises had disappeared, swept into the fog by a current or swallowed by the waves. Every time Nigel missed someone in the gloom he felt sick with guilt.

He returned to shore to take a short break and watched as one man landed on the beach next to him. The man looked around quickly, stripped off his wet clothes and removed dry ones from a plastic bag tied around his ankle. Then he disappeared into the residential streets of Breezy Point without uttering a word. The police, busy shepherding their growing flock, failed to notice him go.

More police were arriving and Nigel heard a helicopter approaching the immobile ship. A power boat shot by as well, with a large spotlight on the front, illuminating the heads of dozens more people in the water. Nigel leaped up and was about to dive back in when he was struck from behind by the body of a massive policeman.

The next thing Nigel knew, he was spitting out sand and squawking in protest while handcuffs were slapped on his wrists. The officer must have mistaken him for one of the Chinese men, but there were a few key differences between him and them. He was clearly in a better state of health, being neither emaciated nor exhibiting a distended belly, he was not vomiting seawater, his clothes were in better shape and he had been trying to enter the water, rather than attempting to leave it, all aside from the fact that he was Japanese. The man should have happily let him go. Nigel knew he could have broken free of the cuffs with little effort but was held just as firmly by the desire to keep from revealing himself as the super-powered person he was.

"Take these off," he demanded. "I'm not with them. I'm trying to help save lives." The use of English should trigger the officer to release him at least, although he did speak with a slight Japanese accent. The officer hauled Nigel to his feet and began walking him over to a huddle of passengers, some wearing handcuffs, presided over by another uniformed officer.

The officer leading him chuckled dryly and said, "The only reason you're on this beach tonight, soaking wet, is because you came off that ship."

"Ask the officer over there," said Nigel, jerking his head toward one of those he had first encountered. "He found me sleeping in a sand dune more than an hour ago."

"Just sit tight," said the burly policeman, "and we'll sort it all out once everyone is safe." Depositing Nigel on the sand beside the passengers, he turned and hurried away. And just like that, Nigel was out of the rescue effort. He sighed, listening to the crackling radio calls about the *Golden Venture*, the ship that had run aground with its human cargo. It seemed as though it would be a very long night.

# 🌼 9 🌼

# THE PROBLEM WITH LOGIC

Karissa had only been asleep for an hour when her pager began vibrating. It rattled on her night table and toppled off, continuing its buzzing on the wooden floorboards of her apartment bedroom in Tribeca. She switched on her lamp and groped around for the device, found it and checked the number on the display. It was an emergency of some kind, which was unusual in her line of work at the INS. Day in, day out she was buried up to her eyeballs in paperwork and sometimes she even forgot she had the pager. A smile played on her lips as she dialed the number from the tiny screen; this was probably something worth her while. The phone rang and rang in the receiver and finally someone picked up.

"Dispatch. Can you hold please?"

Karissa's eyebrows rose in surprise. "Yes, I'll hold." Very unusual indeed.

After a while the dispatcher returned. "Thanks for holding." The man's voice sounded strained.

"Uh huh, what's going on?"

"A ship full of illegal aliens beached itself off Rockaway Peninsula in Queens at zero one hundred forty-five. A rescue and detain operation is underway, with first responders and coast guard already on site."

Karissa's mind was reeling. This was happening now, all the way over in Queens. What would be the fastest way for her to get there, she wondered?

"Have the coast guard choppers gone out yet?" Karissa asked, unsuccessfully attempting to gather her badge and gun from the night table, while simultaneously trying to slide her head through the neck of a t-shirt.

"They're just about to leave."

Karissa felt a sense of relief. She was friends with a coast guard captain who led most helicopter search and rescue operations in and around the Five Boroughs.

"Perfect, can you tell Buck Williams to pick me up from the helipad on top of the Javits building in," and she checked her watch, "ten minutes?"

"I wouldn't know how to reach him, I—"

"Just call the heliport and ask for him," said Karissa through gritted teeth. "He'll want me riding with him on this one."

After a moment of hesitation, the dispatcher agreed and hung up and Karissa scrambled to ready herself. Ten minutes would be pushing it and she didn't want to be late, not to this party.

Nine minutes later, she was hurtling through the foggy night sky in a US Coast Guard Dolphin helicopter, speaking with Buck through her headset. Buck was solid gold and a professional to boot and, like her, helping fellow human beings would be his top priority once they reached their destination, rather than detaining people. She wondered why the district director would have given the order to detain the aliens at all, when the usual INS protocol was to question, process and release, pending a court date. She thought that he must be seizing the opportunity to enact the new, stricter protocol that he had been vocally promoting for years, but which had fallen on deaf ears in Washington, so far.

The fog was clearing as Buck banked the helicopter right and the scene came into startling detail. The beach was swarming with people and still more were in the ocean, their heads dots in the surf. Buck hit the spotlight and revealed the hulking mass of a ship, jammed onto a sandbar several hundred yards offshore. The propeller was still spinning.

As the helicopter worked its way around the side of the ship, Karissa made out the name, hastily stenciled on the rusting prow – the *Golden Venture*. The spotlight swept the deck of the ship where clusters of people were huddled, their hair and clothes whipped by the rotor wash. Some were emerging from the deeper recesses of the ship. A few of these people took one look at the helicopter and jumped over the side.

Karissa reached over and hit the switch for the loudspeaker. She pressed the button on the handset and her voice boomed out: "DO NOT JUMP." She saw a man, clutching his clothes tight to his chest, leap over the other side and out of sight. "STAY ON BOARD." It was doing no good.

"These guys probably don't speak English," Buck pointed out.

"Can you get in a little closer?" she asked him.

Buck looked skeptical but dutifully brought the helicopter in about seventy feet closer to the ship. She tried waving her arms and making halting motions with her hands but nobody was paying her any attention. People were too busy fleeing the high-velocity wind coming from the rotor blades to take heed. Buck flew the chopper up and away from the vessel a few hundred feet and Karissa saw that three coast guard boats had approached the ship but were having difficulty maneuvering in close, due to the relentless surf. A 22-foot Boston Whaler succeeded in coming alongside the *Golden Venture* and the crew were now attempting to coax passengers to jump into the boat rather than into the ocean. Her breath caught as a mammoth wave descended on the Boston Whaler and the smaller boat was tossed like a toy in a bathtub, capsizing in an instant and throwing the three crew members into the water.

Buck was on the radio immediately. "The twenty-two just flipped over," he barked. "We need a visual on our guys." Using the spotlight, Buck swept the sea for his men but was temporarily distracted by the appearance of a second coast guard helicopter (a larger JH-60 Jayhawk) and two police helicopters, which arrived on the scene in quick succession. Buck clicked his tongue in frustration. "Keep an eye out for the crew in the water," he said to Karissa, "I have to alert the airport in case these choppers are on a flightpath." He grabbed for the radio again, transmitting a message about the location of the rescue operation to air traffic control at JFK and requesting that flights be diverted from the area.

Karissa saw rescue swimmers drop from the other coast guard helicopter and plunge into the water, trying to locate the crew from the Boston Whaler, she guessed. As she watched, they loaded an unconscious man into a cage attached to the helicopter by a steel cable.

"We got one crew member," one of the swimmers radioed from his helmet headset. "He has a head wound and requires an ambulance." The injured man was taken into the other helicopter and it circled back to the beach to drop him off with some of the paramedics who were now swarming the area. Karissa counted over fifty ambulances parked on roads and side streets up and down the peninsula.

"Got another crew member here," came another call, "swam himself to the beach."

There was still no sign of the third crew member. The rescue helicopter took off again and joined Buck and Karissa's chopper near the *Golden Venture* and, once again, the rescue swimmers dropped down into the angry sea to look for the third man.

Another call came through. "Two of the ship's passengers here on the beach just went into cardiac arrest. These guys need to get to the hospital fast. Requesting air evac."

Buck grabbed the radio transmitter. "I'm inbound." He turned to Karissa. "I'm going to drop you off on the beach so I can take those two to the hospital."

"Absolutely," said Karissa. "Hell of a job as usual, Buck."

"Thanks. But no way is this usual."

Standing on the beach, covering her ears against the roar of the helicopter, Karissa watched as the two Chinese men were loaded inside. It was her first time seeing them up close and they were a pitiful sight. Clad only in white cotton underpants, their limbs were spindly and their bodies gaunt, ribs jutting like shovels under the woolen blankets that had been hastily tucked around them, their skin sickly and translucent. It looked like they hadn't eaten proper food or stood in daylight for a very long time. She thought that with no fat on their bodies, their blood vessels must have constricted when they hit the water, causing their hearts to stop.

The door slid closed and she jogged away, covering her face with her arm as the helicopter took off, sand flying in every direction. She turned and watched as the Dolphin made a beeline for the hospital on mainland Queens and then she walked off down the beach, flashing her badge at a few cops who were corralling a group of shivering *Golden Venture* passengers draped in metallic emergency blankets. She could smell the passengers' fetid breath, which was shocking, given that she was six or more feet away.

Karissa seethed at the cruelty of the smugglers and at the injustice of it all. Most of these people would not have embarked on such a dangerous journey if the alternative had been better where they came from. How was it that she could live in the same world as they did and never be forced to contemplate making such a journey herself? She found she could not simply chalk this up to luck and have done with it, not being so close to these people.

Tonight would be a turning point for her, she realized, because even though human smuggling was her assignment at the INS, she hadn't encountered very many of the true victims of the industry and she had inadvertently allowed herself to stop caring. But here they were in front of her, huddled masses receiving a welcome far from the one advocated in *The New Colossus*, the famous poem by Emma Lazarus that Karissa had been forced to recite in high school.

It seemed to her that America's immigration problems were the same as they had been back in Emma Lazarus' day. There were still plenty of storms to weather in the world and, in 1993, the sentiment in the US was to shelter only the very few. To justify this practice, the people on the beach would be maligned and dehumanized. In the press, the passengers would be portrayed as criminals which, under current immigration law, they were. Most of them would probably claim asylum, some legitimately fleeing political persecution and starvation conditions in China but few, if any, would be granted visas. The others would be placed on the first boat back and would face an extremely angry government upon their return. The debacle might even serve to undermine existing refugee policies in the US and it might become even harder for people to claim asylum. Maybe asylum would no longer be offered. It was hard to say.

At first, as Karissa considered the implications, she felt irate. Tonight, the score had jumped tenfold in favor of evil; this was how she saw it, and the thought made her want to punch someone, a familiar and reassuring desire for her. But as she mulled the problem over in her mind, she began to experience a creeping sense of paralysis, steadily sapping the power that always accompanied her anger.

On some level, she understood that the event here tonight was at the centre of a very complicated and interconnected web of cause and effect, with globalism, immigration politics, greed and the baffling, utterly mixed reception given to human suffering, all influencing the proceedings. A part of her knew all of this and it was that part that rebelled at the idea of simply reducing the problem to good and evil, for that was not the whole story. But the other part, the angry, defensive part, fought back. It saw the complexity as the source of her paralysis. Because the situation was grey, with so many layers and no perfect person to blame, it would be extremely difficult to act in a righteous fashion, impossible perhaps. *I am a doer*, this part of her seemed to say, and it demanded that she act, for in the absence of action, the world was truly a terrifying place.

So, the angry part of her beat back the thoughtful part, whose arguments were only half-formed, and the thoughtful part hid away inside her and she breathed a deep sigh of relief. This internal struggle happened all in a moment and in that moment, she decided to put the responsibility for the *Golden Venture* disaster entirely on the smugglers, who at least were flesh and blood.

She gritted her teeth and scanned the faces of the bewildered boat people nearby, looking for crew members, hypothesizing that the smugglers would probably be better clothed and better fed than their customers. If she could interrogate one of them then maybe she could find out who was behind all of this and then he would become her target.

She spotted a young Asian man sitting with a group of survivors nearby. He stood out to her right away. His clothes were new and not ragged and he was stocky, well-fed and might not be Chinese. She knew that many smugglers of Chinese nationals were Thai and Malaysian, but she didn't think that this youth was from either country. He couldn't be Japanese, could he? She approached and caught his eye. He looked angry and it seemed to her that he was straining at the handcuffs behind his back. *Bingo*. After flashing her badge to the cop standing watch, she crouched down beside the young man.

"Do you speak English?" she asked.

"Yes."

"Out for a late-night dip I take it? It's clear you're not like the others." She realized that she had clenched her right hand into a fist. He noticed this too and his eyes narrowed a fraction.

"Is it my calm disposition or is it the fact that I'm Japanese?"

So, he was Japanese, and not what she had expected of a human smuggler. There was even a remote chance that he wasn't one but he was certainly out of place. She thought she'd try to rile him up a bit and see if she could shake some facts loose: "How long have you been in the human smuggling trade? Not long I'd guess, by your age. What are you, fourteen, fifteen?"

"I'm eighteen. And I'm no smuggler."

"What are you then?"

"A good Samaritan."

"Cute. Look, I'm going to take you to our holding centre and my partner and I will have good long go at you tonight before you can find yourself a lawyer, unless you can tell me something to change my mind." Karissa looked around for her partner, Benny Wu, who she thought should be arriving any minute.

"I'll tell you what I already told *him*." The Japanese man jerked his head at the cop standing to his left. "I was walking on the beach and I fell asleep. When I woke up there were people in the water. I swam out with two officers and saved several from drowning. But I was mistaken for a passenger and they put me in these handcuffs."

"Where are the two officers you were with?"

He craned his neck, looking around. "I haven't seen them recently."

"Right," she said and, hooking an arm through the crook of his elbow, she stood him up and frog marched him up the beach toward the waiting emergency vehicles. "Let's see if we can find them, shall we?" Partly she wanted an excuse to bring him over to the waiting police cruisers, so she could take him away without a fuss, and partly she needed to leave the beach and its cowering people behind her. She wasn't sure if she bought his story about rescuing people with the police but it would be easy to prove or disprove; either he was bad at inventing alibis or he was telling the truth. They walked in silence for a hundred yards or so and then he spoke.

"What will happen to these people?"

She glanced at him sideways. "What do you care?"

"I care. I told you, I'm no smuggler."

She sighed. "After a visit to the hospital, these people will be detained and then most will be sent home."

"Without due process? These people are clearly refugees."

"There will be legal proceedings, certainly. A judge will ultimately decide what to do with them." She sniffed. The reek of rotting kelp was palpable. "And maybe some of them *are* refugees," she said, "but some of them are likely to be economic migrants and my guess is that if it's difficult for the judge to tell which are which, then the lot of them will be sent packing."

"Economic migrants. Are there any other kind?" he asked.

Karissa raised her eyebrows at him. He seemed also to be asking, '*What's wrong with that?*' And he had a fair point.

"People think that foreigners are taking their jobs," she said, embarrassed by the fact.

"We'd do it anyway," he said, "whether we're here in the US or not. It's called the global supply chain. What are you anyway, police?"

She flashed her INS badge at him.

"Ah, I've encountered your colleagues a few times now, INS gate-keepers."

"We uphold the law. The gatekeepers are the American people." She was becoming more and more bothered by his accusatory tone. "What's your business in the US?" she demanded.

"I'll be attending Tammany College in September."

"What are you doing here so early?"

"That's just what your suspicious colleagues asked me," he replied.

"Listen you little punk, I'm the one who gets to decide whether I believe your story. Having a student visa is not going to save you if I decide you're a human smuggler, so you better think about curbing that sarcasm."

"You'll have to excuse me," he said, undeterred, "the sarcasm is the effect of being tackled, restrained and falsely accused of human smuggling." He glared at her.

She had opened her mouth to deliver a retort, when Karissa heard her name shouted from behind them. She turned and spotted Benny standing with a handful of uniformed police some fifty yards away. He motioned for her to come and join them.

"Sit tight," she said, and roughly sat the young Japanese man down in a dune. He sprawled in an undignified way, toppling briefly onto his side before jerkily righting himself, staring daggers at her all the while. She turned her back on him and strolled over to Benny and the cops.

Karissa liked Benny and relied on his sardonic wit to help her through the day at the INS, though she had begun to suspect that lately the feeling might not be as mutual as she had once supposed.

"Three washed up dead so far," one of the cops was saying.

"Three dead?" Karissa asked as she approached, a sinking sensation in her guts.

"Sounds like," said Benny, who was calmly smoking a cigarette. "Just on the beach though. Word came through that the two from the chopper medevac were dead on arrival."

"Where are the survivors being taken?" she asked.

"About thirty or so went to hospitals in Queens and Brooklyn. And those who aren't hypothermic or injured are headed to 201 Varick," Benny replied.

Karissa thought about that for moment. "The holding centre only has 225 beds. Will there be enough room?"

"It's going to be tight," said Benny.

"Lots of room for 'em in Kings County Jail," said a uniformed cop from the Sheriff's Office in Brooklyn.

"I think we'll hold off on jail for now," replied Karissa.

"Plenty of jail to go around later," agreed Benny. "Picked a favorite?" he asked, nodding over in the direction of the Japanese man seated in the sand.

"Might be one of the smugglers," she said.

"Goodie," he said, rubbing his hands together with mock enthusiasm.

"What a clusterfuck," declared one of the policemen and the uniformed policewoman beside him sagely nodded, arms crossed. Probably she felt obliged to agree with every dumb thing her male counterpart said. Karissa felt for her.

"So what are we standing around here for?" Karissa asked, checking her watch. "Don't tell me it's the official NYPD union coffee break at 2:57 a.m."

"Coast guard's still rounding up the last of the swimmers," the policewoman said sullenly.

Karissa noticed that some nearby police were busy cuffing a group of Chinese men together in twos and ushering them toward waiting buses. News crews from several major channels were capturing the scene and the dejected prisoners on camera. As she had suspected, the incident would be big news. She looked around and saw that the beach was mostly empty now, save for a variety of discarded belongings and refuse, including waterlogged cardboard suitcases, random articles of clothing and empty containers of Taiwanese frying oil, which she had seen some of the Chinese people using ineffectively as flotation devices while she was in the helicopter. Here and there were bits of stationary she guessed had been intended for writing letters home. She sighed.

"Well, well, Lacey and Wu, our dynamic duo."

Karissa whipped around and beheld the towering, gloomy figure of Dick Lamphere, the district director of the INS in New York City. The cops excused themselves, leaving the three of them to confer. She had expected to see the director an hour earlier, at least. He liked to lead from the front during important fieldwork, though this was not always necessary or welcome, as far as she was concerned. Tonight, given the magnitude of events, he must have been busy taking calls directly from Washington. Since the election of the country's new president, the INS had been leaderless, with the appointment of a new commissioner still pending and Lamphere was their go-to man.

"What a clusterfuck," Lamphere grunted sourly, peering beneath deeply furrowed brows at the last of the aliens as they boarded the buses.

Karissa forced herself to refrain from nodding along with the remark. The fact was that she saw eye to eye with Lamphere on almost nothing; she strongly disagreed with his politics and with the way he treated other people and found his methods tedious, repellent, or both. She respected his title though, believing in the hierarchical philosophy that orders should come from the top, or at least she believed in it when it suited her.

"We're about to wrap up here sir," Benny said, motioning to the deserted beach. "Just waiting on a few stragglers, potentially still in the water."

"Good. Listen, I'm going to make a statement to the press. I need you two," and Lamphere thrust a meaty finger at Karissa and Benny, "to make sure that none of these bastards leave our custody. And head over to Varick and prevent any lawyers from gaining access to the site. I don't want any of those vultures getting at the poor wretches before we find out if we can put 'em on the next boat back."

Karissa wanted to ask him why he was electing to detain the aliens when it was against current protocol, and she wished she could press him on the issue of lawyer access as well, but she had learned over the last few years never to question the director. He could be a frightening man.

"Copy that," Karissa said. "I didn't bring wheels though. Benny?" Benny gave an almost imperceptible nod.

"See you both in the morning at my office, 9:00 a.m. sharp. Shit, here's the mayor," the director growled and he stalked off toward the waiting cameras.

"I'm going to collect my prisoner," Karissa said to Benny. "In the meantime, why don't you take that shiny head of yours over to the shoreline and see if you can signal to the last of the passengers." She patted the side of Benny's bald head and jogged away. He chuckled good-naturedly but didn't move, watching her as she trotted off.

Karissa squinted into the darkness as she picked her way over the dune where she had left the Japanese man. Looking around, she saw no sign of the bastard. *Goddammit, he must have run off*, she thought, cursing herself for her inattention.

His escape was highly incriminating. She knew she should have followed her first instinct about him. Well, he wouldn't get far in the bracelets. Then she spotted a glint of metal in the sand and stooped to see what it was: a mangled pair of handcuffs. They were bent at an impossible angle and one of the cuffs had been snapped in two. She narrowed her eyes, scanning the surrounding dunes and the brush beyond. Picking up the pieces, she stuffed them into the pocket of her overcoat and stood up, brushing off her pants. So far tonight, she had accumulated more questions than answers.

## ✺ 10 ✺

# NIGHT FLIGHT

After the INS woman tripped him and left him in the sand, Nigel had decided to take some time to think. Since he landed in New York, he had felt like a passive participant in his own life, going through the motions of being a superhero, while at the same time feeling like a castaway, marooned on an island far from home, and far from where he felt he could do any good. The incident of the other night had not improved matters, rather, when he had heard the body of Lin Little hit the ground, he had felt the last remnant of control slip away from him like a fish through a hole in a net, leaving him with an overwhelming sense of powerlessness.

Sitting there in the sand, he had the sharp experience of feeling trapped, manifested now in the handcuffs on his wrists, but an old feeling too, linked with the cult, his duty, and the longstanding inability to make sense of his own life. Confronted with this feeling, he was surprised to notice a cold anger moving inside him, turning in his stomach, creeping up the inside of his chest and oozing through his veins, accompanying the languid *Resident* in its ceaseless rounds of his body.

The anger had first bubbled up out of nowhere when the INS woman had looked in his eyes, their cold stare stirring something within him, something he had worked his whole life to keep at bay. She infuriated Nigel and, despite the courtesy ingrained in him from his strict Japanese upbringing, he had not been able to bring himself to be civil to the woman. Oddly, she reminded him of his mother, but Nigel did not have to answer to this person who seemed like his mother because he was not beholden to her. A part of him knew that he should be more respectful, if only for his own good, for she was a person with some power, but his anger would not be denied. The emotion was like a wedge with which he could ever so slightly shift the boulder sitting on his independence. He thought he could see a corner of it, peeking out from beneath the heavy stone.

Watching as the woman spoke to her colleague and the uniformed officers, he wondered if they would be able to track him down if he left of his own accord. He knew that he could easily prove his story; it would simply be a matter of finding those officers who had first encountered him and asking them to provide corroboration, but he felt like he couldn't wait any longer. He was bursting to move, to run, to escape. He considered the repercussions of removing himself from custody, which he guessed might ultimately be deportation if they caught him, and he found that he didn't much care. Also, he had a sense that the woman from the INS was somewhat unconventional in her methods and, once she checked into his story, which she would probably do first, she might not bother to arrest him for escaping, choosing instead perhaps to concentrate on the real problem, finding those responsible for the *Golden Venture*.

He hesitated. They were looking over in his direction. The INS woman gestured at him, speaking rapidly, then turned back to the conversation and soon was occupied with a big, important-looking man, who scattered the police when he joined their circle. He scowled mightily, waving a meaty hand around, gesturing with self-importance. Now was Nigel's chance.

He frowned in concentration as his fingers probed the metal of the handcuffs behind his back. They were joined together by three links of chain and the bracelets themselves had a solid feel to them, as though they were meant to be a permanent fixture on blameworthy wrists. He could easily have snapped the chain and freed his hands but he wanted to keep the cuffs intact. With his right forefinger and thumb, he took hold of the single strand of metal inserted into the housing on the left cuff and began tugging, hoping to apply just enough force to pull the strand out of its housing without snapping it. It gave with a tiny squeal and his left hand was free. He brought his hands around front and examined the cuffs. Some of the metal teeth had been broken from the metal strand, obviously subjected to strong force.

Damn, he had wanted to make it look like the handcuffs had been opened with a key, maintaining the secret of his superhuman strength, but his hunch was that if the INS woman found the broken cuffs she would be unlikely to report him, given the awkwardness around losing him in such a fashion, plus he wanted to leave her a little something to remember him by. He growled softly in his throat as he snapped the second bracelet in two pieces, feeling his anger dissipate a little and, dropping the wrecked cuffs in the sand, he slipped into the night.


IT WAS A LONG TRIP HOME. NIGEL COULD HAVE WAITED FOR THE MTA to begin its morning service but he felt the need to quickly distance himself from the Rockaway Peninsula, worried that a search party might still be sent for him. Rather than taking the bridge, where he would surely be seen, he ran toward the subway station at 116th Street, using the darkened beach for cover, hiding from the commotion on the roads, which were mobbed with emergency vehicles and news vans.

Hurtling along, he marvelled at the increased stamina he had from the *Resident,* noting how the act of running had changed since when he was a boy, before the bonding took place. Now, at full speed, each stride was a gravity-defying leap that carried him twenty or thirty feet in a single bound. He imagined what it might look like: sprinting combined with long jumping but with an incredible momentum that carried him from point to point, leaving behind a series of craters in the sand.

When he reached the subway, he ran onto the tracks, carefully avoiding the metal rails where he could be exposed to high voltage current. He thought he might fare poorly if that happened, given that his body was infused with living metal, but he wasn't sure.

He decided to follow the subway line toward Brooklyn and then assess his options from there, wondering if he would be able use landmarks to guide himself home. This part of the line was above ground and soon became a bridge, running out over the water, heading toward Broad Channel.

His eyes were slits against the buffeting wind as he ran. He flexed an internal muscle, a sensation that felt like consciously operating an inner organ, massaging it into motion, into overdrive. He could feel the cool *Resident* material seeping out his pores, joining with itself, enveloping his body as he pulled the nylon Zorro mask out of his back pocket, becoming Kintarō, the Golden Boy.

Unbuckling his belt, he belatedly shrugged off his shirt, tossing it over the side of the bridge and looked down at his pants, which had sagged in front, hindering his progress. Ripping through them with a few extra pumps of his legs, he tore the material away with his hands, leaving it behind him on the tracks. He hurried forward, the night air whipping in his face, the station platform at Broad Channel passing by him in a blur.

After about ten more minutes of running, his breath coming in short, easy pants, the tracks passed overland. There was JFK airport off to the right, its lights twinkling over the flat expanse between, several planes taxiing on the tarmac, coming or going, he couldn't guess. He passed several more subway stations and then, after a few more miles, the tracks turned sharply left and he came to an area under construction.

Ahead he saw several MTA employees hard at work, at the tail end of a graveyard shift, installing a new section of track. One of the men spotted him and let out a whoop as Nigel sped by. In the near distance, the tracks were partially blocked and he realized the other workers were shouting at him to stop. He changed course, leaping up onto the awning above the station platform and continued at speed. From there, the tracks went underground, toward what must be Brooklyn, while off to his right he saw the lights and buildings of lower Manhattan, though they were still a long way off, the structures appearing in miniature at this distance. He decided to abandon the subway line and try his luck traversing rooftops. The shouts of the MTA workers followed him as he dropped from the awning onto one of the roofs below, their voices lost in the pre-dawn gloom.

The roof belonged to a residence and he thought the thump he made when he landed would surely rouse any sleeping occupants. He was there only a split second though, before he took off again, bounding roof to roof, cutting through the neighborhood on a diagonal at an even faster pace than the one he had maintained on the subway tracks. Adrenaline coursed through him and he felt a thrill that even the *Resident* could not deny him, interfering as it often did with the inner workings of his body. He clipped a few television antennae as he went by, possibly breaking them, not caring much, feeling the hydraulic pumping of the muscles in his legs, the pounding of metallic blood in his ears, the damp night air catching in his nostrils. He had never run such a distance before, never pushed himself this much and he felt unstoppable.

On he went, shadowing Rockaway Boulevard, hopping clear across a street here, flipping himself onto and then off a commercial building there, chipping bricks, showering mortar and grinning all the while. He sailed across Atlantic Avenue and almost didn't make the jump. Laughing, he scrambled up onto the roof of the deli he had almost missed and ran on.

By and by he came to a treed area on a hill. He hopped down to the pavement, crossed the street at a dead run and passed into the park, the Manhattan buildings that served as his beacon disappearing for a time, then reappearing as he crested the hill. They beckoned to him, peeking through the gaps in the trees, their presence an unexpected comfort as he traversed the shadowy alien landscape. The air here was cool and calm, fresh in a way he had not thought possible in the city, inviting and intoxicating, producing in him an almost animal sense of freedom, a freedom he suddenly worried might slip away from him before this night was done.

He ran past one cemetery then another, marble and granite monoliths standing guard over the sleeping dead. The gravestones and mausoleums were intensely familiar to him, reminding him of helping to bury the village dead when their time had come.

When he came to the edge of the park, he stopped for a moment to catch his breath and gazed up at the night sky. It was clear and cloudless and a few stars could be seen, despite the glow from the city. He smiled faintly. He hadn't had this much fun since playing in the craggy mountain plateaus of Nagano in his youth, accompanied by his father, bounding from rock to rock, laughing together sometimes, far from his mother and the village. He felt sad then and an unexpected wave of nostalgia swelled in his chest, leaving his eyes slightly damp.

He wondered where Aika was at that moment. It was the beginning of summer in the village and there would be much to do. He supposed she might still think of him sometimes, a prospect which usually depressed him, because it was unlikely he would ever see her again, but here in the darkness of early morning, under the amber glow from a nearby streetlamp, a long-dormant hope shifted and murmured inside him. Maybe he would find a way to free himself from the tangled web of the cult and lead an ordinary life. Maybe he *would* see her again.

He traversed Bushwick in much the same way as he had those parts of Queens, briefly touching down on every other rooftop as he went, causing slightly less property damage this time. He imagined this was what the American Santa Claus must feel on Christmas Eve, leaving his boot prints behind him as he made his yearly rounds. Nigel chuckled to himself, his voice lost to the rushing of the wind.

When he hit the Williamsburg area, he encountered the subway line again. Here it overshadowed Broadway, creating a tunnel-like overhang atop the major street. He paused on a rooftop, overlooking an intersection where a series of large transport trucks was merging onto Broadway, bound for Manhattan via the Williamsburg Bridge. Groups of trucks stopped at the light and then moved on again, rumbling off under the overhang. It was almost five in the morning and the dawn was breaking behind him. He would become visible to onlookers soon and all his leaping and running should end, lest he attract unwanted attention. Nigel chewed a nail and tasted metal instead, spitting with disgust when he realized he had bitten down on the *Resident* covering his fingers.

Watching the trucks, he had an idea. Without giving it much thought, he threw himself up onto the awning over the subway tracks and, as the latest batch of semi-trucks sputtered into motion, he dropped the fifteen feet onto the roof of one as it passed under the overhang. Instantly lying flat, he felt the rush of the wind as the over-hang passed within a few feet of his prone body. He clung tightly to the metal bands riveted to the roof of the truck as they sped off toward the bridge.

Nigel felt pleased with himself as he hunkered down low on the roof of the truck. His getaway had been flawless and now he was almost home. After the bridge, the street became Delancey and the truck continued straight, maintaining its speed as it moved onto the Bowery. He clung on, thinking that maybe he could hop off the truck when it stopped near some cover. He peeked over the side. There were quite a few people walking on the street so early on a Sunday morning and he was surprised. Maybe in the next block.

The truck rumbled on, making a right on Bowery Street, heading toward Midtown Manhattan. Now he was moving away from where he wanted to go. He looked around frantically for a place to jump but there was simply too much activity for him to do so. They went along for another five minutes and then he spotted a building under construction. It was encased in scaffolding and had a walkway for workers around the perimeter, just above the street. The walkway ended in a platform that looked like it might be strong enough to take his weight. The truck was in the right lane, close enough for him to jump the gap and the building site appeared to be free from workers. It would have to do.

The truck slowed with the traffic and he prepared himself, calcu-lating the force it would take to make the jump without punching through the plastic mesh separating the walkway from the interior of the construction site and without landing short.

He was in the process of launching himself when vertigo struck him. It came out of nowhere and for a moment, he was severely disori-ented, the world going sideways and a sudden shrill ringing erupting in his ears, like a burglar alarm. Unfortunately, he was in mid-stride and was forced to desperately hurl himself toward what he thought was the landing area, on a corner of the building through a gap in the scaffolding. He missed, bouncing off the scaffolding with a resounding *PING* and dropped into a waiting industrial junk bin, filled with discarded construction material. A puff of white dust went up and then all was still.

Nigel coughed. His head hurt. He shakily picked himself up from the floor of the bin, gingerly moving his limbs. Nothing seemed broken. *What the hell was that?* He glanced over the side. Nobody was around and the truck had gone. If anyone had seen the spectacle, they hadn't stayed around to check on him. He clambered over the lip of the bin and dropped to the pavement, his legs wobbling a little on impact, almost betraying him. As he regained his balance, a tremendous fatigue settled over him like a heavy coat. Nigel looked around and, taking a deep shuddering breath, he walked back down Bowery in the direction of Chinatown, neither noticing, nor caring to notice the stares he received from passersby as he trudged down the sidewalk, his strange metal suit shining in the morning sun.

## ⚜ 11 ⚜

## PICKING UP THE PIECES

arissa yawned and stretched, rotating her hands in the air
above her head, hearing her wrists click. Benny wore a stony
expression on his face. He was not in his usual good humor
this morning and neither was she.

They had been up all night, first attending hospitals in Queens and
Brooklyn to check on *Golden Venture* passengers, ensuring they were
handcuffed to hospital beds and posting cops to watch over them. The
bewildered people had not been expecting the handcuffs, having been
told they would be processed and released and the haunted look in
their eyes, as they listened to the translator explain what was
happening to them, had remained with Karissa throughout the
morning.

Next, they had paid a visit to the Varick Street holding centre at
the south end of Greenwich Village. The centre was stuffed to capac-
ity, as she had anticipated, but she was somewhat comforted by the
thought that the less than adequate accommodations were probably
heaven compared to the hold of that ship. Benny posted a plastic sign
at the front of the building, declaring the site off limits to attorneys
until further notice, with the caveat that they would be permitted
entry once retained by the passengers. Karissa had complained to

Benny that the people would have serious difficulty retaining lawyers without access to them in the first place. He had said he supposed that might be the point.

Finally, they had made their way to the Civic Centre, where the INS made its headquarters in the Jacob K. Javits Federal Building, and here they were now in the district director's office, their waiting time going on thirty minutes.

Sitting there, Karissa began to think on the current state of the INS. Although one could argue that the organization was crucial to maintaining the integrity of America's borders, the INS was chronically underfunded, which severely reduced its ability to collect meaningful intelligence. Instead, INS agents spent their time responding to individual incidents, which did next to nothing to combat the smuggling of illegal Chinese immigrants, widely considered to be the most sophisticated level of criminal activity the INS encountered.

This had been pointed out in a recent proposal the New York INS office had made, requesting a national task force targeting snakehead smugglers. Unfortunately, the request had been turned down in Washington, quashing hopes for any higher-level intelligence gathering. And now here they were, dealing with a ship-full of almost three hundred Chinese aliens without the faintest idea of who was behind it all.

"How're you holding up after last night?" Karissa asked, slouching lower in her chair.

Benny smoothed some wrinkles in his coat, which was draped across his lap. "Just another day," he said, with what she thought was probably feigned nonchalance.

Benny was a second-generation Chinese-American. His parents had immigrated from Beijing in the late 1950s, fleeing communist China, and had succeeded in preserving their wealth and status from their home country with their move. Benny's father was a businessman and his mother an intellectual and, from the outset, they had refused to live in a concentrated ethnic community. They shared little in common with poor Chinese immigrants forced to live and work in Chinatown, where cheap labor was abundant and a lack of English was not a hindrance to success. Upon arrival, they had purchased a three-floor brownstone uptown and Benny had been raised and educated in a predominantly white social sphere.

Although Karissa knew that Benny had never been to China and had few Asian friends, she wondered if it chafed him even more than it did her to see his countrymen in such a difficult position.

"Any plans for the week?" she asked.

Benny grunted.

"Getting sick of me yet?" she demanded, prodding the bare skin of his forearm beneath his white short-sleeved button-up, half aware that the more run-down she was, the more annoying she became.

Before he had a chance to reply, the door banged open and in strode Dick Lamphere, looking surprisingly kempt. He was wearing a fresh suit, his dark hair slicked back and the smell of aftershave pervaded the room. *Must have squeezed in a shower*, she thought, jealous.

"Don't get up," he barked, sitting heavily into the high-backed swivel chair behind his desk. He cleared some papers out of the way and leaned back.

"Holy jumping Jesus Christ," he declared, "this day keeps getting better and better. Ten people drowned. Injured coast guard. And now I'm under fire from the press about what we're going to do with the detainees."

"Any word from Washington on that?" Karissa asked, settling back into her chair.

"They're going to follow my lead," Lamphere replied, rubbing his hands together with a soft whisper of skin.

Karissa said nothing for a few moments and then, to her surprise, Benny spoke up.

"Was it you who gave the order to detain them?" he asked.

"Damn straight," said Lamphere, brushing an imaginary speck of dirt from the lapel of his suit jacket.

"Won't that cause a problem, considering refugees are usually released before trial?" Benny asked, his hands folded carefully in his lap.

Karissa inwardly cringed and prepared herself for the onslaught. Lamphere looked as though he'd swallowed a bar of soap.

"Did I hear that correctly Wu?" Benny stared back, outwardly impassive, leaning ever so slightly away from the desk. "When they cross the Southern border we have no problem calling them 'illegal aliens,' but when they show up in a boat, now they're 'refugees?' It's that kind of talk that leads to the bogus asylum claims we've been seeing, which as you know, can prevent the few truly deserving, genocide-fleeing foreigners from finding safe haven. And, if we release them, then what? I'll tell you what: they'll all immediately find jobs in the black market in Chinatown, trying to pay off the thirty-thousand-dollar transport fee. We might as well just give nine million in cash to organized crime and have done with it." He stared at Benny, his eyes boring holes in the back of his head.

"My mistake," was all Benny said in reply.

All three were silent a few moments. Karissa could hear the *tick-tock* of the pendulum clock on the wall, an outmoded choice for an office these days, in her opinion.

"Did you communicate with any of the aliens?" Lamphere demanded.

"Through a translator," Benny replied. "I speak Mandarin and a bit of Cantonese, but these speak a local dialect."

"Local dialect? From where?"

"Fujianese. The passengers are all from Fujian province."

"Most Chinese aliens are Fujianese these days," added Karissa.

"I know that," Lamphere said, impatient. "And it's hardly a local dialect. Millions of people speak Fujianese, don't they? Come on you two, I'd give my left testicle for some new information."

Karissa cleared her throat. "We suspect the smuggling of aliens into Chinatown is far more extensive than we can prove."

"I know it is Goddamn it. It's a well-known fact."

"Right, but because of funding issues we haven't been able to pursue the case in the way we'd like—"

"In the way you'd like, you mean," he growled reproachfully. She faltered, regarding him. He made a mollifying gesture with his hands. "I'm under a lot of pressure, continue."

"Anyway," she said, eyeing Benny who was busy checking his nail cuticles, "as you know, most illegal Chinese immigrants we've picked up over the last three years seem to have filtered through one part of

Chinatown, and we believe that one individual, one snakehead, is behind the smuggling." She paused for breath. "I think it's that individual who is responsible for the *Golden Venture* landing this morning."

"It would take a massive organization to pull off such an endeavor," Lamphere scoffed. "It has to be more than one person."

"Not necessarily." Benny cut in. "My informants tell me there is a certain restaurant on East Broadway, owned and operated by a forty-four-year-old Fujianese woman, known as 'Sister Ping,' who is believed to have smuggled hundreds of people from Fujian province into New York, as far-fetched as that sounds."

Karissa gawped at Benny. "This is the first I've heard of it. Why didn't you tell me?"

He gave a shrug. "It's only a rumor I heard recently. I still haven't had the time to check it out."

"But that's absurd," she said. "she doesn't fit the profile at all."

"One thing's for sure," said Lamphere, "we're going to need a hell of a lot more than unsubstantiated rumors to go on and the clock is ticking. You two will go and investigate the woman on East Broadway, today. And if nothing comes of it, shake a few trees in Chinatown, see what falls out."

"Yes sir," Karissa and Benny both murmured.

As she and Benny were headed out the door, Karissa remembered the Japanese man from the beach. She turned and opened her mouth to inform Lamphere about him but he was already on the phone. He held up a hand to her and made a shooing motion. The meeting was over and probably that was just as well; she realized she would have seemed foolish if she'd told him she'd let her prisoner escape. But if this mysterious woman on Broadway was a dead-end, at least she had another avenue to pursue. The Japanese man must be wrapped up in all of this, somehow.

KARISSA WAS QUIET ON THE SHORT DRIVE OVER TO EAST BROADWAY in Chinatown, travelling in the black INS issue cruiser she shared with Benny. They stopped the car at the address Benny had written in his small leather-bound notebook and they stepped out into the sunlight.

The building was a five-story brick tenement that housed a Chinese seafood restaurant on the main floor, advertised by one sign in English and one with giant, red, three-dimensional Chinese characters. The restaurant was closed but they could see that a light was on in the back.

They approached the glass door and Benny loudly rapped his knuckles on the metal frame. A tired-looking Chinese woman approached, unlatching and opening the door a crack.

"We need to see the owner," Benny said.

The woman peered suspiciously at them with heavily lidded eyes.

"Owner not here," she said.

Benny said something to the woman in Mandarin and she replied in a short rapid burst of words.

"She doesn't speak Mandarin," said Benny. "Want to bet she speaks only Fujianese?" He tried again in Cantonese. The woman made another cursory reply.

"Yep," he said. He tried in English: "We are with the Immigration and Naturalization Service. We need to look around your restaurant."

"Owner not here," the woman said again.

Karissa shouldered the door open and the woman, startled, stepped back a pace, her eyes flashing; indignation and distrust mingling on her face. Benny's brows went up in mild surprise at Karissa's breach of protocol. She gestured for Benny to step inside.

"You go," she said, "I have to make a few calls. I'm sure you can handle this on your own."

She could tell Benny wasn't happy about it. He probably thought there could be real danger inside, considering the tip he'd received, but all he said was, "Fine. Keep 'er running." He flashed a mirthless grin and went in.

Karissa spotted a payphone across the street and, looking both ways for traffic, she jogged over to it. The area was busy for a Sunday and there was a steady stream of cars and people coming and going. A delivery truck honked, beeping as it backed into a parking space on the street next to the phone booth. She plugged her right ear with her index finger as she dialed the number, cradling the receiver against her left ear with her shoulder.

First, she telephoned the receptionist at the INS, asking if there were any messages. In the fifteen minutes since she had left, there had been two calls for her: one from an NYPD sergeant wondering what to do with the detainees at the hospital; he reported that several attorneys had made contact with the Fujianese there and were demanding their release; and one from a journalist, requesting more details about the investigation. Karissa wished she had more details to offer, but alas, the newspaper woman probably knew more about what was happening regarding the *Golden Venture* than she did.

She thanked the receptionist and hung up. Then, she called the front desk at the Bowery flophouse where Admiral Rat, her father's old informant, was a regular. The clerk reported that he hadn't seen the pint-sized man in over a week. She'd have to try more of his haunts later. She hung up and plugged the machine with another quarter, dialing the number for her friend Charity Ng in the visa office at the INS. She picked up on the first ring.

"Charity, Karissa Lacey here."

"Karissa, what a surprise! I bet you're in the shit today." The Singaporean woman had a foul mouth on her, which Karissa appreciated.

"You have no idea. Listen, I need you to do a search for me on a young Japanese gentleman. He applied for a student visa on the basis of attending Tammany College in the fall."

"What's his name?"

"The name's what I need. And an address here in New York."

"Christ. Okay, hold the line."

While she waited, Karissa shed her overcoat and fumbled in the pocket for the pack of nicotine gum she kept there. She popped out a piece, which promptly fell on the ground. Cursing, she lifted the pack to her mouth and ejected another piece directly inside it, chewing mechanically and grumbling to herself.

Charity came back on the line, laughing. "You okay over there? I could hear you bitching after I parked the receiver on the desk."

"It's a day of malfunctions," Karissa replied. "What have you got for me?"

"Got a hit. Lucky for you there's only one that matches your criteria."

Karissa tucked the gum under her tongue, feeling pleasantly keyed up from the nicotine. She got out a pen and prepared to write on her hand. "And?"

"Name's Nigel Nakagawa. Arrived second week of May; port of entry, JFK. He's been to the office twice to follow up about his student visa."

"Address?"

"61 Mott Street, in Chinatown." Karissa hurriedly scribbled the address on her palm, suddenly realizing the location was less than a half mile from where she now stood. "What's a Japanese college student doing living in Chinatown anyway? Doesn't he know about Little Tokyo?"

"Beats the hell out of me," Karissa replied, removing the gum from her mouth and sticking it under the pay phone box. "Thanks Charity, you're a pal."

"You're a swell guy," Charity shot back. "Cheery bye." And she hung up.

Karissa stood for a moment with the dial tone sounding in her ear, thinking. After a moment, she dialed one more number. The NYPD staff sergeant who had left her a message at the INS answered, half shouting over the din at his precinct.

"This is Agent Lacey, returning your call from earlier."

"Yeah, the lieutenant is requesting direction regarding the refugees in hospital in Queens and Brooklyn."

"The INS wants the aliens detained until further notice. You can transport them to our holding centre at 201 Varick Street when they've been cleared by the hospital."

"Their lawyers are demanding their release."

"Tell them no dice. They can call our office if they want further clarification or they can take it up with the DA. Those people are not considered refugees yet and they're not getting out anytime soon." Playing the bad guy left a bitter taste in her mouth.

"Copy that."

"Listen, while I have you on the line, can you put me through to one of the two officers first on the scene this morning?"

"I believe those were Park Service patrolmen. I can probably connect you. Hey Nancy!" he shouted. "How the heck do I transfer the line to Park Service? One sec."

Karissa spoke with both officers who had first reported the landing of the *Golden Venture* and they not only confirmed Nakagawa's story, that he had been sleeping on the beach, but also that he had bravely swum out and had probably saved the lives of at least six of the Fujianese in the water. *Damn.* Well, that solved one mystery; he was no smuggler. This fact made her life a whole lot easier today because she would not have to go to the trouble of booking him. Easier and harder, for he had been her only direct line on the smugglers. But something still niggled at her. The broken handcuffs.

Karissa exited the phone booth and crossed the street again, narrowly missing a speeding cab. *Prick.* She opened the front door of the cruiser and rummaged around in the glove box for some paper. She found an old takeout receipt and jotted down a note to Benny, explaining that she was off to investigate a lead. He was probably busy going through the restaurant's records and she didn't want to have to explain herself further. She felt a twinge of guilt. It wasn't really a lead, strictly speaking, but her curiosity was piqued. She slapped the note down under one of the windshield wipers and took off at a brisk trot, mulling over what she would say to Nakagawa when she saw him.

## 12

# CHINATOWN

The buzzer rang and Nigel's eyelids slowly opened. They felt like they had been glued shut. He was terribly thirsty, as if someone had poured Sahara Desert sand down his throat while he slept.

"Just a minute," he croaked absurdly, only partially aware of the fact that the person doing the buzzing would be downstairs on the sidewalk.

He checked the time. It was just past 10:30 a.m. It felt like he had been sleeping for an eternity, and for much less time than he needed, when in fact it had been about five hours since he had flung himself onto his bed. The buzzer sounded again and made his head hurt. He shambled over to the intercom on the wall, naked. Though he had managed to shed his suit in the shower this time, he had failed to locate his pyjamas before lapsing into unconsciousness. He pressed the button and managed a quavering, "Yes?"

"Delivery."

He paused. He hadn't ordered anything, and the only people he could think of who knew this address were from the cult. Something from home then.

"Come in," he said and pressed the entry button, hearing the faint counter buzz in the intercom, wondering how long he had.

He stumped back into the bedroom, a little faster this time and pulled some pyjama pants out of the laundry hamper, wrinkled and stale-smelling. They would have to do for now. Then he went to the kitchen and downed a glass of tap water, the cool liquid running over the back of his chafed throat, causing him to splutter. He felt hungover, a bitter, depleted sensation, his limbs feeling like they were made of jelly, his guts churning, his head stuffed with a sodden mass of cotton balls. *What was happening to him?*

A sharp knock came at the door, causing a muffled echo inside his swollen head. He pulled a blanket off the couch and wrapped it around his shoulders and upper body for modesty and then opened the door.

His jaw fell open. Through bleary eyes, he regarded the unmistakable form of the INS woman from the beach. After all the trouble he had gone through to put distance between the two of them that morning, here she was, standing outside his door, a Cheshire grin on her face. He was speechless.

"Mind if I come in?" she asked.

There was a pregnant pause.

"I'd rather not."

The woman sighed. "Look, you're going to have to cooperate with me. You're wanted for questioning in connection with the smuggling of 286 illegal immigrants, ten of whom are now dead."

Her tone was hard and any part of the elation he had experienced while in transit earlier that morning evaporated like dew in harsh sun. *Ten dead and he hadn't fought to keep saving them. Damn him then.* He stood there uncertainly, not knowing what to do or say.

The woman's eyes softened a fraction. "Why don't we go for a little walk around the neighborhood, sort some things out?"

The last thing he wanted was a walk but he didn't have the energy to disagree, the effects of the recent dizzy spell lingering in a troubling way. He nodded, turning for the bedroom in search of proper clothes.

"My name's Karissa by the way," she said after him. "But you can call me Agent Lacey."

. . .

DOWN ON THE STREET, UNSYMPATHETIC SUNLIGHT SLASHED AT Nigel's eyes, intensifying his dizziness as he walked reluctantly beside Karissa. He had been expecting a grilling, or their stroll to end inside a squad car, but if that was her intention, she gave no sign, striding amiably along, allowing him to keep his silence.

By this time, throngs of people milled about on Mott Street and the clamor was building in volume. Though it was Sunday, there were laborers, delivery men, grocers and housewives, all coming and going, heedless of the fact that, at least in some parts of the city, the work week was temporarily on hold.

Many of the men wore dusty blue jeans and faded flannel shirts, polo short-sleeve shirts tucked into grey or brown pleated slacks, baggy cargo shorts, pockets bulging with who knew what; their heads down, moving at speed, stopping only to call a few words to those whom they knew or pausing at shops to buy or sell or chat.

Nigel saw two elderly Chinese women picking their way through the mass of people. Lingering at a stall selling crockery, they fingered the wares, conversing loudly with each other. The one nearest was sporting an oversize white t-shirt with the words, "New York City Marathon 1991," emblazoned atop a silhouette of Manhattan buildings in green, yellow and maroon. The woman's companion made a rapid exchange with the stall owner, holding out a teapot, then she replaced it on the shelf with a shake of her head, perhaps dissatisfied with the price.

Nigel and Karissa walked on, saying nothing, passing under green, red and white market canopies, which cast shade over fresh produce in every colour of the rainbow. Nigel spotted okra, persimmons, melons, radishes and bulbous red, ripe strawberries, all familiar, yet all distinctly different from what he remembered from back home.

They came upon a fish monger where there were tanks on display, filled with squirming eel and flashing sea bass, the fish packed so tightly together they could barely maneuver themselves around. There were clams, oysters, muscles and scallops, packed into ice, their shells tightly closed against the glare from the street and the noise and the heat. Nigel breathed deeply, the salty fish smell clearing away some of the haze in his mind, taking him back to Sundays in the village when fresh seafood was delivered from Toyama and the Noto Peninsula. Karissa wrinkled her nose.

"How much do the clams cost?" he asked the shop attendant.

The man opened his mouth to reply but was interrupted by a shrill ringing. He reached down and removed a grey cell phone, about a hand long, from a leather pouch on his hip. Holding up a finger to Nigel, he answered in Mandarin. Karissa shrugged and they walked away.

"Chinatown seems to be thriving," he said to break the silence. He still wasn't sure what she wanted from him.

"Appearances can be deceiving," she said. "The Chinese everyman is poorer than most people realize." She curled her tongue and shot out a hard, white lump of gum, which sailed onto the street, rolling down a storm drain.

"How so?" he asked, reaching a hand to rub at his temple.

"Take your typical waiter. He works maybe sixty hours a week for about two hundred dollars a month. He's living in a dilapidated, three-room flat, fending off cockroaches, while supporting three generations; no overtime pay, no benefits, and no job security."

Karissa paused to regard a fire hydrant, which had been opened some time before, probably by neighborhood kids, dribbling its last onto the pavement.

"The thing is," she went on, "the associations and societies imported from China to help immigrants, are fundamentally positioned to exploit workers. Chinese immigrants coming to the States, looking for fairer wages, political stability and equality, find themselves at the mercy of powerful players, in bed with big Hong Kong investors, all exploiting cheap labor here in Chinatown."

She motioned and they went on, his dizziness abating slightly as he listened to her. It sounded as though she genuinely cared.

"Surely the kind of job you're talking about is just a stepping stone?" he suggested. "Maybe some of these people are saving up to go back to school? Chinese immigrants are overrepresented in many top colleges from what I understand."

She scoffed. "You don't think *he* will end up in Harvard, do you?" She pointed at a young man with a pock-marked face, hefting a crate of chickens off a delivery truck, a lit cigarette drooping from the corner of his mouth. "Or her." She motioned to a shopkeeper, clad in a frumpy, dusty dress, beating a carpet for all she was worth.

"Why not?" he asked, feeling a flush of anger rising in his cheeks.

"You're thinking of the uptown Chinese. They come from a much different background, with higher status and wealth accumulated in China before they came. Many downtown Chinese will never assimilate. It's a myth."

"What about activism?" he asked. "I read that ten or fifteen years ago, thousands of Chinatown residents successfully demonstrated against the low minimum wages paid by factory owners."

"That's true," she agreed, "but on the other hand, labor unions are losing their power all over the country, not just here, and political parties are becoming less and less able to deal with corporate developers. My bet is that soon enough, it'll be too late for Chinatown to organize itself, if it's not already." She seemed angry as she popped a fresh piece of gum into her mouth, chomping down on it fiercely.

"Then there's the rise of the tongs," she said darkly. "It used to be that Chinese crime bosses employed foot soldiers directly. But they're smart, right? Now they hire middle men, 'dai low,' to coordinate their operations and gun violence has peaked. Did you know that before you moved here?" She glanced sideways at him. "Of course the police mostly stay out of Chinatown, preferring to spend their effort where they understand the system, leaving the thugs, no more than boys really; younger even than you," she added, "to completely run amok. They roam around in gangs, cool as you like, threatening, intimidating, pulling in money from racketeering, gambling, adult theatres, massage parlors, the works. But nobody will point a finger, so the police stay away, because ultimately, it's a waste of their time. Until some white civilian catches a bullet, then the place is crawling with cops for a couple of days. Then it's back to business as usual and the rest of the city grumbles about the crime wave and goes back to sipping lattes." She paused to catch her breath. "Like two nights ago, when a white college senior got shot along with a prostitute and her pimp, just a few blocks from here. You hear about that?"

Nigel nodded, stifling a gulp, recalling his own involvement in the affair.

"In a Chinatown where organized crime rules the streets and the rest of New York turns a blind eye, allowing and even encouraging exploitation to happen, how can immigrants make a go of it? It makes you wonder, even if the *Golden Venture* passengers had made it onto the streets, what kind of life would they have?"

He stopped walking and regarded her steadily. "Immigrants grow up in difficult circumstances, otherwise they wouldn't come here in the first place. They stick together so they can make it, whatever the odds." He spotted a food co-op across the street and next to it, an independent restaurant workers' union. He pointed past her, indicating the storefronts, attempting to prove his point. "See?"

"I wish that was true Mr. Nakagawa," she said, sadly shaking her head, "but I just can't believe it. Where did you get all your optimism from anyway?"

Nigel found that he was tired of the conversation. "What is all this about Agent Lacey? Am I under arrest?"

She grinned at him. "No. I checked your story with the cops who found you on the beach and I have a mind to let your escape from custody slide."

He was taken aback, feeling somewhat relieved, but somehow he doubted she was finished with him.

"Why bother finding me then?" he asked.

She produced a set of broken handcuffs from the pocket of her folded overcoat. He stared at them, the memory of snapping them like they were made of balsa wood coming back to him in a rush.

"Oh. Yes, I broke those," he said.

"Uh huh, how?"

Nigel had opened his mouth to reply when the unmistakable sound of automatic gunfire erupted to their right.

KARISSA JERKED HER HEAD AROUND AS THE FIRST SHOTS RANG OUT, feeling annoyed that they had been interrupted just when she was getting somewhere with Nigel, then chilled when she realized what the sound was. It wasn't so unusual, gunfire in broad daylight on the streets of Chinatown, even on a Sunday, though she had never been present for such an incident before.

Her first thought was for Nigel's safety, moving to shield him with her body, drawing her weapon and motioning for him to get down behind the nearest parked car. She glanced at Nigel, who had crouched beside her and was looking worriedly down the street. She followed his gaze.

From around the corner spun a youth, about sixteen or seventeen, dressed in a black suit and tie, his eyes covered by wrap-around mirror shades, uselessly clicking the trigger of a spent machine pistol, still smoking. He ducked into a nearby shop, causing Karissa to wince and Nigel to stand up.

"Sit down," Karissa hissed, tugging on his leg. "You're going to get yourself shot."

He threw her a look, startling Karissa with the hardness in his eyes, making her feel unaccountably silly for her concern.

A moment later, six more youths ran around the corner, a ragtag bunch in comparison, clad in faded, ripped jeans and sleeveless white t-shirts, whooping and shouting, jeering at the one who had taken refuge in the shop. Just then, the shopfront window exploded outward, a hail of bullets bursting forth from the machine pistol within, causing the youths on the street to dive in all directions. They shot back and several civilians screamed and ran, coming dangerously close to running into the line of fire.

Karissa was up and off down the street, sprinting, shouting, "Down! Everybody down!" She realized with a shock that Nigel was close behind her, easily keeping pace, a look of grim determination on his face. As the firefight continued, rounds pinging and whizzing past her, she tried desperately to shepherd the panicking people, ushering a white-faced woman pushing a stroller with an infant behind a nearby parked car.

Then she spotted a young girl, frozen with terror, standing in the middle of the road, staring wide-eyed as the youth emerged from the shop, just clicking a new magazine into place at the base of his pistol. Karissa screamed as he ran sideways along the sidewalk, a burst erupting from the gun, aiming back at the other boys but now with the little girl directly between them.

A blur passed her, a figure moving so quickly it was tough to make him out. It was Nigel she realized. Moving at great speed, he managed to scoop up the girl in his arms before she was struck by the oncoming bullets. He faltered, tripping on the rough asphalt, just managing to tuck the girl away, protecting her from the impact with his body as he sprawled spectacularly on the pavement. Karissa had never seen such a brave and unbelievable act of heroism in her life. There he lay, motionless, curled around the girl, who was sobbing into his chest, the rain of bullets falling ceaselessly around them. They were pinned down.

Checking that the mother and infant still had good cover beside her, Karissa raised her service weapon and squeezed off two quick rounds in the direction of the clump of boys, who were hidden behind parked cars on one side of the street. The two bullets broke the windshield of a mini-van and perforated its hood. The youth in the suit poked his head up and she shot at him too, causing him to duck out of sight, the bullet ricocheting off the concrete wall behind him. She swivelled her upper body back to face the others, scanning for them among the vehicles, then she spotted them running up the street, staying low, now a half block away. The one in the suit was running too she saw, making his escape in the opposite direction, back toward the market down at the end of Mott Street. Her eyes fell again on Nigel.

The girl extracted herself from his rigid grasp, turned and fled back to her mother, who turned out to be the woman with the stroller. Karissa passed the girl as she jogged over to Nigel, panting as she approached. He lay unmoving on the pavement, eyes closed, mouth hanging open, dribbling a grey foamy substance onto his shirt, a gaping bullet hole in his throat.

## 13

# HOSTING IS SUCH AN EFFORT

K arissa swished the last of her wine around the bottom of the stemmed wine glass, absently rubbing the soft material of her blouse between forefinger and thumb, the events of that day playing out in her mind.

As if the *Golden Venture* hadn't been enough, she had been forced to participate in a gun battle on the streets of Chinatown, like it was the wild west. Moreover, she had watched a man shot, a man surrounded by the biggest mystery she had yet encountered. Now, running on little sleep and less food, she attempted to piece together the events as they had unfolded, still not knowing if she could believe what her eyes had seen.

After realizing Nigel had been hit, Karissa had cast about her, looking around for help. He was dead, surely. Nobody could survive a wound like that. But the streets were empty and she carried no cellphone. She cursed herself for leaving her radio back in her vehicle, her lifeline to backup and help for him. She was filling her lungs with air, about to scream for anybody to come and assist her, when a flicker of movement caught her eye. A dark metallic substance was slithering out the hole in Nigel's neck; oozing, moving almost lazily, it coated the area around the wound, fixing itself to the young man's skin. Then, a small metal object protruded from the hole, inching its way ever so slowly out.

She crouched and peered at it, trying to determine what the object was. Then it fell, pinging to the concrete – the bullet. Karissa's eyes went wide, watching as the substance plugged the gap, like liquid tar used to seal a pothole, sitting on Nigel's skin for a moment, stagnant, like a malignant growth. The patch glinted in the sunlight before dissolving, draining onto the street, becoming a small, dark stain beside Nigel's now unbroken throat. She could see that he was breathing shallowly, his chest rising and falling in small, intermittent heaves that were painful to look at.

His eyelids suddenly flickered and he stared up at her, looking dazed. She bit her lip and looked around. A middle-aged Chinese man had emerged from the doorway of the shop next to the one whose window had been shot out. Beside him, a younger man who looked like his son appeared, his face wrinkled with concern, placing a hand on his father's shoulder as though to draw him back inside.

"Wait," Karissa called, "this man needs help."

"I'll call an ambulance," the younger man said, turning away.

"No! It's okay, he fainted in the excitement." The man looked skeptical. "Help me take him to his apartment. It's just down the street."

Karissa ended up paying the two men to help Nigel back down Mott Street and up to his apartment, narrowly missing the droves of police that swarmed the corner a few minutes later, looking for the gunmen. She paid them to help him and to keep them quiet, for she knew that they were deeply suspicious about her decision to bypass the hospital. She wasn't quite sure herself why she had convinced them not to call for an ambulance, except that her gut told her that Nigel was not in need of any medical attention, only rest, and that behind his miraculous recovery lay a secret she didn't fully understand, but which she thought best to keep between the two of them, for now.

After dumping Nigel unceremoniously on his bed, the men left and Karissa stood there studying him. He seemed tremendously fatigued, having fallen asleep almost immediately, but otherwise alright, his breathing regular, his body shifting occasionally on the mattress. Her gut told her that he would probably pull through with a few hours of rest and, at this point, she felt fine leaving him on his own. Besides, she needed a shower and some time to calm herself down. She scribbled a note to him on the back of a bank statement she found on the kitchen counter:

*'No need to explain the handcuffs. I know your secret and I'm sure you don't want me blabbing it around. Let's discuss more over dinner tonight if you're well enough. I cordially invite you to my apartment at 249 Church St, corner of Leonard and Church, at 9:00pm. You have some explaining to do.'*

She'd placed the note on the dresser across from Nigel's bed where she had known he would see it, momentarily reconsidering its implied threat of exposure. She probably wouldn't tell anyone about his unusual abilities but it never hurt to give a man extra motivation to be on time for dinner and she'd chosen to leave the note where it lay.

Now, sitting in the fading light of the day, in her sixth-floor apartment, Karissa felt uneasy as she anticipated his arrival, not because she thought he would do anything to harm her but because she knew that hosting him would probably implicate her in whatever it was he was involved with.

Something was bothering her about the way the metallic substance had looked after it had spilled from the hole in his neck. She recalled the news story, describing a man dressed in a metallic suit, who was supposed to have been involved in the shooting of three people in Chinatown a few nights ago. Nigel and the man might be one and the same and, if this was so, the question was, what were his motivations? Why was he gallivanting around Chinatown at night? And what was the material on his skin? It had seemed to be alive.

She reflected on Nigel's actions, first on the beach, then on the street in Chinatown. Brave to be sure, selfless, maybe even heroic. Could it be that he was an actual superhero? She almost dismissed the idea out of hand but found she could not fully do so, knowing what she had seen and having read so many comic stories herself. Smiling unexpectedly, she thought about Nigel's optimism regarding immigrant prospects and their strength of character and wondered when she had become so jaded.

She looked at the time – almost 10 p.m. Where was he? She had been sure he would at least show up. *Give him time*, she thought and, heading to the kitchen, she poured herself another glass from the bottle of *pinot gris*, sitting in a ring of condensation on the corner of the counter. She surveyed her modest dining room table, set with a full complement of cutlery and dishes, lit candles and paper serviettes. It looked ready for the meal, which she had managed to cook despite the recent mayhem, the roast now emitting an inviting aroma from her convection oven. *Damn she was hungry.*

She glanced up and the glass of wine fell from her hand, shattering on the hardwood floor. In front of her was Nigel Nakagawa, sitting in the frame of the open window, his mercurial suit dully reflecting the light from the candles, his eyes glinting darkly beneath his mask, full of anger and questions.

"You're late," she said.

He said nothing in reply.

"I was expecting you to buzz, or at least use the stairs. Come on in, unless you're also a vampire." She moved to grab the mop she kept behind the pantry door, clearing the glass and the liquid off the hardwood, moving the debris across the boundary onto the linoleum in the kitchen. "I'll deal with that later. How the Christ did you get up here?"

"I climbed."

"I see that. Want a glass of wine?"

He shook his head.

"What about food? I've got a rump roast in the oven. Time I took it out I think."

He shook his head again.

"Any chance you want to take that mask off and talk like normal people?"

A silence stretched.

Karissa was annoyed. Considering she'd helped him when he was shot, let his flight from custody slide, and went to all the trouble of cooking him dinner, the least he could do was show some manners, she thought. She stalked over to the kitchen, jerking a pair of oven mitts over her hands and, throwing open the oven door, she removed the perfectly cooked roast.

"What's your game, Agent Lacey?" came his cold voice from behind her.

She set the roast down on the stovetop and, as she shed the oven mitts, an impudent note crept into her voice.

"Can't a girl just ask a guy for dinner?"

She walked over and, because she knew it would irritate him, she reached out to touch his arm, hesitating when she saw the liquid metal crawling there, folding in on itself, growing and shrinking, causing her empty stomach to churn with revulsion.

He flinched away from her touch, anger boiling over. "Blackmail, is that it? Or some other scheme? Maybe outrageous demands, pending the release of my identity?"

Karissa paused for a moment, taken aback. He had it all wrong of course, her intentions for him, who she was at heart, what she stood for. A part of her supposed she could hardly blame him, thinking back on the trouble she'd caused him, the way she'd manipulated him into coming out to speak with her, twice.

But tonight, as it had many times before, her equanimity failed her, abandoning her when all it would have taken was a simple apology and a calm explanation of her behavior. Instead, she laughed, emitting a series of great hacking guffaws, bending double to catch her breath and then she laughed some more. She wasn't quite sure where the laughter came from, except that she simply couldn't hold it in. It was shot through with bitterness, for all that she tried and failed to do for others, for all her good intentions and wasted effort, for all the times she reached out and came away empty-handed, disappointed.

After a while, her laughter abated and Nigel's figure swam back into view through the tears in her eyes. He stood rigidly, clenching his fists tight, his cheeks pink, eyes narrowed to slits beneath his mask, his outfit swirling and pulsing almost angrily, more alive than ever. He must not have understood the despair behind her laughter, misinterpreting it awfully, because he suddenly lunged at her, quick as lightning, crashing into her and bringing them both to the floor.

Hitting the hardwood on her back, Karissa used their momentum to keep him going, rounding her shoulders, rolling backward with the weight of his body and, planting her bare foot in his chest, she propelled him over her head and into the dining room beyond. He crashed through the dining room table, unfortunately, shattering plates, splintering the wood and sending cutlery spinning and clattering in all directions.

She was up again in an instant, taking a fighting stance, her laughter gone. He leaped up again too, inhumanly fast, stumbling and slipping in the wreckage before righting himself, looking even angrier than before. He bellowed, charging at her, hands outstretched. She grabbed his wrists on the way, spinning him off balance, but he managed to catch her arm and they both stumbled sideways into a bookshelf, books showering on them, a particularly heavy volume coming down on the crown of Karissa's head, point first.

"Mother fucker!" she exclaimed, her anger flaring up red hot.

She reached for a hardback, spinning around as he came charging at her again, both of them snorting with frustration and rage. She struck him in the face with the edge of the book, once, twice, three times, his head snapping back. He shook his head, growling, the book-beating leaving no mark. She sprinted into the kitchen, pulling a long knife from the block, brandishing it blade down, the way her father had taught her.

Nigel cleared the distance between them in a single fifteen-foot dive, flying across the room, skidding over the counter, spearing her into the oven, a spidery crack spreading across the glass front of the door. She gasped, feeling a sharp pain in her back, as it bent the wrong way over the stovetop. With a herculean effort, she managed to right herself, shocked at his incredible strength bearing down on her.

She stabbed him with the knife in the side, her hand jarring, feeling the blade snap without penetrating his suit. He took ahold of her wrist, slamming her hand against the microwave, denting its side, and she let go of the broken knife. Then he backhanded her across the face, sending her toppling to the floor. The room spun and lights flashed and twinkled in her vision, blotting out his face as he loomed over her. Then he was gone.

She groaned, picking herself up from the floor, shaking her head a little, wincing at the pain. She stood up with some effort, unsteady, spotting him sitting on the only dining room chair that remained untouched by the melee, his back to her.

A broad, toothy grin split her face. "Fuck," she said, cracking her neck and rotating her wrist around. Nothing felt broken. "I haven't fought like that in a long time!" A trickle of blood reached the top of her mouth from her nose and she stuck her tongue out to catch it, smacking her lips at the ferrous taste. "Jesus you're strong. Technique's a little off."

She saw his back moving up and down, his shoulders shaking and realized that he was crying. "Hey, it's okay," she said, approaching him. "I don't hold it against you. I probably would have attacked me too." She placed a hand on his shoulder, her heart skipping a beat as her fingers sunk into the cold surface there, the material oozing around her digits, covering part of her skin. She jerked her hand back with a sucking noise.

There came a knock at the door.

"Hang on," she said to Nigel.

She strode over to the apartment door and opened it a hand's width. Outside stood her neighbor, his forehead creased with concern, holding a wooden baseball bat. She imagined how she must look, her clothes torn, knees and elbows scuffed, her nose bloody, a purple bruise already forming on her cheek. Her neighbor peered past her at the place in shambles, the broken table, the toppled bookshelf, books strewn over the floor, the pieces of broken china radiating outward in a chaotic pattern, the sound of a man's crying audible in the room beyond.

"It's okay Larry," she said.

"B-b-but."

"Just doing a little combat practice."

"I called the police."

"Call them back. Say you checked on me and that I'm an INS agent and in no danger whatsoever." Larry nodded, a little shakily. "See you on Thursday for squash, right?" He nodded again and she gently closed the door in his face.

She sighed and tiptoed back over to Nigel, through the debris, feeling light on her feet, the rush of the tussle having released the pent-up frustrations and tensions of the day.

She righted a chair and sat down beside him. After a few minutes his tears stopped flowing and, for a time, the two of them sat quietly, gazing out the window, thinking, brooding.

"I've never hit anyone before," he said eventually, in a melancholy way. "I was afraid of what might happen." He stared at his hands, claw-like and shaking.

"Guess you're new at this."

He nodded. "I'm supposed to be a crime fighter but I can't seem to get it right."

"A superhero?"

He nodded again. "It's what my mother wants."

She thought about that for a moment. "Your mother wants you to be a superhero?"

"Yes."

"Where is your mother now?"

"In our village in Japan, with everyone I know." His shoulders slumped a little more, if such a thing was possible.

"The homesickness must be a bitch," she said, scratching her head. "Listen, I think you're doing a great job. Think of the people you saved in the last day and a half, that girl on the street, and who knows how many of the passengers from the boat."

"Six from the boat, I think."

"There you go! Your mother would be proud." She moved to place a hand on his shoulder again but thought better of it.

"What were you doing the other night in Chinatown, when those people were shot?" she asked, trying to keep her voice sort of light. He silently put his head in his hands, grimacing and clenching his teeth. "How the hell did that happen anyway?"

"There was a man with a gun. He emptied the magazine into my stomach and those people were hit by the bullets that bounced off my suit." Every word seemed to be an effort for him. "I can't control my powers. Lately I've been having these dizzy spells and this morning I missed a jump. I think the *Resident* might hurting me."

She wrinkled her forehead. "The resident?"

"*Resident*. It makes up this suit," and he raised an arm, rubbing his hand along it with a soft shriek of metal on metal, the sound defying the liquidness of the material, as though he was stroking an iron blancmange. "To be honest I know almost nothing about it, except that it's old, very old, and probably not of this world."

"Ah, the saga of the sentient, super powered, possibly evil suit of alien origin," said Karissa, her eyes glinting as she considered Nigel, sitting there like an underwater explorer, about to sink into the deep.

"You're half-right," he said. "but I suspect the *Resident* isn't sentient, rather it's more like a parasite, acting by instinct, unknowingly harming me in its occupation of my body."

"It seems like it has some benefits though," she suggested.

"I suppose," he said. "Most people would probably covet power like I have."

*Too true,* she thought.

"But ever since the *Resident* was bonded to me, all I've thought about is ridding myself of it. The truth is, I want nothing to do with the power and I wish it was bonded to someone else."

"A reluctant hero."

"Exactly."

She thought for a moment. "Maybe you need a cause?"

"I'd rather *not* have one." He put his chin in his hands, gloomy eyes trained out the window, staring out at the building lights beyond.

She leaned forward a few inches, entering his periphery. "What about the *Golden Venture?*" she asked.

He sat up, swivelling his head to look at her. "What about it?" he asked.

She leaned forward a bit more. "I'm going to find those human smugglers and I sure could use your help doing it. Wouldn't you want to put a stop to them if you could?"

"Of course." He hesitated. "But I'm not sure that I'm fit for any heroics."

"You said the *Resident* is old, right?" she asked.

"That's right."

"How old?"

"I think it predates the cult, which has been around for about eight hundred years."

"The cult?"

"Yes, I'm the Champion of a Japanese cult called 'Hitsujikai.' The cult's mandate for the better part of a millennium has been to shape human life for the better, by sheltering people from the evils in the world. Where required, the cult inserts its Champion into the mix, a crime fighter with the ability to tip the scales in favor of good at pivotal moments in history."

"Sounds like my kind of organization."

"You'd probably fit right in."

"That's a lot of pressure on you though."

He said that he guessed it was.

"If the *Resident* is as old as you think it is, then it might appear at other points in the historical record. As far as I know, the myth of the superhero dates back some four thousand years to *The Epic of Gilgamesh* and crops up again and again in literature from all over the world.

"Listen, why don't I introduce you to a friend of mine, Amy Kang. She works as a night janitor at several major archives, housing all kinds of records and artifacts. You might find something about the *Resident's* origin and what it might mean for you to be carrying it around inside your body. I'm sure Amy would agree to help you with the research."

"She's a janitor?"

"Not just any janitor." Karissa's eyebrows rose and her voice took on a hushed tone. "Amy Kang is widely considered to be the best janitor in New York. Her reputation is due to her meticulous cleaning techniques, a keen interest in maintaining the condition of ancient documents, and discretion when it comes to the sensitive materials she encounters. She has access to resources and information that even university academics and researchers can only dream of laying their hands on. And she's only sixteen."

"Really," he said flatly, "a sixteen-year-old janitor has that level of access."

She shrugged. "Someone has to fight the dust."

"And what about her famous discretion? Why would she help me?"

"She owes me a favor."

"Ah," he said.

She winked. "I'll tell her you're coming. In the meantime, I'll contact you when I have more information about the *Golden Venture* and the scumbags behind it."

He nodded then stood up, stepping over to the window. He braced one hand on the top of the frame, turning his torso to face her, yellow city light spilling from behind him, shadowing his face. All Karissa could see were the two dark coals of his eyes, inscrutable behind the black Zorro mask he wore.

"I call myself Kintarō, the Golden Boy," he said, standing motion-less, waiting as though for a response.

"Nice to meet you Kintarō," she said, smiling and nodding to him.

"I look forward to hearing from you," he said, then he was gone, out the window and into the night, the curtains shifting almost imper-ceptibly in his wake.

❦ III ❧

## 14

## A SHEEP IN WOLF'S CLOTHING

"I don't know who the f—k to vote for right now." The mayor's voice was husky and thick with drink in the low-quality audio recording, blaring from the television in its cubby-hole recess in the wood-paneled restaurant wall. "I might vote Democrat."

"You're a Republican mayor though dude. You own a business. How can you vote anything but right?" The other man's voice was louder than the mayor's, though also muffled and slurred, occasionally obscured by the clink of a glass or a drunken hyena laugh, flaring up then abruptly cutting off.

"I f—ing hate the corruption at the State level," the mayor blurted, irrelevantly.

"What about Jessica Marionetti for State Senator?"

"The one with the huge tits? F—k, I shouldn't say that stuff, not with a lady present. Sorry about that sweetheart." A break in the tape, then the mayor's braying voice cut back in, close to the microphone, the audio distorted. "Heavy is the head that wears the crown man, know what I mean? F—ing sick of this city dude."

There was a muffled question or comment from a third man on the tape, the tone rowdy, challenging, seeming to insist on a point made unintelligible by the background noise, by the man's distant proximity to the microphone and, presumably, by the botched delivery of mangled, drunken words.

"If you don't finish your drink for that, I'll rip your f—ing arm off," the mayor bawled, words all coming together like the cars of a derailing freight train. "No, no, I want that f—ing spic down there to slam his drink."

"Did you just call me a spic?"

There was another break in the tape, the audio coming in again in the middle of another of the mayor's boasts. "...can do whatever the f— I want and I'm still gonna come out on top." The tape ended and the news anchor came back on, bug-eyed and rigid in his seat, as though he was too nervous to be on television.

"There you have it. That was the voice of Mayor Rusty Kincaid, recorded at a bar in Brooklyn a week ago, the mayor's sexist remarks and racial slurs going public at a crucial time in his re-election campaign. The tape, which was leaked to the press by an unknown source, has not changed public approval for mayor Kincaid however, according to the latest polls." The video feed cut to a man in a pin-striped suit, possibly a handler of some kind.

"We are deeply disturbed that a special interest group would stoop to taping the mayor, with the clear intention of preventing him from continuing his fabulous run in our city. He was there on his own time, blowing off steam in the same way as the average New Yorker does. As for his remarks, never has there been a man so quick to admit his faults, a man so willing to change when he knows he's wrong." The feed cut again to the news anchor.

"This statement from Mark Hendricks, Mayor Kincaid's chief of staff, seems to imply the mayor will retract his offensive statements in due course, however an apology has not yet been issued." The news anchor went on, detailing some of the upcoming proceedings of the 1993 New York mayoral race.

Losing interest, Karissa cut a slab of seared meat off the ribeye steak, carefully folding the speared, succulent accordion into her mouth; chewing methodically, filling both cheeks, she slurped a little to prevent the juices from running down her chin.

The steakhouse was noisy, noisier than Karissa preferred, with its rowdy Thursday night crowd of patrons, most here for the discounted 'steak n' suds,' served before six o'clock. The volume on the television sounded like it had been turned all the way up, contributing in no small part to the uproar. She removed a hunk of gristle from her mouth with her fingers and flicked it onto the edge of her plate, as if attempting to discard the disgust she felt after watching the news bulletin; though it was satisfying, in a way, to have her opinion about the politician validated.

Mayor Rusty Kincaid. What an ass. She had voted against him in the previous election, which he had unfortunately won by a landslide, carried to office on the creaking backs of an army of Republican blue-collar workers and immigrants and not a few conservative white-collar salarymen. The thing that reputedly connected them all to Kincaid, making them believe that he truly cared, was that he spent almost all his time with his constituents. Not only did he hold a huge number of rallies, even when he was not campaigning, but he showed up at street festivals, holiday events, celebrations, weddings, even the occasional Bar or Bat Mitzvah. New York was a party city and people loved to party with the famously accessible mayor.

Of course, the media had a field day with the mayor's constant carousing, drinking and frequent bad behavior, taking every opportunity to expose him for the dangerous buffoon he was. But none of his followers paid any attention to this, rather they rallied more strongly around him, thumbing their nose at the leftist establishment and the elite.

On the other side of the party line, the no-nonsense and upstanding citizens of New York spent much of their waking hours being appalled at the mayor's antics and laissez-fair attitude toward governing but their outrage fell on deaf ears. According to the tally from the last election, 42% of the city's total population voted for Kincaid – plenty enough voters, if the turnout was similar this time around, to keep the mayor in office for years to come.

Aside from reporting on his questionable methods of governance, the media loved to poke fun at the mayor's broad oval face, which, like the curved visage of a Halloween pumpkin, stood almost apart from the rest of his head; his cheekbones so wide and jutting that, when he looked straight at you, they partially blocked his tiny cauliflower ears and the sides of his fiery red hair from view. Karissa had at first found the public mockery petty and distasteful but as problems with the mayor mounted and Karissa's fury at him grew, she began to relish ridiculing the man's unusual distinguishing features.

Karissa shook her head, thinking of the sideshow that the most important office in the city had become. The one consolation was that Kincaid was so obviously incompetent, so outrageously bumbling, so flagrantly inept, that Karissa could, on her good days, write him off and carry on without becoming too depressed. On other days though, such a feat was impossible and she wallowed in her hatred of Moon Face and fumed at his neglect of her city.

To make matters even worse, in the three weeks since the *Golden Venture* disaster, the mayor had made several public appearances, condemning the actions of human smugglers and, *surprise, surprise*, denouncing 'illegals,' attempting to settle in New York. The mayor's stance on the *Golden Venture* was gaining him even more votes, as an increasing number of New Yorkers rallied around the perceived threat from illegal immigrants.

The way Karissa saw it, the opportunistic mayor was using the divisive nature of the incident to extend his tentacles into new territory, winning over the racists of the upper echelon, who had previously written off the blue-collar mayor, the son of a clam fisherman turned shipping baron, and his working-class hordes. Karissa found it both terrifying and hilarious that in the next election, only four months away, the mayor would have Somali immigrants working three jobs apiece and racist administrative service managers, earning well above six figures, all casting ballots for him. It was ludicrous.

She cursed as a drop of gravy skirted the napkin on her lap and plopped onto her pants, a grease spot forming, mostly concealed by the hue of the material but occasionally glinting wetly in the light.

Her thoughts drifted to the meeting scheduled for the next morning at 1 Police Plaza with Dick Lamphere, Benny Wu and the police chief, along with several of his captains and lieutenants. The INS was supposed to bring the NYPD up to speed on its progress with the *Golden Venture* investigation and would discuss the coordination of joint operations in the city. Grimacing, she remembered that she had what amounted to squat to report. Perhaps Benny would offer some information tidbits that could save her from scrutiny, but she doubted it.

It bothered her, because she knew that if she could just track down Admiral Rat, she might gain some information to keep the INS director and the police chief at bay, but Rat had been particularly elusive lately, as he often was when he heard she was looking for him. She didn't know why but he seemed to view her as a threat. Maybe it was because she saw through his eccentric façade and knew him for what he was: a shrewd and dangerous man, which, on the Bowery, was not a widely-held opinion, to say the least.

Sighing, she fished in her clutch for the small fold of bills she kept there, frowning as her fingertips brushed the cool metal of the old brass knuckles her father had given her many years before. She had been carrying the heavy things around in case of emergency (a girl couldn't be too careful in this city). She wondered where her father was now and what he was doing, then she pushed the thoughts away. Now was hardly the time for nostalgia.

Karissa paid for the meal and strode out of the noisy restaurant, the tumult from its insatiable patrons fading behind her, replaced by the clicking of her heels as she stepped down the golden sidewalk, bathed in the rich light from a dying summer sun.

THE THREE INS PERSONNEL STOOD AS ELEVEN OF THE NYPD'S TOP brass filed in, all mustaches and stubble, all stripes and deep blues, their creaseless uniforms trimmed with gold, their starched cuffs and white collars immaculate, their expansive, flat-topped hats tucked under their arms; hats that, like foot stools, could have the effect of making the men appear taller, more imposing than they had any right to be.

As they took their seats in a horseshoe around the raised, carpeted platform at the centre of the room, Karissa became keenly aware that she was the only woman present. Dick Lamphere, who was standing a few feet to her left, motioned for her and Benny to sit. They did so,

Benny folding his hands on the table before him, Karissa crossing her arms defensively beneath her breasts.

She didn't regret her decision to leave the NYPD but, with such a show of organizational force on display today, she was reminded of how impotent the INS had become and felt an irrational sense of inferiority, though she knew she could match any of those present in everything but their bravado.

The police chief entered a few moments later, eliciting a flurry of movement from his majors and lieutenants as they stood to pay him his due respects. He gestured for them to take their seats with the casual ease of a man well used to his position. Ascending the platform, about a foot from the ground, he centred himself behind the wooden lectern, the NYPD crest carved into the front.

"I'd like to welcome our guests from the Immigration and Naturalization Service: District Director Dick Lamphere, Agent Karissa Lacey and Agent Benny Wu." Karissa made a small nod of acknowledgment as her name was announced. "Considering the recent rise of human smuggling in general and the *Golden Venture* incident in particular, we're here this morning to talk about coordinating our efforts and sharing intelligence between the NYPD and the INS. Director Lamphere and I spoke over the phone about the importance of better operational coordination. This briefing is the first step toward that.

"I know the Director would like to kick things off by providing an update about the status of the *Golden Venture* aliens and I understand his agents have been hard at work gathering information and may have some leads to share with us." He gestured for Lamphere to approach the podium.

"Thanks Tom," Lamphere said, standing up from his chair. "I'll speak from over here if that's okay." He bent over and picked up a yellow Duo-Tang from the table and began leafing through its pages, then, finding the information he wanted, he opened his mouth to begin.

Just then there was a muffled commotion in the corridor and suddenly a woman in dark-rimmed glasses opened the door a crack and poked her head through. She looked and sounded mortified.

"I'm so sorry for the interruption Chief," she said, "but the mayor is here."

"The mayor?" The chief sounded confused. "Is something wrong?"

"Sir, I—"

The door banged open and in strode none other than Mayor Rusty Kincaid with two of his staffers following in his wake. He smiled emphatically, taking in the room with his beady blue eyes, his enormous pale face exhibiting a layer of sweat, which glistened in the fluorescent light from the ceiling. He tramped through the middle of the room, bellowing, "Don't let me interrupt!" his tenor more than filling the space. He sprawled in a chair at the back of the room, forcing his staffers to stand, there being no other seating nearby.

"Mr. Mayor," said the chief, "surely an operational meeting is beneath your notice. I'll have someone send a report to your office."

"Nonsense!" exclaimed the mayor, leaning back, his hands clasped behind his head, seemingly intent on presiding over the meeting anyway. "Don't stop on my account."

"We were just about to hear from Director Lamphere of the INS on the status of the detainees from the *Golden Venture*," said the chief.

Kincaid vigorously gestured for them to continue.

Lamphere cleared his throat and launched into an update on the fate of the *Golden Venture* passengers. He spoke about where they were being held and what new protocols had been enacted to keep them there. The passengers had been divided up along gender lines, the men sent to a prison in York County and the women and children to a special holding facility in New Orleans...

Karissa stopped listening to Lamphere's words, choosing instead to study the mayor, who seemed to be listening intently, periodically mopping his expansive face with a plush cloth the size of child's bath towel. His presence here was a mystery to her. As the chief had implied, Kincaid should have had more important things to do than attending this meeting. He could easily have been briefed on everything that was said, yet here he was, perhaps with some vested interest in how the police and the INS were dealing with the aftermath of the *Golden Venture*. But what could the fool's interest be? With a sniff, she directed her attention back to what the director was saying.

"I'll turn the floor over to Agent Wu, who has the latest on Sister Ping, our lead suspect in the *Golden Venture* smuggling operation." Karissa leaned back in her seat. Benny had previously tried to arrange a time to bring her up to speed on his investigation but she had been too busy. She'd hear about his progress now she supposed.

"Thank you sir," Benny said, rising and turning to address the uniformed policemen seated around the room. "The name Cheng Chui Ping was given to us by one Dickson Yao, also known as the Fat Man, a reliable informant who has been working for the DEA for decades in Southeast Asia and who knows all there is to know about human smuggling." He paused, flipping open the cover of a black binder and peering at the typed lettering on the front page.

"Sister Ping, as she is known locally, immigrated from a village in Fujian Province in 1981. Ping owns Yung Sun Seafood Restaurant at 47 East Broadway and the Tak Shun Variety Store on Hester Street with her husband Cheung Yick Tak, catering to Fujianese newcomers. We asked around and learned that Sister Ping is revered in Chinatown for her efforts to assist fellow immigrants with matters of settlement, hence the 'Sister' honorific. Because of the widespread affection for Sister Ping, it has been extremely difficult to gather information about any illegal activities, apart from the information we received from the Fat Man." Benny paused again, turning the pages of his report.

Karissa was beginning to bristle as she realized the extent to which she was out of the loop. She knew her availability had been slim lately but she thought Benny could have made more of an effort to brief her. She ground her teeth a little as he continued.

"Fortunately, we've discovered key information linking Sister Ping to the smuggling of Chinese nationals. First, we intercepted several parcels, addressed to Yick Tak, containing multiple Chinese passports, and we also found her name on at least twenty airline manifests, correlating with more than two hundred illegal immigrants who arrived on the same flights. We had the telephone company produce their toll records for both of Sister Ping's businesses and noticed an unusual pattern of international calling to locations in Fujian Province, as well as to Hong Kong, Mexico City, Honduras, El Salvador and Guatemala. And, a few days ago, a small craft bound for Florida from the Bahamas was apprehended with twelve undocumented Fujianese men aboard. That morning, the pilot of the boat had made a telephone call to the Tak Shun Variety Store, owned by Ping. Most importantly, the Fat Man puts Sister Ping behind the *Golden Venture*.

"We had a talk with Sister Ping and her husband in their restaurant." He cleared his throat. "The meeting was brief. Sister Ping, who did all the talking, categorically denied any involvement with the *Golden Venture* but as much as admitted to human smuggling. In fact, she went as far as telling us outright that she didn't believe we have the resources to catch her." Benny eyed Lamphere, who shrugged. "And at this point she's right. That's where you come in. We need anything you can give us on Sister Ping, particularly any information tying her to the *Golden Venture*."

Karissa had to hand it Benny; it was a neat piece of work but, as he had indicated, the evidence they had at present would not be enough to convict and a chasm remained between Sister Ping and the *Golden Venture*. Apparently, the mayor was more optimistic about it than she, for he jumped to his feet, hot on the heels of Benny's brief.

"Amazing work, incredible! Sounds like we have our woman. Chief, you'll let me know when you have enough to make an arrest, won't you? We can't have another *Golden Venture* incident." He snatched his towel from the seat of his chair with a flourish. "Just can't have it." And with that, the mayor swept out of the room, as abruptly as he had come, his tired-looking staffers in tow.

The police chief watched him go and then asked with a sigh, "Is that everything for this morning director?"

"That's it from us," Lamphere replied, gathering his printed materials. "Let's be in touch," and he snapped his briefcase closed as if to emphasize the suggestion. Benny began to clear up too and Karissa, having nothing to gather, produced her pack of nicotine gum and popped a piece in her mouth, the flavor contrasting with a sour taste she hadn't noticed before.

As soon as the elevator doors were closed, Karissa turned to Benny, who was leaning against the back wall opposite her. Lamphere stood facing away from them, as silent as a tree, seemingly lost in his own thoughts.

"Sounds like you're well on your way without me," she whispered, chewing sullenly at her cheek-full of gum.

He ignored her for a moment then turned his head, hissing, "You're damn right I am. I had to piece all that together on my own. Where the hell were you anyway?"

She threw a surreptitious look at Lamphere, silently listening to the quarrel. "Tracking down an informant, that's where. My leads are just as viable as yours."

He gaped at her. "Did you hear a word I said in there? We're this close to tying Sister Ping to the *Golden Venture*." He shook his head. "I'm sick of this. You always think you know better, shutting me out, and I'm left to do all the real work by myself."

She was taken aback. She had always thought theirs was a decent working relationship and had no idea that Benny had been harboring secret resentment toward her. The thought hurt and she opened her mouth to hit him with a defensive retort but Lamphere spoke first.

"You two better sort this out right now," he said, without turning around. "We don't have time for bickering. Lacey, you are to immediately drop your line of investigation and come on board with Benny's. Clear?"

She squirmed with frustration, finally managing a, "Yes sir."

Benny stared at the ceiling of the elevator, his face still flushed with emotion. A silence stretched. Karissa, now feeling vaguely guilty and resenting the fact, decided to switch topics.

"How about Rusty Kincaid crashing the meeting?" she asked. "Strange, right?"

"Not really," said Lamphere tiredly. "He's the mayor. He can attend any meeting he wants."

"I thought he seemed overly interested in the *Golden Venture*," she mumbled.

"It's political," said Benny through clenched teeth. "He's gaining voters every day by flogging the immigration issue."

"Sure," she said, "but why was he at a private operational meeting with the police? It doesn't make sense."

"Drop it Lacey," growled Lamphere.

And as far as they knew, she did.

## ✣ 15 ✣

## DUSTY WORDS

B eneath the star encrusted midnight sky, beneath the misty
humming streets, beneath concrete, gravel and earth, beneath
live wires and sewer lines, subways and maintenance tunnels,
beneath the heat and the noise and the grit; as if removed from time
and space, silent and brooding, the gloomy archival room lay, as though
waiting for something. *Or someone*, Nigel thought, as he crawled, upside
down, clinging to the metal apparatus supporting the ceiling of the
museum's secret subterranean archives. Fine dust particles danced in
the air, passing unobtrusively in and out of his lungs, swept along with
his breath.

Below him, the space was dominated by twenty-six shelving units,
each about twelve feet high, supporting a series of identical, jet-black
storage boxes. The shelves fanned out in a semi-circle, a long table
flanked by wooden chairs at their epicentre. Against the back wall, was
a cubicle containing a tiny desk and several filing cabinets. It looked as
though a curator or librarian spent their days here, far from the bright
lights and the hustle and bustle of the city. There was also a custodial
station nearby, complete with a bucket, a mop, a garbage bin, a tap and
a floor drain.

Suited and masked, Nigel had waited until the museum was closed and, carefully avoiding the eyes of security cameras, he had passed through a maintenance door that had been left unlocked for him. He had then followed the map he carried through a labyrinthine network of narrow staircases and passages, past mysterious unmarked doors, through a rock tunnel, lit with naked bulbs and down a trapdoor into the chamber. The map had been sketched in the spidery hand of Amy Kang, the best janitor in New York.

He fished for his watch inside the flap of cloth that held his belongings, found it and checked the time. It was 7 p.m., still five hours to go before he expected Amy Kang and he was growing peckish. Rummaging around in the bundle again, he produced a package of hard, brown *senbei* rice crackers. He tore open the plastic and took a bite from one, wishing he had brought something more substantial with him for dinner. The crunching noises he emitted were immediately swallowed by the chamber, as though the walls were hungry for all sound. Finishing the food and stowing the wrapper, he checked his watch again and, with nothing else to do, he decided to indulge the urge to explore.

Having climbed down the ladder, Nigel walked between the shelves, peering up at the vast array of black banker's boxes, all with small, white labels on the front. He slid one of the boxes toward him and was removing its sturdy lid when he heard a female voice behind him.

"Don't touch that."

He jumped, jerking his hands away from the box. It teetered for a split second on the edge of the shelf, then fell to the floor with a thump, its corner crumpling, contents spilling out over the floor. In the pile was a sheaf of fragile onion skin papers, along with a small ink pot and quill, a glass vial with gold flakes suspended in solution and a pebble with a face carved into it. The ink pot had smashed and a black puddle was forming, seeping into the grooves of the stone floor, a mercifully safe distance from the fallen papers. Fortunately, the glass vial had remained intact, its golden contents swirling angrily.

Nigel looked up and saw an adolescent woman standing before him. She was not very tall, her body hidden within the folds of a pair of black, tearaway track pants and a bulky, light-grey hooded sweatshirt, her hands stuffed inside the kangaroo pouch in front. Her features hinted at her Korean ancestry – Amy Kang.

"My sincere apologies for the mess," he said, formally.

Amy Kang said nothing, expressionless, staring down at the spilled contents of the box at Nigel's feet. Then she ordered, "Don't move. Stay there," and walked away, disappearing around the corner at the end of the row of shelves.

Obediently, he stayed where he was, listening to the faint sound of her soft soled shoes, *scuff, scuff, scuff,* on the stone floor. He heard water running and the squeak of a tap being shut off, then he heard her return. *Scuff, scuff, scuff.* She rounded the corner again, toting a bucket of warm soapy water and the mop he had seen. The bucket steamed faintly, emitting a pleasant chemical smell of citrus. Nigel wondered how there could be hot water in this place, apparently so far from the rest of the city.

She stuck out an arm and, as though clearing away cobwebs, gently moved him to the side, away from the fallen papers and ink. She knelt and began to carefully gather the thin parchment, righting the damaged box and placing the papers inside. He crouched to help her but she raised a hand, stopping him and, without saying a word, continued to replace the contents of the box.

When all the items were inside, the vial and the pebble placed carefully alongside the parchment, she returned the box to the shelf, then deftly gathered the broken pieces of glass with blue-gloved hands and placed them in a thick plastic bag, taking care not to spread the ink as she did so. She tied off the bag and placed it next to the box then, with brisk strokes, cleared the ink from the floor, the mop handle almost a blur; yet she was careful and methodical for all her speed.

"I dusted twenty hours ago," Amy Kang said out of the blue, surprising Nigel. He waited for more but nothing followed the statement.

"All the surfaces look very clean," he said respectfully.

"Yes," she said, without looking at him and kept mopping.

"You arrived here sooner than I expected," he said, shifting uncomfortably. She made no reply, still not looking at him. It occurred to him that she didn't seem to mind or even notice how he was dressed.

"Maybe I should change," he muttered to himself.

She stopped mopping. "What for?"

"Some people feel uncomfortable around this." He held up an arm, its grey metallic surface crawling and oozing in a stomach-churning way, reflecting faint golden rays absent in the room's lighting.

She went back to her mopping. "It doesn't matter to me." Her tone was flat, convincingly indifferent and he marvelled at this young woman, girl really, who was so skilled at her solitary work in this silent place. But he was still uncertain if she could help him.

Clearing his throat, he said, "Good. Well, as you know, Agent Lacey recommended I ask for your help with some research."

"Yes," she said.

Nigel paused, considering how best to express his position. "I think that my suit, what I call the *Resident*, is harming me."

Amy Kang set her mop against a shelf and, moving up close to him, she grabbed his hand, turning it over and examining the palm, as though attempting to read his fortune. She stared intently at the shifting lines of black and grey, like veins of iron ore shot through its surface, head cocked to one side like a magpie.

"What gives you that impression?" she asked.

"I've been having dizzy spells, headaches. About three weeks ago I was struck with vertigo and missed a jump. And the symptoms have been followed by a quality of deep fatigue I've never experienced before."

"Maybe you should consult a physician?" she offered, dropping his hand and pinching off excess moisture from the mop in the press mounted on the side of the bucket.

"Maybe," replied Nigel, doubtfully. He wondered what he was doing here. Amy Kang seemed nice enough but his doubts about her usefulness were mounting.

"You acquired the *Resident* from Hitsujikai," Amy Kang said suddenly.

Nigel gawped at her. "How did you know that?"

Amy Kang pushed her mop into the bucket and left it there,

sticking out at a jaunty angle and motioned for him to follow. They walked out the end of the aisle and stopped at the centre of the room where the long table stood with its fleet of sturdy, wooden chairs. From that position, they had a clear view of the rows of shelves and the panels displaying filing ranges: 'AAA-AZZ,' 'BAA-BZZ' and so on. After a moment of scanning the panels, Amy Kang set off again, shuffling down an aisle to their left, with Nigel in tow. She stopped suddenly, staring up at a box a few feet out of reach and paused, considering.

"I'll go and get the ladder," she said at last.

"No need," said Nigel and he hopped up to stand on the first shelf, sliding the black banker's box toward him, taking care to balance it in one hand as he descended to the ground. He felt the need to prove himself after the recent mishap. Extracting the box from his grasp and, without a word and without looking him in the eye, Amy Kang turned and made her way back toward the centre of the chamber.

"After Karissa told me about your situation, I took the liberty of researching your cult," she said, surprising Nigel again. She placed the box on the long table and he peered over her shoulder, not knowing what to expect. Removing the lid, she revealed a single scroll with wooden handles, nested in a bed of fine cedar shavings, and a small envelope. The scroll was thin, with a diameter of only a few centimeters and the envelope that lay beside it was faded, displaying a New York address and exhibiting a large, curling postage stamp in one corner.

From inside the front pouch of her hooded sweatshirt, Amy Kang produced a pair of small white cotton gloves, worn but obviously very clean. Donning the gloves, she lifted the scroll with the utmost care, gently unfurling it and laying it tenderly on the table in front of them. She removed the envelope and placed it beside the scroll. Nigel noticed that the top had been slit and what looked like a letter was tucked inside.

The scroll was written in Japanese but, as Nigel scanned the characters, he noticed from the syntax and vowels that the language differed slightly from modern Japanese, though it was not difficult for him to discern its meaning.

"The language is Middle Japanese, dating from the late twelfth century," Amy Kang said, slightly breathless, her cool demeanor altered for the first time that evening.

He began to read the Hiragana on the scroll, written with a calligrapher's brush:

*'In response to the call comes Hitsujikai.*
*From the heavens came the call, like rain from the sky.*
*Black rain on black earth; black rain on the body of the Champion.*
*No fire will burn him but inner fire; no blade will pierce but the blades within.*
*Only lightning will be his undoing; only lightning will be his salvation.*
*His will be the hand to carry us all, through the black night to the shining dawn.*
*To other lands will he travel; all are the sheep of Hitsujikai.*
*He will preserve the world of our ancestors, and lay a guiding hand.*
*On the shoulders of the enemies of Hitsujikai, his gauntlet will rest.*
*Woe be to the darkness; woe be to the enemies of the light.*
*Careful hammer blows on the gossamer world, until the shining dawn.*
*Though time will be short for him, the Resident will live on.*
*Hammer blows on the gossamer world.'*

Someone had scrawled a note at the bottom in English:

*-From the first oratory of Grandmaster Ota, Hitsujikai, after thirty years.*

Nigel had barely finished reading the scroll when Amy Kang reached for the envelope with the letter inside, drew out the folded papers and thrust them into his hands:

*November 12, 1911*

*Dear Dr. Okamura,*
*I acquired the enclosed scroll during my recent encounter with Hitsujikai. I will confess that the cult leaders did not grant permission for its removal. My only excuse for possessing it now is that my stay in Village Ryūiki ended abruptly two weeks ago and I was forced to pack my things and return to Stockholm in a most hurried manner. I was studying the scroll just prior to my depar-*

*ture and it became inadvertently mixed with my things when I was all but ejected from the village.*

*The reason for the terse and un-Japanese ousting from my lodging at Ryūiki was the demise of the cult's Champion. As I suspected, the parasite, also known as the 'Resident,' had caused catastrophic internal damage to the body of the host. And, as the leading and perhaps only physician in the known world with expertise in the area, the cult leaders presumed that I might be able to forestall the decay that had taken root in the Champion's very bones. Certainly, I might have done so if I had been called upon earlier.*

*I have been convinced by scattered accounts that it should be possible to mitigate the parasite by running high-voltage electrical current through the tissue of the host. This I tried but, due to the host's advanced state of deterioration, his body ultimately could not handle the strain and he succumbed, though not before I could learn some new and intriguing information.*

*When electricity was applied, I observed that the twenty-nine-year-old host became more lucid and regained some of his formerly enhanced strength. And, at one point, near the end of the treatment, I noticed that some of the parasite had begun to leak away, at first coalescing on the skin of the host, like the protective covering he could previously extrude, then falling away from his body in great treacly drops, which the cult members rushed to collect.*

*The host's recovery, albeit temporary, fits with what I have read concerning other carriers. I hypothesize that electricity may be the key to unlocking the secrets of the parasite and, in addition, might behave as medicine for any poor soul stricken with its destructive effects, though I should think it could never cure what is most likely a terminal condition. Truly the host is both blessed and cursed.*

*I fear that the missing scroll, when added to the death of their Champion, may cause the cult to close their society permanently to the likes of me. This may prove to be a grave error on their part, for if I were granted more prolonged access to the parasitic substance, I should be able to develop additional methods of prolonging the lives of future hosts, whom they hold in such esteem.*

*I am entrusting the scroll to you, for although you were banished from the cult, at least you know its whereabouts in the high Nagano mountains and, depending on shifting loyalties and changing leadership, you may yet regain contact with Hitsujikai. Until then, it eases my mind to know you will keep the enclosed document safe. Relinquishing it to you almost allows me to believe that I have returned what I inadvertently stole.*

    *Yours truly,*

    *Mikael Karlsson, MD; Ph.D.*

Nigel's eyes flew across the pages, which Amy Kang had spread on the table for him to view. He looked between the letter and the scroll, his future laid out before him like some terrible proclamation, dreadfully abridged and seeming trivial of a sudden, as if he had skipped to the last sentence of a mediocre book. The documents, which she had revealed to him almost casually, seemed to confirm what he feared most – that his relationship with the *Resident* was hazardous and was rapidly shortening his life.

Inside him, the feeling of uncertainty about the future had been replaced with... with what? It wasn't resignation; he realized that he had a strong urge to live, to fight the *Resident*, to beat it, and his mind rebelled at the thought that his life should take such a course, with him having little say in the outcome. It was anger he felt.

He spread his hands out before him, staring hard at their metallic surface, fighting the urge to violently shake away the cloying substance, then he turned to his new companion and stared at her for a long moment.

"What now?" he asked, his voice wavering a little.

Amy Kang smiled for the first time that evening, her small white teeth gleaming dully in the harsh light from the ceiling. "More research," she said.

## ❧ 16 ❧

## DIVE

Someone was singing, the sound of it echoing strangely in the dank, narrow space of the hallway with the quality of an old recording limping out the mouth of a gramophone on the fritz. Karissa thought she knew that voice, her brows knitting together as she made her way toward it.

The entry, which was unusually lengthy for the size of the establishment, led to Lazy Dane McCain's, a small and notorious Lower East Side dive in the heart of the Bowery. It was well known but not particularly remarkable in Karissa's opinion; what with the stink of old booze and fresh urine, the penetrating scarlet light and the cloying, swampy quality of a men's locker room, the place could be any of the hundreds of rundown old bars in Lower Manhattan.

She rounded the corner and beheld Admiral Rat, standing before a small and motley crowd, solemnly singing his heart out. *About time.* Karissa had spent the better part of the last week looking for him and now here he was. Clearly, he had given up on eluding her.

In the audience were grey-haired down-and-outers, with no other place to go on a Thursday, dressed in faded blue jeans and nearly identical plaid button-up shirts, clutching dented and tarnished pewter mugs that would be hung on designated wall hooks at the end of the night. And a younger crowd was present, equally dirty but with an eclectic fashion, wearing an assortment of outsize thrift store clothes, including stained, billowing t-shirts with crazy, scribbly designs, and ripped and baggy pants modified with chains, metal studs and spikes.

When asked, Rat liked to sing old Bowery tunes from the turn of the century. He was old-timey in his way. On this occasion, he was dressed in a cream-colored shirt with French cuffs, a threadbare double-breasted vest with a matching bowler hat and dark moth-eaten slacks folded over the tops of worn leather boots. His singing was plaintive and raspy, somewhat reminiscent of the 1920s hillbilly folk icon Harry McClintock, but with each note sung at least a semitone off the mark.

> *The Bow'ry, the Bow'ry!*
> *They say such things,*
> *And they do strange things*
> *On the Bow'ry! The Bow'ry!*
> *I'll never go there anymore!*

The rest of these bums never seemed to notice that Rat was off-key or at least were content to suffer his discordant performances because the jukebox was broken, which it had been off and on since it was installed in the seventies. Inevitably though, the mood of the room would shift and somebody would creep up behind Rat and light his shoelaces on fire. It was an old joke, a hotfoot, mean-spirited and only perpetrated on those occupying the lowest tier of the barroom hierarchy: the goofballs, the clowns, the official butts.

Admiral Rat was the butt of many, many jokes; he was widely known for it. His name was a prime example – 'Admiral Rat of the Bowery navy,' courtesy of some wise-ass more than forty years ago. But you had to be careful what you said around Rat because someone important might find out, and they often did.

Rat had a well-earned reputation as the top informer on the Bowery. He kept both eyes open and had an almost preternatural ability to be in the right place at the right time. He had a knack for remembering and squirreling away conversations he heard and regurgitating them later, word for word. And he had an aptitude for distilling truth from rumors, and for piecing together a patchwork of seemingly unrelated happenings to form a larger picture, delivering it whole to his patrons. In addition, Karissa could think of nobody with such a detailed understanding of the Bowery and the adjacent neighborhoods of the Lower East Side, East Village, Chinatown, Little Italy, and the Five Points as Rat had, nobody close. He knew every corner, every alley and every drinking establishment, existing seemingly everywhere at once.

Traveling from place to place, Rat kept tabs on important business deals, political maneuverings, personal disputes and the workings of organized crime. He was a champion ear-bender and enjoyed loitering in the Bowery police precinct, chatting up the highest-ranking officers available. He regularly slipped in and out of the offices of key district politicians at City Hall and inserted himself into the back rooms of bars and nightclubs where local celebrities rubbed shoulders with mob bosses and drug lords. Most were at least a little fond of Rat, perhaps harboring a splinter of respect for his brazen schmoozing, but the real reason they tolerated his presence was the high-quality information he offered in exchange for a pittance; just enough pocket money, free food and free booze to keep him going.

She wondered, as she often did, how he avoided the dangers associated with such high-level gossiping. One thing he seemed to do extraordinarily well was navigating an often-treacherous landscape of competing interests. For example, in the recent turf war between the White Tigers and the Flying Cranes in Chinatown, she knew he had kept both youth gangs' parent tongs appraised of the situation throughout the bloody conflict, while somehow escaping the notice of gang members who had begun to resent the tongs' meddling. And she knew for a fact that Rat informed on Italian mob bosses to the police and vice versa. It was almost comical how blissfully unaware they all were of Rat's status as a multiple double agent. Across the board, key players failed to look past his antics and shabby exterior to the wily man beneath and though they called him 'Rat,' they never saw him as a danger. *Big mistake*, Karissa thought.

Rat howled as a gout of flame from a rapidly combusting boot lace singed his pant leg. The malnourished drunk who had lit the lace cackled and scuttled off to the bar, tucking his orange plastic lighter into the back pocket of a pair of grimy jeans and calling for a shot of rye. Making a show of it, Admiral Rat hobbled back to his seat at a table of guffawing grey-haired regulars. Attempting to mask her wolf's grin, Karissa approached the table and pulled out a wooden chair with a sharp *rrrk*. Rat's face was drawn, with an increasing number of lines and a leathery, weather-beaten appearance that had become more pronounced since she was a youth.

"Hiya Rat," she said, tossing her overcoat on the table and motioning to the bartender to bring her over a glass.

"Agent Lacey!" Rat was suddenly all smiles. As usual his words came in a jumbled, anxious rush. "Saw your old man the other day."

If Rat had loyalty to anyone, it was to her father. He had always been his man. She noticed Rat's grin never reached his eyes, which were filled with caution and mistrust.

Karissa accepted a glass from the bartender as he stumped past and she snatched the whiskey bottle belonging to the other men at the table before they could protest.

"That makes one of us," she said, the cork coming free with a gentle *thwop* and she poured herself two thick fingers of the amber liquid, rotating the glass so its greasy smudge faced away from her.

"Where the hell have you been?" she asked Rat, unclasping her shoulder holster and dropping it on the table, along with her gun. The other men eyed the objects and they silently rose as one, finding other places to continue their drinking.

"Here n' there." He smiled, revealing an uneven row of shit-colored teeth. "What can I do for you?"

She eyed him closely. "What do you know about the *Golden Venture?*"

His lip twitched. "Not much t' say on that score, nothing new, not a peep."

"Nothing at all?" she demanded, taking a burning swallow of whiskey.

He looked down at the table. "Just that the *Golden Venture* landed way off target. Either the dock boys got cold feet and shoed 'er away or the ringleader made a bad choice on crew." He took a sip from his own glass of whiskey, coughed, spluttered and, teeth bared in a grimace of displeasure, called out, "C'n anyone get the Rat a beer?" There being no immediate reply, he emitted a sigh and turned his beady eyes back to Karissa.

She leaned forward. "Know where the *Golden Venture* was supposed to land?"

"Just the docks in Brooklyn, that's it," he said, taking a cautious sip of the whiskey.

"Anything new in the world of human smuggling?" she asked.

"Sounds like your partner's on track to bust Sister Ping over there on East Broadway," he said a little hoarsely, grinning cheekily at her. He was infuriatingly up to date, as usual.

"Waste of time," she said. "No way Ping's behind something as big as the *Golden Venture.*"

"You think the INS is barkin' up the wrong tree?" he asked, small eyes glinting as he watched her.

Her eyes narrowed a fraction. "What do you think Rat?"

"Could be," he said, sucking his teeth, "but then again, I try not to judge books by their covers." He paused, seeming to consider the matter. "Hard to say."

Karissa sighed. "I'll keep it in mind. That all you have for me?" she asked, a yawn creeping into her voice.

"Yes ma'am."

"Come on Rat. It took me all week to find you and you're really going to let me leave empty-handed?" She tried to look intimidating but found her heart wasn't in it. Talking with Admiral Rat always left her feeling vaguely drained.

He shrugged, the picture of remorse.

"Fine." She tipped her head back, summarily downing the rest of the whiskey. "I'll be back early next week. Hope you'll be available." She handed him a crumpled ten-dollar bill.

"Course," he replied, unconvincingly.

"Why avoid me Rat? You know we'll cross paths sooner or later."

He just looked at her, a grin half-formed on his cracked, purplish lips.

She turned to go and was striding toward the exit when Rat spoke up again, unexpectedly, his unmistakable gravelly voice reaching her from across the room.

"Heard the mayor crashed your meeting at the precinct the other day," he said.

She stopped and made her way back over, lowering herself into the chair she'd left pulled out from the table.

"What about it?" she asked, fixing him with a penetrating stare.

"Not a big fan of his, are you?" he asked, smugness leaking around the edges of feigned deference as if from a badly patched sewer line.

She waited, wondering where this was going.

He looked around him for potential listeners, his stubby fingers playing with themselves on the surface of the table. "Thought you might like to know he's been in to see the Hip Sing a dozen times or so over the last year."

Karissa's eyebrows rose. Hip Sing was one of the largest of the Chinatown tongs. Although the organization had officially distanced itself from organized crime, taking the time to rebrand itself the "Hip Sing Public Association," everyone knew Hip Sing was still behind most of the crime in the Chinese community. *What was Rusty Kincaid doing meeting with them?*

She asked Rat as much.

"Beats the hell outta me Agent Lacey," he said, giving her his widest, most revolting grin yet. "let me know when you find out will you?"


THE NEXT DAY, KARISSA SAT ALONE IN HER QUIET OFFICE AT THE INS, staring at the screen saver on her computer monitor, silent and brooding. She felt hungover, though she had drunk only two more glasses of whisky after departing Lazy Dane's and abandoning Admiral Rat to whatever mischief he had planned for the rest of the evening. She silently lamented the fact that three drinks could cause her this level of discomfort, when she used to be able to power through the day after a full-on bender, running on nothing but nicotine and strong black coffee.

Today, amid the haze in her mind, she found herself consumed with thoughts about the mayor and the Hip Sing. She wished the INS could investigate the mayor's connection to organized crime but this wasn't the FBI and Kincaid had to be connected with something related to immigration before Dick Lamphere would even consider letting her open a case on him.

She frowned, thinking about the mayor. *How dare he?* It was bad enough that he badly neglected an ailing New York, slashing public programs and handing out breaks on taxes that should be going toward solving the city's problems; homelessness, rampant addiction, and a rapidly failing transit system were only some of the issues on the list. Kincaid failed to build anything meaningful, only tore things down and now it looked like he was probably mixed up in something. The question was, how should she go about bringing his shady dealings to light?

Shaking her head, she stood up and made her way to the breakroom down the hall, where she discovered her friend Charity sitting at the small circular table there, watching the television. The breakroom had the only television in five floors and it was this configuration that had allowed her to meet Charity, who worked in the visa office three floors up, in the first place. She snuck up and flicked her earlobe.

"Jesus!" exclaimed Charity, turning her head to regard Karissa.

"Guess who?" said Karissa, spreading her arms wide.

"Shhh," replied Charity, increasing the volume on the television with the remote. She pulled out another chair from the table and motioned for Karissa to sit beside her. On screen, a news bulletin was in progress. Charity glanced over. "Big news regarding the mayor," she said and an electric thrill ran up Karissa's spine.

A female anchor was on screen. "Late last night in Red Hook, a dry dock registered to New York mayor, Rusty Kincaid was raided by police. Sources say that at the time of the raid, a party was in full swing. Not only was the mayor reported to have been hosting, he was apparently participating in the festivities. Reports are that, after a brief exchange with police, Mayor Kincaid was taken into custody for possession of methamphetamine. The following scene occurred minutes ago outside the NYPD's seventy-second precinct, as the mayor was released, pending further investigation."

The camera cut to a swarm of reporters clustered around the doors of the police precinct. The mayor appeared a moment later, his moon face flushed a ruddy crimson, sweat glistening on his forehead, bloodshot eyes darting wildly about him.

"Mister Mayor, will you be charged with possession of methamphetamine?"

"How long have you been using crystal meth?"

A microphone was thrust under the mayor's nose. He panted into it for a few moments before members of his staff ushered him off to a waiting vehicle.

The anchor came back on, "We have also received reports this morning that thirteen illegal Chinese immigrants were apprehended from the mayor's company premises. The mayor's office has yet to comment on the presence of these alleged aliens, who were apparently staffing the event and who are now being held by police until their status in the U.S. can be confirmed. For Channel 6 News, I'm Rachel McCloud."

"Ho-lee-shit," said Charity.

Karissa sat stunned in her chair, staring at the television. Kincaid was a crook. The meth alone proved it. Not only that, he had been caught employing illegal Chinese immigrants, which was definitely an immigration issue.

Charity locked eyes with her. "What a scandal," she said gleefully, "and right before the election!"

Neglecting to reply, Karissa stood up and bolted out the door of the breakroom, the sound of Charity calling her name echoing in the corridor behind.

Twenty seconds later she was standing outside Dick Lamphere's closed door, fist poised to knock, trying to calm herself by taking deep, measured breaths, willing her heartbeat to slow down. Then she knocked.

"Come."

"Morning sir," she said, attempting to infuse her voice with a chipper tone.

"Out with it Lacey. I'm probably too busy for whatever it is anyway." She noticed there were dark circles under his eyes and saw a cluster of used paper coffee cups at his elbow on the desk. He had probably been at the office since the small hours of the morning and appeared to be in an even worse mood than usual. *Great.*

"Sir, did you hear the news?"

He rolled his eyes ostentatiously. "News, Lacey?"

She paused, fighting to keep her face as neutral as possible. "The mayor was arrested last night for drug possession and is alleged to have been employing more than a dozen illegal Chinese immigrants."

A long silence stretched.

"And?" he finally said.

She goggled at him. "And I want to investigate him."

"On what fucking basis?" he hissed.

Her words came out in a breathy rush: "On the basis that he might be a human smuggler."

The INS director was so still she wondered if his heart had stopped and he had died with his eyes open. She pressed on. "Kincaid crashed the *Golden Venture* meeting with the NYPD." She held up her hands defensively. "And I was ready to let it go like you said, until I received a reliable tip that the mayor's been meeting with Chinatown tongs. And five minutes ago, a major news channel broke the story that he's into drugs and involved with illegal immigrants. So—"

"So nothing!" Lamphere roared. "The mayor is *not*, I repeat *not*, a human smuggler."

"But sir, I–"

"And if I hear even a whisper you're after him, I'll have your badge." He smiled nastily at her. "Are we clear?" She nodded and he gazed at her for a moment, eyes narrowed. Then he stretched, his hairy arms protruding from the cuffs of his starched white shirt as he raised them over his head. "You watch," he said in a milder tone, "he'll shed this trouble and be back on the campaign trail by the end of next week. It's Rusty Kincaid. He's made of fucking Teflon."

## ✣ 17 ✣

## HEAD TO TOE

The prophetic words of Dick Lamphere held true; it wasn't a week before the news of the mayor's scandal had dissipated, remaining only as a thin sheen of greasy oil on the water that was the public consciousness.

Amazingly, the mayor's legal team had orchestrated the dropping of all substance-related charges and had somehow halted the media chatter about the mayor's relationship with illegal immigrants with an injunction, successfully arguing that stories written on this topic were to be considered libelous. The strategy had proved effective; the incident on the docks hadn't even affected the mayor's approval rating.

Karissa would have been impressed at the near-magical feat of making the mayor's problems disappear if she wasn't so furious. As it was, she could barely eat or sleep for her relentless anxiety, taking her by surprise with its intensity. Regardless, she knew from experience that hot on the heels of the anxiety would come depression, unless she did something about it.

On Wednesday afternoon, she left the Javits Building early, headed for her tailor's in the East Village. Esteban, a Spaniard who had trained with several prominent clothing makers in Italy, had been constructing a special outfit for her under specific directions. She had requested

that the suit be durable and afford her protection during rough spar-
ring. Esteban had been eager to tackle the project and that morning,
after several months of work, he had left her an enthusiastic, heavily
accented message on her answering machine, announcing that the suit
was ready for pickup.

Although it was true she had commissioned the outfit to use with
her martial arts training, which, after a hiatus of more than eight years,
she was pursuing with renewed vigor, a secret part of her had thought
it might come in handy if she ever needed to put on her vigilante's
mask and take to the streets again. For, unbeknownst to her, a frustration had been mounting, akin to the emotion her father must have felt
as a frustrated policeman. It was perhaps a side effect of a worldview
that included the twin beliefs that there were far too many low-lifes
and far too few people who cared about the havoc they wreaked on
law-abiding citizens. And over the last few days, after hearing that the
mayor had ducked the justice he deserved, she had discovered her frustration could not be contained.

A little after 4pm, Karissa took the subway to 1st Avenue station
and walked the five blocks to Esteban's shop at 331 East 9th Street.

Miniature stoneware chimes tinkled pleasantly as she pushed open
the glass-fronted door and Esteban's distinct voice drifted out from
the back room.

"One moment please!" he called.

"Take your time," she replied, surveying the room. It was more of a
costume shop than a traditional tailor's. Esteban worked with several
well-known Chelsea drag queens. He was also a long-time collaborator
with members of the kink community, constructing wondrous,
spiralling outfits in leather and steel, more ornate cages than wearable
garments but she supposed that must be how his clients liked them.
She occupied herself with running her hands over the swaths of
flowing fabric, hanging on hooks and scattered about the room, and
admiring the elaborate gowns displayed alongside colourful, avant-
garde men's suits, all works of art that elicited a pleasant feeling of
spine-tingling awe.

Esteban burst through the red velvet curtain serving as the door to
the back room. His arms spread wide, he moved rapidly toward her, an

enthusiastic smile spread across his tanned face. "Karissa! So happy you're here. I am very excited to show you to your beautiful outfit."

She smiled and gave the man a hug, the brightness of his greeting and the warmth of his body perceptibly lifting her spirits.

"Hi Esteban, thank you. I'm excited to see it."

He guided her into the back room where, in a beam of halogen light, her outfit stood, displayed dramatically on the body of a mannequin. It was a midnight blue, verging on black, made from a tough-looking material that shimmered faintly where it caught the light. The outfit was one piece, with a long mat-black zipper down the back and what looked like stirrups holding the material in place around the bottom of the mannequin's feet and in the crook where its thumbs met its hands. At intervals across the chest, down the torso, and at arm and leg joints, were bands of tough, richly-dyed, brown leather, carefully stitched and integrated with the fabric, with handcrafted steel buckles for adjusting the diameter of the bands. She could see that the leather would protect the wearer's most vulnerable points.

"The material is a variant of Kevlar, a ceramic," said Esteban, "It is flexible and extremely breathable. I added the leather for extra protection, as you requested, and both materials are resistant to edge weapons, in case you are practicing with knives." He winked. "As a bonus, the entire garment is flame-resistant, though I hope you will not be requiring that feature." He turned to her expectantly, dry washing his hands in excitement.

Karissa stared at the suit for several long moments, her eyes filling unexpectedly with tears. The little man had somehow captured exactly the outfit she had envisioned as a young girl, dreaming of becoming a real-live superhero in New York, a fantasy that had been forced aside by life's harsh realities. As she stared through the shimmering liquid in her eyes, she dared to allow herself to hope for a new beginning and was nearly overcome.

"Thank you," she breathed.

Esteban nodded meaningfully, a man who knew the power of special clothes. "Let me get you a box," he said.

. . .

When she arrived home to her apartment that evening, Karissa made herself a simple meal of boiled pasta, green peas and canned tuna. She chewed the food thoughtfully, staring out at the dying light. The orange glow of the sun reflecting from the glass of the adjacent buildings filled her with calm certainty about what she would do that night.

After she had finished her dinner, she methodically washed the dishes and the pan, meticulously drying them and replacing them in the cupboard. She padded into the bedroom, rummaging in the back of her closet for the grey steel box she had lugged with her from place to place over the years, reminiscent of her father's old arms box.

Sliding the box toward her, careful not to scrape the hardwood floor, she produced the key and opened the lid. Inside was an assortment of cruel-looking items. She selected a pair of tough leather gloves and placed them to the side. In addition, she removed a compact black stun gun and an ASP telescopic baton, which she had borrowed from work. The weapon evoked the wooden baton she had been forced to leave behind when she left her father's apartment. Finally, she withdrew a slim black flashlight and closed the box.

Arranging the items in a fan around her, she pondered the collection. Finally nodding with approval, she thrust the box back into its hiding place in the closet and cast about for her old police service belt, with its brown leather pouches and, finding it in a drawer, she filled it with the items from the box. Then she walked into the other room and opened the package Esteban had given her. Slipping out of her clothes, she donned the midnight-blue suit, stepping into it through the back, reverently sliding the material over her bare legs and arms and adjusting the leather bands so they fit snuggly over her chest.

She admired herself in the full-length hallway mirror, standing proudly, hands on her hips. Grinning at herself, she bared her teeth in mock ferocity, then headed back into the bedroom, pulling thick woolen socks over the hardy suit material covering her ankles. She shoved her feet into a pair of worn, heavy-duty combat boots and, clipping the bulging police belt around her middle, she threw her tan overcoat atop the ensemble, stuffing her old sky-blue balaclava deep in the coat's inner pocket. She clicked off the hall light and left the apartment silent behind her.


THE TWO NIGHT SECURITY MEN WERE ON BREAK AT THE SAME TIME. They had paused their outside rounds and were smoking and talking quietly together, seated on the concrete stop behind one in a row of empty parking stalls. The lot bordered the mayor's company dry dock, a massive red brick structure with a high vaulted roof, situated along the waterfront at Red Hook.

Karissa could see the guards from her high vantage point, which she had gained after successfully negotiating a barbed wire fence on the northeast corner of the lot and climbing up a long, sturdy fire escape to the roof of the building. She peered over the edge, down at the two men. Not the best time to take a break she would have said and, especially given the recent attention this warehouse had received in the media, she would have expected a greater number of security personnel. She was grateful for the oversight though, because it meant she would have an easier time slipping in and out unnoticed. A thrill of excitement travelled up her spine. Here she was, in direct opposition to Lamphere's orders to refrain from investigating the mayor, though she supposed if she was caught breaking into the building, the Director's wrath would be the least of her worries.

She turned and stepped lightly up to the nearby skylight, offering a view of the cavernous interior of the building. The space was dominated by a ship about 150 feet long, raised on an enormous, rust-encrusted platform with slats in various places, through which she could see ocean water sloshing and glimmering in the moonlight. At one end of the space there was a white-painted steel staircase leading to a platform and a row of closed office doors. She guessed that at least one of the offices might house something of interest to her.

Peering around, she looked for a way in. Inside there was a series of scaffold-supported platforms, connected by ladders, running around the perimeter at various heights above the ground, the nearest of which was only about six feet down. The problem was that none of the skylight panels were hinged and there was no way to enter aside from breaking the glass. She sighed, sliding the telescopic baton from its loop at her side. Hefting the weapon, she removed the balaclava from her head and wrapped the blue material around the end of the collapsed baton. Then, as though crushing pepper corns with a mortar and pestle, she bumped the padded end of the baton against the glass surface with short, firm strokes.

It began to crack and then broke, pieces of glass falling into space, tinkling faintly, leaving behind a jagged hole. She withdrew the baton, unwrapping the balaclava and shaking it free of excess shards. She hoped she wouldn't get any glass in her eyes for her trouble. She re-stowed the baton and, taking a deep breath, she vaulted through the hole, landing with a muted *clank* on the platform below.

She checked her arm, which had scraped the jutting glass on the way down. Not even a scratch. She silently thanked Esteban for the second time that evening for using such remarkably tough material in her suit. The scent of stale sea water and faint odors of creosote and engine fuel wafted up to her.

Carefully, quietly, she slipped down the various ladders until she reached the floor. She stared up at the ship, looming over her, silent and brooding, silhouetted in the moonlight cascading through the newly perforated skylight where she had come in. The vessel was probably about the same size and class as the *Golden Venture* she guessed, diesel fuelled, with one enormous propeller protruding from the stern.

She recalled that the INS had experienced difficulty with tracing the history of the *Golden Venture,* which had probably been physically altered and renamed at some point in a facility very much like this one. They had recovered the twelve-digit serial number from the vessel, known in the shipping world as the 'Hull Identification Number' or HIN, but the ship's history was spotty. Knowing nothing aside from where it had been manufactured and that it had previously been called the *Najd II,* the INS was in the dark about the ship's previous owners and the specific nature of its operations before it had arrived like a phantom at Rockaway Beach.

Turning away from the ominous mass of the ship, Karissa hurried over to the staircase leading up to the offices on the far side of the room, carefully avoiding the bottles and plastic cups still scattered on the floor from the infamous party two nights before. Looking at the debris, she thought of Amy Kang and wondered how she and Nigel were getting on with their research regarding the nature of his powers.

Her boots rang softly on the metal as she ascended the stairs, her gloved hands making a soft hiss as they slid along the rail. She paused outside the first office and peered through the glass window set in the door. Inside was a bare desk, an empty shelf and a lonely-looking office chair. Moving on to the next office, she spotted a desk coated in a carpet of papers, a computer on screen saver, and several tall filing cabinets in the back corner of the room.

Karissa tried the handle. Locked. Raising her elbow, she shattered the office window, reached in and opened the door from the inside. *Always wanted to do that*, she thought. Broken glass crunching under her feet, she moved swiftly into the room, wondering what she should be looking for. She pawed through the papers on the desk, scanning without interest the shipping manifests, parts and equipment invoices and overdue bills.

Rummaging through the drawers of the desk, she grimaced with disgust as she turned up a collection of old fast food wrappers and suspicious-looking used tissues. Then she spotted a small black safe, innocently wedged under the right side of the desk. Its door was slightly ajar and she reached inside, her hands closing on several items, which she withdrew and placed on the desktop. These included a wad of bills, maybe $800 worth, a 9-mm handgun, not loaded, and a sizable notebook, which was bound in plush white leather.

In the beam of her flashlight, she eagerly flipped through the foolscap pages of the notebook, which appeared to be a ledger of some kind, but her face fell as she realized that the contents were completely indecipherable. The notebook contained page after page of a kind of shorthand or code she didn't recognize. She did notice however, that the document contained dozens of twelve character sequences, which she guessed were Hull Identification Numbers.

One of the numbers caught her eye: CQD 67A79 F1 71, scrawled next to a date from the previous year, 05/28/1992. She blinked and her jaw fell open. She always memorized important details about her cases, which, this time, included the *Golden Venture's* HIN. And here was that number again, in a coded ledger, sitting in a dry-dock safe owned by the mayor of New York City. Not only was the mayor connected to illegal Chinese immigrants, she realized, but this tied him directly to the *Golden Venture*. The ledger might even contain the details of an elaborate human smuggling operation, for why else would it be in code?

She jerked her head up at a sound outside the office and froze, clicking off her flashlight. There were voices coming from below the platform. The two security men. *Shit, shit, shit.* She had thought they would stay outside the building. Maybe they had heard her shatter the glass of the office door. *Sloppy.* She strained her ears, listening, hardly daring to breathe. Then came the faint metallic ringing as the two men began to climb the metal stairs.

Adjusting her balaclava, she hastily drew the telescopic baton, extending it with a quick flick of her wrist, the heavy, segmented rod snapping into place with a solid click. *I wasn't going to hurt anyone tonight*, she thought, with a surge of anxiety. She placed the baton on the desk and drew the stun gun. She considered it, turning the weapon over in her hands; tasers were known to cause cardiac arrhythmia and occasionally, sudden death.

Deciding she couldn't take the risk (these were innocent men after all), she stowed the weapons at her belt, took up the flashlight and tiptoed across the room, putting her back to the wall next to the door. She heard voices, then a cry of surprise as one of the guards noticed the door's broken glass panel. The room was flooded with the light of two roving flashlight beams, then the door creaked open. The two security men entered, cautiously surveying the scene. One was short, bulky and young, with pants that rode low on his plump ass. The other was older and thin, with a grey braid poking out from under the back of his official-looking cap.

The two were partway into the room when she hit them with the beam of her flashlight. They spun around, throwing up hands to shade their eyes from the glare of the high intensity beam. And, in the moment of their disorientation, Karissa turned and ran out the door, clutching the ledger close to her chest. "Stop!" shouted the older guard hoarsely and they gave chase, only a few feet behind her.

She came to the stairs and hurled herself down them three at a time. Hearing a crash from behind her, she stole a backward glance, noting that the younger guard had tripped and fallen down most of the flight of steep metal stairs and was moaning in a heap at the bottom.

Her eyes widened and the guard with the braid was suddenly on her, having closed the distance between them despite being at least twice her age. He grabbed her arms, yanking her toward him, panting stale smoky breath into her face. His grip was like iron and the intensity in his eyes startling, but fortunately it didn't seem as though he'd had much combat training.

Karissa shifted her weight and propelled him sideways, using the force of his tugging against him. He stumbled and released his grip on her arms but managed to tear the ledger away from her. It flew into the air and landed next to the edge of a large gap in the metal grate over the ocean water below. She hadn't seen the gap before, and held her breath as the aging security guard staggered backward toward it, flailing his arms, still off balance. Then there was a splash as he fell through the gap into the square of oily sea.

He surfaced a moment later, having lost his hat and looking irate. Then his eyes settled on the ledger, just above him. He swam a few strokes, hoisted himself partially up onto the lip of the grate and groped for the notebook. Karissa was there in an instant, her boot pressing firmly into his hand. He cringed, trying unsuccessfully to withdraw the hand, and she bent down, scooping up the ledger.

"Finders keepers," she said and gave him a shove with her foot. He toppled back into the ocean, coughing and spluttering. On her way out of the building she checked over her shoulder. He was clambering out of the water again, swearing loudly, and his compatriot, now seated, was clutching his ankle and moaning. The one would help the other. She knew there would be no lasting harm done, but she felt a guilty pang in her stomach as she scaled the chain-link fence and made her getaway.

IV

## ❧ 18 ❧

## THE THING ABOUT FAVORS

A chill autumn breeze caressed the skin of Nigel's face, causing his eyes to water slightly as he walked sinuously along, traversing the campus at Tammany College. He paused as he neared the opposite end of the rectangle patch of lawn, humped in the middle, which the students called *The Knoll*, and which separated the north from the south end of campus. For a moment, he stood with his eyes closed, inhaling the earthy gunpowder scent of late October deep into his lungs, feeling somehow intact, despite everything.

It had been nearly three months since the encounter with Amy Kang in the museum archives, three months since he had learned of his probable premature death from the *Resident*, which he suspected was quietly killing him, sapping him of an essential something he didn't understand. The thought that he might die had at first elicited panic in him but, as it happened, the six weeks since the beginning of the September term had been the most enjoyable of his life.

Each morning he woke up feeling rested, having shirked his super-hero's duty the night before and made the relaxing one-hour commute to the campus, which was located in the Bronx, overlooking the north end of Manhattan and the Midtown skyline beyond. And each evening, having consumed his fill of lectures and having absorbed the liveliness of hundreds of his laughing, carefree peers, he would travel home again to immerse himself in more hours of study.

During those tranquil fall days as a student, thoughts about his demise rarely entered Nigel's head; however, he was never fully relaxed. He sometimes found himself brooding when night fell, staring out the window into the gathering darkness, unable to concentrate. As the days grew shorter and the dusk came earlier, he found it more and more difficult to retain a positive state of mind.

It wasn't dread he felt but rather guilt – guilt because he was indoors with his nose buried in books when there might be people somewhere who needed his help. At such times, he reminded himself that since his time was now limited, it should belong to him, and to him alone.

Today however, as the icy eastern breeze blew against his face, carrying with it a faint hint of salt from the Atlantic, he felt neither guilt nor dread, simply an eager anticipation of his final lecture of the day, Nicomachean Ethics, which was to begin in five minutes. He was about to head in the direction of the classroom, whose windows were visible on the third floor of the building ahead, when a woman's voice made him stop in his tracks.

"Nice backpack."

He whirled around and beheld Agent Karissa Lacey, standing with her back to a tree, her Cheshire grin on her face. She looked the same as she had when they first crossed paths almost six months before. Her sandy blond hair was loose and blowing in the wind; her tan overcoat, which partially obscured her compact frame, was buttoned up to her pointed chin against the chill, and her deep-set green eyes were partly lidded as if on the verge of sleep, but were nevertheless alert and appraising, seeming to search him for something.

He recovered from his surprise, wondering what she was doing here, aware that he'd probably rather not know the answer. Her presence could only mean that she wanted something from him; or rather from Kintarō, the Golden Boy. Recalling that he was done playing the hero, he stood still, waiting for her to speak.

"You're not around your apartment much these days," she said, folding her arms in front of her chest, visibly suppressing a shiver as the chill wind rose again.

"Usually only in the evening," he replied impassively.

She cocked an eyebrow. "That's surprising. I thought you'd be out then, making the rounds."

"Not lately," he said, shifting his backpack on his shoulder.

She shrugged. "I hear Chinatown's been pretty quiet anyway."

"What can I do for you Agent Lacey?"

"Walk with me."

He checked his watch. There were less than three minutes to go before his class began. "Maybe another time," he said, "I have a lecture right now."

"Go ahead. We can meet after. I saw a sign for a basement pub in the student union complex as I came in. What time's the class finished?"

He hesitated, several potential excuses flashing through his mind, though none seemed convincing enough to voice. He sighed inwardly.

"6 o'clock," he said.

THE ETHICS LECTURE PASSED IN RARE TEDIUM. NIGEL STARED OUT the window, watching the thin ruddy light as it slowly flattened, shadows stretching as the sun slid through the last finger of horizon. He realized that he was only half listening as the professor explained how one could apply Aristotle's moral virtues, courage and temperance to daily life. He found, to his surprise, that he didn't much care, either about the content of the lecture or that he might be perceived as neglecting to pay attention.

Nigel had little idea what Karissa would propose for him when he met her in thirty minutes' time. Regardless, he hoped he would have the nerve to decline to participate in whatever it was. He was content to let his super alter ego slip away, noting the relief that came from imagining at least that part of himself dying. He also felt the decision to focus on his studies was the correct one for him. And yet the enthusiasm he had felt, striding purposefully toward his class this evening had vanished with Karissa's reappearance, replaced now by a vague anxiety that gnawed, like a sightless rodent, at his insides, heedless of the discomfort it caused him.

From Karissa, he anticipated the kind of request he had always found difficult to refuse. She would probably ask for help, playing on his sense of responsibility, which, over the course of years, had been honed to a sharpened point. Once aroused, he knew that it would prick at his conscience, causing enormous pressure for him to divert his attention away from locating his heart, which he had begun to unearth as if on some archeological dig. In recent weeks, he had enjoyed letting the underused organ guide his actions, despite the guilt he felt at doing so.

Why was it, he wondered, that he always felt so guilty when he tried to look out for himself? Perhaps his Japanese upbringing was to blame. Loyalty, discipline, self-sacrifice – these were the key principles on which Japanese society rested. It could be argued that such values explained the widespread prosperity, and the fact that many people in Japan led good and fulfilling lives. Because the system was turned inward, oriented toward the collective, individuals tended to benefit even if some of their needs went unmet.

The problem was that when Nigel was removed from his home and country, the connections between him and other Japanese had been broken as he was cast adrift. And, with no support system, it had been extremely difficult to uphold the Japanese principles and values he had been taught.

Then there was the problem of the cult, which continued to keep him in line, even in absentia. One of its main goals was to rectify some of the issues of wider society, making a show of attending closely to individual needs and prioritizing recreation and rest alongside hard work. Predictably however, the cult demanded its members relinquish their self-determination, which could ultimately be viewed as the biggest self-sacrifice of all.

Nigel recalled how his own attempts at self-determination had been quashed, by his mother and father, by the Grandmaster, by his chaperones, by his teachers and by the parents of his few friends, at critical moments in his young life. He guessed it was these moments which together had constituted a subtle overturning of his freedom.

But, in an unexpected way, the experience of having been faced with early death had initiated a new drive toward self-determination and he found that he was preparing himself to fight for more.

A flurry of movement caught his eye, redirecting his attention to his surroundings. His classmates were packing up, talking in moderated tones, some walking toward the door, and he realized that the class must have been dismissed. He stood, stifling a yawn with the back of his hand and, gathering his things, he reluctantly shuffled out the door.

Nigel had never been to the pub in the student union complex and had to wander around until he spotted a hand-painted sign with white lettering that read, 'The Sepulcher, Student Pub.' The sign displayed a chubby red arrow, directing him down a dimly lit flight of stairs.

As its name suggested, The Sepulcher was dark and silent as a tomb. Devoid of windows, the cavernous interior was partially lit by small lamps set at widely spaced tables and at secluded booths, which fringed the room. Lamp chords snaked hazardously in the gloom, drawing their power from outlets installed at various intervals along the wall. Attached to the ceiling was an enormous vintage chandelier, offering a small quantity of illumination from above. In addition, light leaked from fluorescent tubes fixed beneath the bar. Nobody, not even a bartender was to be seen.

Nigel paused on the threshold, wondering if the place was closed. Then he spotted Karissa, mostly hidden behind the tall back of a booth, with only the top of her head, eyes and nose visible. She wiggled her eyebrows at him and he approached, weaving in and out of the tables, forcing a smile onto his face. She had somehow procured a bottle of beer and took a long swallow of it as he sat, sliding his rear along the vinyl seat cushion and stowing his backpack beneath the table at his feet.

"Can I buy you a drink?" she offered, sliding a cardboard coaster over to him and replacing her bottle on her own cardboard disc.

"No thanks," he replied, though in fact he was inexplicably craving a cold beer. He rarely drank alcohol since the *Resident* negated its effects.

"Are you sure?" she asked.

He nodded.

She rummaged around in the pocket of her balled-up coat, which had been dumped unceremoniously on the seat beside her.

"Mind if I smoke?"

Nigel glanced around, wondering if she was allowed to smoke in here, or if she should, considering there were no air vents nearby. He heard the rasping sound of a flint as she lit up. As far as he remembered, she had never smoked around him before, although she often seemed to be chewing a wad of gum.

Karissa placed the pack of cigarettes on the table next to her elbow and a sky-blue plastic lighter atop the tiny box. He noticed a camel on the front, picked out in gold on an idyllic Egyptian landscape, pyramids in repose under a late afternoon sun, a grove of palm trees standing over a desert oasis.

"I have a favor to ask you," she said, tapping ash onto a third cardboard coaster. She kept her cigarette pinched between two fingers, the blueish smoke curling and dissipating in a localized cloud. Through the haze, her features were very slightly obscured, giving Nigel the impression that he was sitting across from a vaguely altered version of the woman.

She leaned toward him. "I get the feeling you're trying to give up the cape, and I say fair enough. But hear me out, okay?"

He nodded his assent, fiddling with his coaster on the table.

Settling back, she dragged thoughtfully on her cigarette. "I'm trying to think of the best place to start." She tapped off more excess ash, drank a mouthful of beer and said, "Remember the beach in June?" Her eyes took on a faraway look. "All those people in the water."

"How could I forget?" he said, shifting uncomfortably in his seat as an image of heads bobbing in the waves came to him unbidden.

"He was there."

"Who was there?"

"The mayor."

Nigel hesitated. "I don't remember that," he said after a moment, offering her a small shrug.

Karissa went on as though she hadn't heard him. "Even at the time I thought it was strange. When big public incidents like the *Golden*

*Venture* have happened in the past, Rusty Kincaid barely managed to put out press releases. But this time there he was, looking for all the world like he gave a shit."

Nigel felt confused. He was about to voice a question when a waitress suddenly appeared at their booth.

"Can I get you something?" she asked, directing the question at Nigel. He looked up and was surprised to see that the waitress, who looked like a college student, might also be Japanese, or at least of Japanese descent. She immediately reminded him of Aika.

"That's okay, we're fine," said Karissa, somewhat impatiently.

The waitress turned to go but Nigel spoke up. "Actually," he said, "I'll have a lager please." The beer might quench his thirst, he thought, even if it wouldn't inebriate him.

Karissa looked surprised for a moment, then said, "Make it two." She stubbed out her cigarette on the coaster, the burning ember charring the cardboard and, lifting the side of the coaster with a fingernail, she checked to make sure the cigarette hadn't burned through to the table.

The waitress looked unimpressed. "Can I get you an ashtray?"

"Uh huh, sure," Karissa replied.

When the waitress had gone, Nigel leaned in. "What's so significant about the mayor's presence on the night of the *Golden Venture* landing?" he asked.

Her voice became hushed. "I think the mayor was involved in the *Golden Venture* smuggling operation."

"How could that be?" he asked, shocked.

"I was first suspicious when Kincaid came unannounced to a meeting between the INS and the police during the *Golden Venture* investigation. I checked with a contact in the mayor's office and apparently, due to a self-proclaimed lack of interest, and because his schedule is so filled with public appearances, the mayor almost never attends meetings like that in person. He's usually handed reports after major police briefings, although he apparently rarely reads them, yet he was unusually interested in the proceedings that day."

Nigel thought for a moment, considering what that might mean.

"It does sound suspicious," he conceded, "but it doesn't connect him firmly to the *Golden Venture*."

"Not by itself," she said, flicking a loose strand of hair from her face. "But, my informant said he'd seen Kincaid coming and going from the building where the Hip Sing coordinates its criminal operations on several occasions over the last year. He seems to be having regular dealings with one of the biggest Chinatown tongs." She swallowed a mouthful of beer. "Of course, I was pissed when I realized that our elected mayor might have ties to organized crime, but I figured I could simply pass the tip on to the FBI and have done with it —" She cut off as the waitress arrived back with their drinks.

After setting Nigel's lager on the coaster he had positioned in front of him, the waitress proffered a fourth, fresh coaster, on top of which she placed the second, sweating bottle for Karissa then added an ashtray to the centre of the table.

"Keep 'em coming, will you?" Karissa requested.

The waitress looked for confirmation from Nigel, who, having just taken his first refreshing swallow of beer, nodded his head in agreement.

Watching after the waitress for a few moments, Karissa went on. "I tried to let it go, but when the news story broke that Kincaid was into drugs and had used illegal Chinese immigrants to help him host parties, I decided to investigate. I had a hunch that if I looked around the mayor's dry dock at Red Hook, the location where he held that party, I might find something. I'm sure you heard about the time he was busted with his pockets full of meth, right?"

Nigel nodded, nursing his beer.

Finishing her first beer, Karissa moved on to the second. She lit another cigarette, puffing on it and left it to smolder, wedged in the side of the ashtray.

"So the INS is investigating the mayor?" he asked.

She looked uncomfortable. "Not exactly," she said, "just me."

"Why is that?" he asked. "I mean, why isn't the INS backing your investigation?"

"The INS is busy chasing a shopkeeper and neither the director nor my partner want to listen to reason." There was a meaningful pause, as she stared intently at him. "I visited the dry dock and found this."

Reaching into the folds of her coat, she removed a large, white notebook bound in what looked like faux leather. She dropped the notebook on the table and, dragging on her cigarette, she motioned for him to take it. The smell of tobacco smoke filled his nose as he slid the notebook toward himself.

Opening the cover and flipping through the first few pages, he found most of the contents to be unintelligible. He could make out a series of entries, one per page, organized in sequence by date. There were dollar figures scribbled next to what appeared to be shorthand and there were multi-digit sequences containing both letters and numbers, but nothing that made any sense.

"What is all this?" he asked, accepting another lager from the waitress who was back with more, though he still hadn't finished his first. Karissa threw a sidelong glance at the waitress' retreating back, gulping down the rest of her second beer as though determined to keep pace with the steady rate at which the drinks were appearing.

"Take a look at this," she said, reaching out and eagerly flipping to a page she had dog-eared near the end. Letting the notebook fall open, she stabbed a finger at a twelve-digit sequence next to a scribbled note and a six-figure dollar amount. "This, right here, is the *Golden Venture's* Hull Identification Number," she said with a note of triumph in her voice. She paused meaningfully, looking at him. "So what is this number doing in a coded ledger, sitting in Rusty Kincaid's company safe?" She emitted a wet chuckle into the neck of her beer bottle before treating herself to a mouthful.

Nigel narrowed his eyes at the page, trying to forget the fact that Karissa had probably broken the law to obtain the ledger. "What's this dollar figure here?" he asked, pointing at the number next to the *Golden Venture* serial.

Karissa smacked her lips. "I think it's the cut Kincaid took from the Hip Sing."

He blinked. "That's quite a small amount, wouldn't you say?" He paused, considering. "What's the typical price for an illegal immigrant to make the passage to America from China?"

She frowned. "About thirty thousand dollars, give or take."

"There were almost three hundred people on that ship, right?" he asked.

"Two hundred and eighty-six, yeah."

He nodded. "So with that number of passengers and at those rates, the profit would be more than eight million dollars. This number is way too low to compensate for the risk Kincaid would have taken on as the shipper." He looked up at her.

She hesitated. "It could be what he paid for the vessel itself."

"That does make more sense," he said, wondering why she hadn't seen that before. She was as sharp an investigator as they came, as far as he could tell.

She sighed and rubbed tiredly at her eyes. "I guess I've been letting my dislike for Kincaid get in the way of thinking through some of these details," she admitted. "But the fact that the ship number shows up in this ledger is damning by itself, and Kincaid's ownership of the *Golden Venture* at the time of its landing in June would be the smoking gun."

He thought about it for a moment, arriving at the conclusion that, as Karissa said, the evidence against the mayor was damning indeed. It made Nigel angry to think that a person in such a position of power should be allowed to take advantage of poor people from another country, to flout the laws and the system he was elected to uphold and be allowed to get away with it. Perhaps Nigel had retained an appetite for justice from his days as a superhero because he heard himself say, "What do you need from me?"

"The ledger's been a dead end. I've spoken with several code breakers in the Bowery underworld and nobody could decipher anything from it, so I was thinking of asking the Hip Sing about it myself."

"What about tracking down one of Kincaid's company employees instead?" he asked.

"I thought of that but his company records are all inside the building at Red Hook and the place is crawling with police and security these days. I think the only play is to confront the Hip Sing leadership about its dealings with the mayor."

He tensed, waiting to hear more about how he fit into the risky-sounding scheme but the waitress was back with more full bottles, adding a third beer to Nigel's queue, despite the fact he had yet to finish his first.

As Nigel contemplated the three bottles before him, one half-empty and the other two full to the brim, all slowly releasing their carbon dioxide into the surrounding air, he realized that he was, once again, in over his head.

"Drink up," said Karissa, and she winked at him, "we have some planning to do."

## ❦ 19 ❦

# FROM THE CRADLE

T he next day was a Friday. Nigel awoke feeling dizzy and vaguely disoriented in his apartment bedroom. Sliding out of bed, he dragged the comforter with him and went to the small window, spreading a section of the dusty metal blinds with one hand and peering out at the grey morning over Mott Street, listlessly thinking of what he might hope to accomplish that day. He felt foggy-headed and physically weak, as if standing up straight required special effort.

Since that time in early June, when he had missed his jump from the roof of the truck, he had experienced a series of aches, pains and other internal maladies, and most especially, recurrent dizziness. These were all new symptoms for Nigel, who had enjoyed unusually stable health for most of his life, and they had increased in frequency and severity over the course of the last four and a half months. He grimaced as a headache flared. It was rapidly propagating itself through the front of his skull when the telephone rang.

He shuffled into the living room, where the old touchtone phone sat on a coffee table. The phone was beige and had come with the apartment, complete with a restrictively short chord and a chronically too-quiet receiver.

"Hello?" he said.

He could hear someone speaking but the words were too muffled for him to understand, due to the shoddy phone.

"Can you speak up please?" he asked, frustrated. "My phone is broken."

"Nigel Nakagawa?" He heard the words more clearly now.

"Yes?"

"This is Amy Kang."

He remembered giving her his telephone number weeks ago. "Amy, hi." Glancing at the wall clock, he saw that it was 8:30 a.m. "I would expect you to be asleep now."

"I finished my night shift thirty minutes ago, or rather, my early morning shift, at New York University. I found some quite interesting historical materials in the special collections section of the university library and thought I would call and arrange a meeting with you before I go to sleep for the day."

Nigel's heart leaped. "Are they relevant to my situation?" he asked.

"Yes, very much so," she replied. He could faintly hear her chewing something. "How about we meet today at 4:30 p.m.? There is a coffee shop across from the courthouse: *On What Grounds*."

"Fine, that's fine," he said, remembering the one. "How will what you found affect me?" he asked, unable to wait until later to ask the question.

"Tough to say," said Amy Kang. "My prediction is that the information will help us deal with your problem, but this talking we are doing would be more effective in person."

"Of course. See you at 4:30," said Nigel, his heart beating with excitement. She hung up the phone without ceremony and he hung up too, wondering how he might kill the eight intervening hours until their meeting.

BY A QUARTER PAST FOUR, THE LEADEN, SEEMINGLY IMMOVABLE clouds had parted, allowing sunlight to stream through cracks in the grey canopy, illuminating wide patches of the street. Tendrils of mist curled from the pavement, which had been spattered by a rain shower earlier that afternoon.

Dressed in black jeans, sunglasses and a grey bomber jacket, Nigel rounded the corner at Centre Street, and emerged into the open space across from Foley Square, a large concrete round, across from the Courthouse. The fastest way to reach *On What Grounds* was to cut directly through the square, but a film shoot seemed to be occupying much of the space, presenting a potential obstacle. Nigel decided to cut through the square anyway, more out of curiosity about what was being filmed, than out of a need for haste; he still had a few minutes before he was supposed to be at the coffee shop.

As he approached, Nigel thought he could hear a chorus of men's voices. Were they singing? And, as he came around the side of a cluster of tents, he confirmed that indeed, four men were singing in what sounded like three-part harmony, plus bass. A cluster of crew members surrounded the quartet, some working a wind machine, some supporting white foam boards, reflecting light at the singers. A pair of shaggy, black-clad cameramen were operating cameras mounted on tripods. They were filming a music video, he realized, though he didn't recognize the group.

He tried to make out the lyrics as he passed by, but the words were carried away on the gusting wind. Nearby, several crew members rushed to hold down metal stands supporting sheets of black fabric as they caught the breeze and became sails, threatening to blow away. With a wry shake of his head, Nigel was about to cross the street in the direction of the café when he suddenly spotted Amy Kang, standing about thirty yards away, staring intently at the film shoot. He made his way over to her.

"Hi," he greeted her, "thanks for meeting me."

She was dressed in an oversize navy blue windbreaker, the hood drawn up over her head and its strings tied in a tight bow at her throat. She had on the same navy tearaway pants from the first time they met, worn over royal blue high-tops, exhibiting the kind of monochromatic look favored by travelling sports teams. She greeted him with a slight nod of her head, remaining strangely fixated on the performers in the square.

"So," he said, after thirty seconds had passed, "do you think they're filming a music video?"

"Yes."

He threw her a sidelong glance. "I don't recognize the band members."

She grunted. "It's Rockapella, the in-house a cappella group for the children's game show, '*Where in the World is Carmen Sandiego?*' on PBS."

"Oh," he said, perplexed. "Is that a famous show?"

Nigel saw that the five men had stopped singing and capering and were retreating to nearby tents. Her trance broken, Amy Kang turned to him, seeming vaguely nonplussed.

"Let's go," she declared, without answering his question.

They crossed the street in silence, arriving at their destination a few moments later, guided by the neon sign, which shone brightly in the window of the tiny café, which was housed in the massive twenty-five-story building at the corner of Duane and Lafayette. Inside they queued for coffee and Nigel, resigned to overseeing the production of polite conversation, asked Amy Kang how she knew the a cappella group from the square.

She hesitated. "I was one of the first contestants."

He thought for a moment. "On the gameshow you mentioned outside?"

Amy Kang stared at the countertop. "Before I took an interest in anthropology, I was fascinated with geography. Much of my childhood was spent reading the 1985 edition of the *Encyclopedia Britannica* and anything else I could find containing facts, figures and oddities from various places in the world. The alluvial composition of Calcutta's substrate, Cambodian festival names, the metric tonnage of the bulk cargo throughput at the port of Amsterdam," she said, pointing to the side of her head, "I memorized it all. When PBS rolled out their geographical game show, I was already in regular correspondence with the executives at PBS regarding their programming, so I was invited to participate in the first episode."

This was more than he had ever heard her say at once and he wasn't sure exactly how to respond. Fortunately, they were interrupted by the barista, asking what she could make for them. Amy Kang ordered a black coffee and Nigel asked for a cup of earl grey tea. Finally lowering the hood of her jacket, Amy Kang shook out her short dark hair then carefully brushed and gathered it into a stubby ponytail that stuck up in the back.

As they stood by the counter, waiting for their hot drinks, Nigel voiced something that had been on his mind, as sensitively as he could: "You're only sixteen, but you could easily be studying at a graduate level, or higher I think. I know that your job offers you special learning opportunities and it must feel good to be considered the best janitor in New York, but why are you a janitor when you could do anything you chose?"

She blinked, hesitating, then said, still without meeting his gaze, "My mother was ill, and she was the sole provider, so it was up to me as the eldest to quit school and find work. She was a janitor, so I used her connections to get a job, which would have been difficult otherwise, since I was only thirteen." And then, as though the two thoughts were connected, she said, "I was fourteen when I was on *Where in the World is Carmen Sandiego*. The grand prize would have been a trip anywhere in the continental United States." She regarded his chin with eyes that were bright, fathomless and perpetually far away. "But I still have yet to leave New York." And with that, she turned, scooping up her coffee and his tea, which had just been placed on the counter for them, and made for a table near the window, cups and saucers clinking.

They sat down and stared into their drinks, blowing cool air over the surface of the steaming liquid in their cups. Wisps of warm vapour and the pleasing aroma of English tea drifted up, caressing Nigel's nose and cheeks. Amy Kang took a gulp of her coffee and, fanning her open mouth with her hand, she exclaimed, "Hot! Hot!!" Nigel gently pushed his own cup aside to allow it to cool.

After she could speak again, Amy Kang launched into the business at hand. "The documents I found were lengthy," she said, "and unfortunately I was unable to remove them from the library or photocopy them due to their fragility, so please allow me to summarize." She waited, as if for permission to continue.

"Of course," he said, gesturing for her to proceed.

"Excellent," said she, warming both small hands by gripping the sides of her coffee cup. "I discovered two parallel accounts of early Spanish explorers around the time of first contact between Europeans and aborigines on the north coast of Mesoamerica in the early part of the sixteenth century. At the time, the Yucatán Peninsula was inhabited by the Maya, an ancient and sophisticated society, living in one of the six cradles of human civilization." She took another sip of her coffee, grimacing again at the temperature. "All this background comes from my own knowledge of the subject, you understand."

"It's appreciated, thank you," he said with sincerity, though he was unsure of where all this was headed.

"The Maya had been highly advanced for millennia, pioneering systematic farming techniques, writing, mathematics, astronomy, and religion. They existed within a vast network of city states, all connected by trade, and made elaborate art and beautiful textiles, enjoyed music and dance, ate a diverse cuisine, and practiced various forms of highly effective medicine." He nodded enthusiastically, blowing again on the surface of his tea then taking a tentative sip.

Seemingly satisfied with the picture she had painted, Amy Kang went on. "Spanish contact was tainted by miscommunication and bloodshed in the early 1500s. The Europeans looted Maya vessels in the waters surrounding the Yucatán Peninsula and the Maya people captured, enslaved and sacrificed several of the early Spanish explorers. However, there were brief periods of friendly relations, during which the explorers were permitted to make land and, in some cases, were invited to view some of the wonders of the Maya.

"The descriptions I found were written by one such explorer – Miguel Juarez de Cordoba, the captain of one of the first Spanish voyages, who kept a detailed log of his encounter with the Maya. He witnessed incredible things: monumental architecture, vast tracts of arable land, large quantities of Aztec gold, brutal human sacrifice, and a phenomenon that would have been dismissed by most as impossible."

Her eyes sparkled. She seemed to be enjoying herself. "Juarez was invited to view a kind of gladiatorial sport, a dangerous game played in the jungle by the esteemed warriors of Mesoamerica, many of whom were war leaders and members of the Maya aristocracy. These champions not only possessed peak athleticism but could also perform feats of a special and wholly fantastical nature."

Staring meaningfully into space, she continued. "According to Juarez, who was permitted to watch the game from on high, the champions possessed inhuman speed, strength and resilience. He watched as the competitors leapt from treetop to treetop, hurled boulders at each other and felled trees like threshing corn."

Nigel's eyes had narrowed and he was leaning so far forward in his seat that his ribs pushed against the edge of the table, though he barely noticed.

"In addition," she continued, "the champions were clothed in a material the explorers had never seen before. Captain Juarez described it as '*a mercurial ooze, both solid and liquid, reflecting all the hues of the sun.*' Sound familiar?"

Nigel was astonished. *And here I thought mine was the only one.*

"Evidently not," said Amy Kang, and Nigel realized he had spoken his thought aloud. "There are some differences though, between your parasite and theirs. Juarez details how only certain parts of the champions' bodies were covered by the material – patches of chests and torsos, knees and elbow joints; some heads and faces were concealed and some were bare. Also, these champions could be hurt or killed by conventional means. Some were injured in combat and at least two died with the explorers looking on."

"So mine is more powerful."

"Possibly. And possibly more lethal over the short term. There is a single mention of a champion with a unique illness, presumably weakened by his parasite. But he was of the same age most people died at that time; somewhere in his late forties or fifties by the sound of it."

Nigel paused, digesting this information. After a few moments, he asked, "So what happened to these *Residents*?"

She winced. "I'm not entirely sure; I would like to do more research."

"Of course," said Nigel, musing. "Though it would be strange if they were lost, considering the importance of the super-powered warriors to the Maya."

"Not really," she countered. "A lot of Mayan records and culture disappeared in the Spanish conquest. Maybe the Spanish actively sought to cover up the champion's presence after losing battles to them." Nigel pictured the champions wreaking havoc on the Spanish lines, making the highly trained and well-equipped European invaders look foolish. "Or perhaps the parasites were secretly taken to Spain for some unknown purpose. But the existence of other parasites is a secondary point, and not the reason why I requested we meet at such short notice."

Nigel looked up. "It's not?"

By way of reply, Amy Kang resumed her story. "On the last day of his visit, Captain Juarez was led by a Mayan lord to a mountain peak where a tall rod had been anchored in the rock. The rod was several times the height of a man, a hand-span in diameter, and made of solid gold. Juarez seems to have been distracted by so much wealth because he barely noticed as the elderly champion, the one who was sick from the parasite, was lashed to it. The captain describes how he watched in horror and fascination as the man was left to bear the full brunt of an enormous thunderstorm, standing on the highest point of ground, lashed to a metal superconductor."

"Was he hit?" asked Nigel breathlessly.

"Many times," said Amy Kang gravely. "Juarez was forced to look away and eventually to take shelter, retreating down the mountain at the urging of the Maya. When they returned, the man was unconscious but alive. At his feet was a shifting pool of dark liquid, which the attendants rushed to collect in a golden basin. Juarez was shocked when they suddenly dumped the fluid over another man, whom he realized was next in line to receive the powers of the parasite. The receiver tipped his head back, the liquid flowing into his eyes, ears and open mouth. Smoke and steam rose as he sank to his knees, silently screaming as his flesh was transformed by the molten material streaming down his body."

As she described this, Nigel flashed back to his own boyhood transformation in shocking, visceral fashion. He could suddenly feel the burning of his skin, could smell the acrid stench and could hear the crackling of his bodily fluids as if it was happening to him all over again.

The last part of the story Amy Kang quoted from memory: "*Then all was still. And through the haze I saw the man as if reborn in hell. Wide tentacles of the substance clutched at his naked body like the talons of a beast, glinting there, strong and dark as iron. Thus, a new champion was born.*"

The café had become quiet. The other patrons had departed and the barista was quietly polishing the chrome espresso machine behind the counter. The only sound was Nigel's quiet gasping as he fought to bring himself under control.

"What's wrong?" Amy Kang asked concernedly, as if realizing for the first time the effect of her words.

"I'm alright," Nigel managed through gritted teeth, the room swimming back into focus as he opened his eyes, beads of sweat glistening on his brow.

She paused, staring at him quizzically for a moment. "Juarez's story tells us two things we didn't know before" she said. "One, a parasite can be fully separated from a host using high-voltage electricity. And two, the parasite can be transferred to another host immediately following. The latter fact, though incredibly interesting, is not highly relevant, I think. But the former?" Her eyebrows rose in excitement. "The former might be the key to your freedom and recovery."

She picked up her cold cup of coffee and thirstily downed its contents. "There are a few details I need to check and we don't know what happened to the older champion in the weeks and months following the separation, but I think I can devise a way for you to undergo a similar treatment as his, if that's what you decide, one that could possibly rid you of the parasite forever." She looked at him expectantly.

Nigel let go of the table, which he had been gripping with both hands, shakily reaching for his own drink. He stared at it for a moment, then drank the room temperature tea in one gulp and, as he lowered the empty cup, now adorned with a few scattered tea leaves, he began to laugh.

## ✣ 20 ✣

# TONG TIED

K arissa leaned against the wall in the entrance of a red brick tenement building kitty-corner from the four-story structure at 16 Pell Street in Chinatown. It was Sunday evening, around seven o'clock and it was Halloween. The sun had set a short time ago and any remaining daylight was swallowed by the surrounding densely packed structures. Street lamps cast an amber glow and the light from apartment and storefront windows, neon signs and the headlights of cars provided enough scattered illumination for a clear view of her surroundings.

The area was livelier than usual for a Sunday, populated, in the early evening, with costumed children, their pillow cases bulging with candy. Later, she predicted, the streets would be filled with older revelers, dressed in a medley of costumes, off to this or that Halloween party, stopping off in Chinatown in pursuit of fireworks, alcohol or drugs. The pops and bangs of Chinatown ordinance echoed off the buildings of the narrow street, reminding Karissa of the one and only firefight of her career, which had occurred in this very neighborhood only a few months before.

She was watchful, having arrived two hours before the prearranged time of seven, and remained intent on soaking in the surroundings, allowing her mind to adjust to the dangerous task ahead. Surveying the area, she had seen few Chinese entering or exiting the Hip Sing Headquarters, and hoped that the right people would be inside. The tong didn't hand out appointments to just anyone, so they weren't expecting her. She was banking on the fact that, once they realized she was a federal agent, they probably wouldn't kill her.

The 1993 New York mayoral election was only two days away. Karissa felt a sinking sensation in her guts at the thought of it. She didn't know what would be worse: another term of that man neglecting the city and its people or another term of him using his power and influence to expand his human smuggling empire. It could be both. It would be a spectacular time to topple Kincaid. In all the excitement, she hoped she would remember to vote.

At that moment, she saw movement on the rooftop at 16 Pell. As she watched, a figure stood, silhouetted against the blackening sky. She flashed him a thumbs-up and he silently ducked out of sight. Despite her being with the INS, she still might require backup, particularly since she would be breaking and entering, and even her credentials might not save her if she angered the Hip Sing gangsters in the process, which was why she had recruited Kintarō, the Golden Boy.

She wondered why Nigel had agreed to help her, knowing that he had decided to leave his superhero persona behind him. Amy Kang had confirmed this, informing Karissa about the plan to extract the parasite from Nigel's body. Perhaps he felt that he should do something meaningful with the time he had left. Karissa thought about Nigel's ingrained sense of duty, which she respected. She mused at the contrast between these virtues and his apparent desire to quit, although she understood that for him, it was matter of life and death. Even so, she still envied him his powers.

The Hip Sing front on Pell Street was a fully functioning massage parlour, designated by an enormous white and red backlit sign, advertising "FOOT RUB," "BACK RUB" and "FOOT HEAVEN," alongside large red characters, presumably corresponding to the English. Hanging in the windows were various massage menus and diagrams of foot meridians, the use of the latter probably an attempt to draw on the mystique surrounding traditional Chinese medicine.

The parlour was open and Karissa knew the back room connected through to the upper levels of the building. She also knew that this passage was carefully watched and the landing on the second floor was always guarded; this according to Admiral Rat, who was in and out of the building semi-regularly, providing the Hip Sing with information. Fortunately, with Nigel's help, she should be able to find another way in.

Following the plan, she crossed the narrow street and entered a Chinese laundry. The space was filled with washing machines, plumbed with exposed pipes jutting from the ceiling. The lone attendant wordlessly stared at her as she walked briskly through and into the back room. The rear door led to an enclosed area, shared by all the businesses on this side of Pell and the Bayard block behind. More of a narrow courtyard than an alley, the space was cut off from foot and vehicle traffic by buildings at either end, closing the rectangle.

Swiftly moving toward the Hip Sing building, she slunk around the trash and debris, her movements as stealthy as a city-hardened rodent, keeping away from watchful eyes. Arriving at her destination, she pressed herself against the side of the building, wary of its narrow windows, grimy though they were.

A rope fell next to her and she looked up. Nigel's masked face peered down at her from the roof, expressionless. She checked that her overcoat was buttoned tight and grabbed hold of the rope, looping it twice around her hips and tying it off in a practiced knot. Then, positioning herself with her feet against the brick, she signalled to Nigel and was jerked upward, her feet running horizontally up the sheer face of the wall.

When she reached the top, he hauled her upright and she toppled into his arms. Setting her on her feet, he cleared his throat, seemingly embarrassed about the bumpy ride he'd given her, but she'd had rougher treatment. She unwound the rope from her middle and dropped it next to the edge of the roof.

Her heart was in her mouth as Nigel ripped the locked stainless steel handle from the stairwell door with a powerful tug. It gave way with a *clank* and there was a faint *clunk* as the inside knob struck the concrete floor within. They looked at each other for a moment, hardly daring to breathe, listening for any sign that the noise had been detected, but the silence held, perforated only by the *zing-pop* of a bottle rocket. The door gave a faint squeak as Nigel swung it open and led the way into the building.

Inside was a flight of concrete stairs. Karissa peered over the railing, seeing nobody below, hearing no sound. Slowly, silently they crept down to the fourth floor. Turning the corner, they paused, considering the darkened hallway beyond. The distance was approximately twenty feet to the next set of stairs, with a sliver of neon light falling on the red-carpeted floor from the only open door, which was at the other end of the hall. They stopped and listened. Nothing.

Nigel slipped into the gloom, leaving her temporarily behind, his outfit blending seamlessly with the darkness. He stopped in the doorway at the end of the hall, standing motionless in the slash of light from the street, gazing at the room's interior.

She joined him then, peeking around the doorframe. The room was unoccupied, its main feature a large desk, resting directly on the hardwood floor, the surface of which was partly covered by a cracked leather writing pad. A green-shaded banker's desk lamp rested on one corner. On either side of the desk were two large grey filing cabinets and above hung an enormous, elaborately framed rendering of a Chinese dragon, the faded browns, blacks and reds of the picture further muted by the yellow light from the street. The sound of fireworks bursting and crackling could be heard faintly, a few blocks away. Flashes of blue, green and red danced over the dragon, inert and oblivious in its frame.

Next they came to the stairs leading to the third floor. Unfortunately, these creaked. No matter how they tiptoed and shifted their weight, they could not prevent the stairs from groaning their presence. Karissa, who was in front this time, tried to get it over all at once, descending rapidly, with a blood-curdling series of creaks and moans issuing from the stairs. Nigel followed close behind, adding to the racket.

The traitorous stairs deposited them in a place like an anteroom, with dark chestnut wood panelling adorning the walls. Karissa stood listening, hoping but hardly daring to believe that they could remain undetected. On the walls was a series of small black and white photographs of Chinese men posing in twos and threes and in larger groups. These were displayed alongside several portrait photos of unsmiling, powerful-looking men. Ahead was a set of double doors and another stairwell descended around to the right. A worn, rose-colored settee was the only piece of furniture in the area.

While Nigel peered at one of the photographs, Karissa stepped up and put her ear to the crack between the two doors, feeling a soft breeze coming from within. There was a faint clink of cutlery, then silence.

"What should we do?" she asked in a whisper.

He turned from the photo. "I think we should go in," he murmured back, his tone surprisingly mild, though he rocked restlessly, back and forth on his feet.

"Just, go in?"

"You go in. I'll wait here," he said. And, after seeing her dubious look, added, "I'll stand guard."

She took a step back, considering the two doors, picturing a crime boss eating his supper, surrounded by armed, trigger-happy guards. She motioned for Nigel to step to the side, positioning herself next to him along the wall. He looked at her for a moment, then moved to her other side, putting himself between her and the door. Her back to the wall, she mouthed 'Ready?' He nodded, crossing his arms in front of his chest. She could feel one of the photographs shift under the pressure of her shoulder blade.

Carefully, gingerly, she leaned out and gripped the handle of the left-hand door. Then she jerked it toward them. It opened almost silently and swung toward them at speed, bouncing off Nigel and swinging back in the other direction. It swung into the room, rebounding a second time, then slowing and finally settling again in the closed position. Karissa and Nigel looked at each other. Nobody seemed to be rushing to attack them.

There was no sound at all until: "Hello?" The voice echoed from deep inside the room, muffled by the doors. "Hello," it said again, this time with a hint of exasperation. Karissa bit her lip and, pushing herself from the wall, she went over to the doors, motioning for Nigel to wait, though he made no move to follow her. She pushed the doors wide, inward this time, and entered a large, dimly-lit room.

The cavernous space was empty except for a long dining table, the messiest she had ever seen; littered with used paper napkins, half-filled glasses, and a variety of partially empty food containers, filled with greasy breaded chicken, vegetables drowning in sauce, chewed pizza and traces of rice. The table was festooned with dirty dishes, these covered with bones and shells. She thanked her lucky stars she had missed the army it must have taken to produce such disarray.

Presiding over it all from the opposite end of the table, was a lone Chinese man, staring at her over the top of an open newspaper. The man appeared to be in his late sixties, with messy silver hair, wire-rim glasses, and wearing a white button-up shirt with a charcoal tie and matching dress pants. He seemed surprised to see her.

"Who are you?" she asked.

The man smiled sardonically at her. "My name is Mr. Johnny. And who are *you*?"

She froze. Mr. Johnny was the leader of the Hip Sing. "Agent Karissa Lacey, INS," she said, flashing her badge at him, willing herself to remain calm.

"Agent Lacey," he said, putting down his paper. "I've heard of you." He sipped coffee from a plain china cup and waited.

"I've heard of you too," she said. "I have some questions to ask you."

"You have? I am not in the habit of answering the questions of federal agents unless there is good reason. Am I under arrest by any chance?"

"No."

"And are these the questions of the Immigration and Naturalization Service or are they yours?" She hesitated. "Yours then," he said, nodding. "Then I'm afraid I cannot help you." He returned to reading his paper.

Her lip curled. "Tell me about your dealings with the mayor."

He looked up at her, surprised. Then, shaking his head, he looked back at the pages spread out before him, his eyes following the words there.

"Who is your companion?" he asked suddenly.

"My companion?" she replied, caught off guard.

"Yes, the man dressed for Halloween in the corridor. I caught a glimpse of him when you opened the door the second time." He looked up again, his face serious. "Please, invite him to join us." Seeing her hesitation, Mr. Johnny clicked his tongue in annoyance, calling out, "You there, standing outside the door. Please come in!"

After a moment, the door swung open and in came Nigel, the surface of his impressive, nauseating suit swirling and shifting as he approached the table.

"Kintarō, the Golden Boy," exclaimed the crime boss. "I am Mr. Johnny, president of the Hip Sing Public Association. I am pleased to meet you, after hearing so much about your exploits in Chinatown." Nigel shifted uncomfortably, saying nothing.

Karissa fixed Mr. Johnny with a hard look. "How long have you and Kincaid been in business?"

Mr. Johnny gazed back at her for a few moments, then said, more than a little scornfully, "I will answer your questions, if he answers mine."

"Me?" asked Nigel, taken aback.

"What kind of questions?" asked Karissa suspiciously.

"I would like to know more about the costumed vigilante who has set up here, in my neighborhood."

Karissa looked over at Nigel, who shrugged.

"Where are you from, young man?" Mr. Johnny asked.

"Japan," Nigel replied, after a moment.

"Ah," said Mr. Johnny, leaning forward. "What region?"

"Nagano Prefecture."

"The mountains then. And from what village?"

"The village is little known, even in Japan. I doubt you've heard the name," said Nigel, rocking almost imperceptibly on his feet.

"You might be surprised," said Mr. Johnny.

"You don't have to answer him," Karissa said to Nigel.

"It isn't Ryūiki, by any chance?" asked Mr. Johnny.

Nigel froze. "Pardon me?" he asked.

"The name of your village, it isn't Ryūiki, is it?" Mr. Johnny's eyes glinted like polished onyx in the dim light.

"How did you—" began Nigel, but he was interrupted.

"So you are the Champion of Hitsujikai. I wanted to be sure." Nigel and Karissa stood speechless. "And you killed Lin Little," said Mr. Johnny, matter-of-factly.

"By accident," said Karissa, "defending himself." She was disturbed by how the scene had turned.

"It's alright," Nigel said to her. And then to Mr. Johnny he asked, "How do you know these things about me?"

The crime boss smiled. "I know your parents. They both worked for me, your father for five years, your mother for less than a month, two decades ago."

Muscles squirmed in Nigel's jaw. "Bullshit," he said.

"I thought your mother might have sent you to be a thorn in my side. The termination of her employment was less than amicable." Mr. Johnny took another sip of coffee.

"Why would you employ Japanese in your organization?" asked Karissa.

"Frank Nakagawa sought us out, after a falling out with the Yakuza, where he had been an enforcer since he was a young man. There was a price on his head and nobody else would take him. I however, have always taken special pleasure in frustrating the Japanese. But they forgot about him after a while, and he went on to do remarkable work for us."

"And my mother?" Nigel asked.

"Your mother was a curse. Though she was extremely useful at first. I hired her to do our books. She was adept at arranging our financial records in such a way that they would be most *transparent* to the government. It is an important tribute to our democracy, keeping legible financial records, wouldn't you say Agent Lacey? Better not to waste the time of federal employees in audit." He turned his attention back to Nigel. "Yet, in hindsight, I think your mother was always only here because of your father." He paused, removing his glasses, cleaning them with a small cloth he produced from somewhere. "Frank Nakagawa was a principled, loyal man. He refused your mother at first, after it became clear that she wanted him to leave the Hip Sing."

Nigel was silent, his face set.

"What made him change his mind?" Karissa asked, curious.

"I fired Fuyuko and had her forcibly removed," said Mr. Johnny. "Of course by then Frank was in love with her and was extremely displeased with her rough treatment. He left."

"And I'm supposed to be a thorn in your side, you said," growled Nigel.

Mr. Johnny looked at him. "I assume your mother sent you to target my businesses. Why else would you be here, in Chinatown?"

"To do some good," said Nigel in a flat voice.

"Is that what she told you?" laughed the mobster. "She didn't lie. I am a bad man after all. Most of the wrongdoings in Chinatown could probably be traced back to me somehow, if law enforcement wasn't preoccupied with other things," and he winked at Karissa, "but I should think your mother's reasons are more complicated than that. I smell a personal vendetta."

"Let's say I believe you," said Nigel. "What do you want from me?"

"Nothing at all. I just wanted to be sure of who it is I am dealing with," Mr. Johnny said, simply.

A silence stretched in the room, punctuated by the boom of a particularly loud firework in the street outside.

"You asked your questions," growled Karissa. "Now tell me what I need to know."

"Regarding my dealings with the mayor?" scoffed Mr. Johnny. "I'm not sure what half-baked theory you have in your head Agent Lacey, but my business with the mayor has ever only been about one thing, and that is permitting."

She gaped at him. "Permitting."

"Correct."

She stood there, her face becoming redder and redder, an angry furnace roaring in her ears. "You lying son of a bitch," she spat. "Deny it then. Deny that you and Kincaid are behind the *Golden Venture*."

The gangster's eyes flashed. "I would open my developer's books to disprove your baseless accusations, but your rudeness has dissuaded me. Now," he said and he stood up. "Get out of my building."

The sound of many running feet could be heard on the stairs from the floors below. "Tell me the truth!" she screamed at him as Nigel tugged her toward the exit. "Snakehead coward!" She caught a last glimpse of the man called Mr. Johnny, standing still as a statue, as she was hauled through the double doors and half-carried up the stairs to the roof.

## ✲ 21 ✲

# A VISIT FROM HIROJI

Nigel's reflection was remarkably clear in the window of the Broadway Line subway car. He could see himself, haggard-looking, over the shoulder of the person sitting across from him. Despite another headache this morning, he had forced himself to attend class at the college, but had soon regretted the decision, the dizziness coming on strong during the first lecture of the day. It had become difficult for him to stay upright in his chair, let alone pay attention to what was being said.

The headache and the dizziness were still present on his commute home, but the discomfort did not prevent him from brooding. Nigel was deeply troubled by what Mr. Johnny had said. If what the gangster had claimed was true, if his mother had cooked the books for the Hip Sing and if his father had cracked skulls for not one, but two New York crime syndicates, then that would change everything. It would make his parents criminals. The problem was that he didn't know how to verify the gangster's claims and wasn't sure he wanted to. His belief in his parents' integrity had remained unshaken up to this point and he was afraid to learn too much about their dealings in New York, lest his opinion change.

On the way home to his apartment, Nigel bought a little flat of steamed buns from a shop outside the Canal Street subway station and an order of dumplings from his favorite Chinese restaurant. He was craving carbohydrates, as he had eaten nothing since the night before, and was now quite fond of the flavorful and convenient cuisine on offer in Chinatown.

As he pushed open the door to his apartment, he smiled in anticipation of the soft buns and warm dumplings, but the bag containing the food dropped from his hand as he crossed the threshold, and he let out a yelp of surprise and alarm. On his sofa, sat a bald man with penetrating black eyes. Nigel squinted in the dim light, realizing that it was not just any man, but his former teacher, Hiroji. What was he doing here, and how had he come in?

They stared at each other for a long moment, then Hiroji smiled, pushing himself to his feet and inclined his head. By reflex, Nigel bowed back, deeper than he would have liked, considering the circumstances, then he straightened, retrieving the bag with his dinner from the floor and closed the door behind him, turning again to face his uninvited guest.

A short while later, the two men were seated in the living room, eating dumplings with chopsticks and tearing hunks off the steamed buns with their teeth. Hiroji seemed hungry, appearing to lack any compunction about eating more than half of Nigel's meal. Fortunately, Nigel had lost much of his appetite.

Hiroji seemed cheerful enough. "Nigel-san, how long has it been since we last shared a meal together?" he asked in Japanese.

Nigel thought back, remembering the simple meals of rice, tofu and steamed vegetables he had eaten in the back room of Hiroji's dusty outpost, sometimes with the bureaucrat, but often alone. Hiroji had seldom kept him company, at least not in the strictest sense.

"Not long Sensei. Six months perhaps," said Nigel.

Hiroji smiled, nodding his head in agreement. "Do you miss Shimokitazawa?" he asked. The Tokyo neighborhood in which Nigel had lived and trained was almost as cramped and esoteric as Hiroji's office had been. He supposed that it might seem a charming place to tourists and young people, with its cozy bars and trendy eateries, its vintage clothing stores, its skinny streets and even narrower, winding alleyways, down which sometimes only scooters and bicycles could travel. But for Nigel, who had been accustomed to wide open sky and the strong, steady rush of the river, it had felt like a cell.

"Sometimes," he said, working his jaw mechanically as he slowly chewed a pork dumpling. "How is it?"

"Much as you left it I would imagine. But I cannot say for sure."

Nigel looked at him. "Haven't you been back?"

Hiroji had initially flown with Nigel from Tokyo to New York, had helped him rent his apartment and had then ostensibly left, back to his branch office in Japan.

"No," he replied. "I have been living nearby, following your movements and activities."

Nigel remained silent, managing to swallow his dumpling, despite the lump that had formed in his throat.

"Come Nigel-san, you are after all, our most valuable asset and the details of your comings and goings are of great importance to our people."

Nigel shook his head. "I am only a figurehead," he said, more than a little bitterly, then seeing Hiroji's surprise, he added, "My apologies Sensei, I have felt ineffectual for quite a while. I thought I was fighting on the side of good against evil, but now I am not sure what I am doing." He looked down at the nail cuticles of his right hand. "And what's this I hear about my parents having worked for the Hip Sing crime syndicate? Such a thing is deeply troubling to me."

Hiroji snorted. "Good and evil are ideas for children. I would have thought that by now you would have moved beyond such basic notions. Our organization believes in the principle of cause and effect. The *Golden Venture* is a clear example. We believe that if left unchecked, despicable acts such as human smuggling, which carry the terrible weight of exploitation, will spread, leading to the gradual erosion of human prosperity, even in the places we have so carefully curated, apart from the rest of the world." He seemed sad as he spoke the last, as though some related thought was weighing him down.

"And what of the Hip Sing?" prompted Nigel. "Speaking of cause and effect."

"There is a war going on," said Hiroji obliquely, "but the sides may be different than you think. Our enemies are those who take much more than their share, to the detriment of every living being on the planet, and you are our best weapon in the fight against them."

Nigel pondered this for a moment, weighing the consequences of telling his former teacher that he planned to resign as Champion, but he dismissed the thought, knowing the older man would never accept his choice.

"I know what you plan to do," said Hiroji, as if reading his thoughts. "I know that you plan to rid yourself of the *Resident*. But trust me when I say this to you: it cannot be done, not without your death following soon afterward."

"That is simply not true Sensei," Nigel said, shaking his head adamantly. "There is convincing evidence that high voltage electricity can be used to safely separate *Resident* from host. I am working with a highly competent researcher who has discovered this information."

"Do you think we have not tried using electricity?" asked Hiroji, waving a dismissive hand. "Long have we wished to save the lives of our Champions. I have always thought we owed them that much. But nothing worked. Even in cases where massive bursts of electricity were used to treat Champions, their bodies disintegrated within days. The only benefit from those experiments was that the *Resident* could be more quickly prepared for the next host. But we have never allowed such a treatment to become common practice. Electrocution and its aftermath is far too painful."

"Instead you let us slowly deteriorate and die anyway," muttered Nigel angrily, Hiroji's final confirmation of what would happen to him coming like a kick to the stomach.

"Yes, well, there is one added benefit of allowing nature to take its course. The *Resident* is far more powerful after slowly curing in chromium, one drop at a time. The importance of cultivating a breed of nearly invulnerable Champions cannot be underestimated." Hiroji sat back, the soft incandescent light from the lamp spilling over him, transforming him into a silhouette. Only the glint of his hard, black eyes was visible.

"Did my parents know about all this?" Nigel asked.

"Yes," replied the other. And then, as Nigel's shoulders slumped, Hiroji leaned forward and laid a hand on his former pupil's arm. "I am deeply sorry you were not told about the potential harmful effects of the *Resident*. It might be better to think of it as your destiny, as your father and mother do."

"Destiny is it?" asked Nigel reproachfully, stripping his arm from Hiroji's grasp. "Was it destiny that made my parents to join your cult? Was it destiny that gave them no choice but to bring me into the world, then keep me apart from everybody else? Was it destiny that dictated they send me all the way to Tokyo, then across the world to America without a friend in the world? Tell me Sensei, was it destiny that consigned me to death?"

Hiroji was silent for a long moment, considering him. "Yes," he finally said, "it was."

"Oh," said Nigel, his words dripping with bitter sarcasm, "what a relief."

Then the bureaucrat changed the subject, continuing, businesslike, as though Nigel's outburst was something to be graciously ignored. "Your mother asks that you continue to assist Karissa Lacey with her investigation into the New York mayor. She believes, as I do, that Agent Lacey shows a promising ability to see through the smokescreen of government to the corruption lying beneath. It is important that you help her verify her leads. Unsolved, the *Golden Venture* mystery sets an unacceptable precedent in today's world. Your mother also told me to inform you to leave Amy Kang alone. She cannot help you." Hiroji scratched the surface of his bare head, sending flakes of his skin into the air, which eventually settled on Nigel's couch.

"Is that why you're here?" Nigel asked. "To communicate my mother's orders to me?"

Hiroji sighed, expelling a puff of cool, dry air, like a desert breeze at night. "I was instructed not to reveal my presence to you unless absolutely necessary." The muscles clenched on the side of his balding head.

"Something has happened." He paused, as if considering where to begin.

"In June, the Japanese government moved ahead with the expansion of its rural electrification project, commencing construction on more than a dozen dams in Nagano Prefecture alone. Over the past several years, we have resisted their efforts to evict the people of Ryūiki to make way for the Toyooka Dam. At first, the project was successfully delayed through the efforts of our legal team, citing the rights of the existing tenants. When this eventually failed, your mother and father went in person to petition on behalf of themselves, their neighbors and their friends." His face grew dark. "But the government found a loophole, which gave them the right to appropriate the land and an eviction notice was issued." He paused meaningfully, pressing together the tips of his fingers in his lap.

"Your mother was furious. She was always a fiery woman," he said, frowning. "I counselled her to obey the government and lead the villagers to another suitable site, but she refused. Instead, on the day the village was supposed to have been emptied, she organized a protest. Unfortunately, the police arrived in force to arrest Fuyuko, Frank and the rest." He watched Nigel's face, gauging his reaction. Nigel wondered what his own expression might reveal to the old man about the resignation he felt, hearing all this.

"The police had no idea what your mother had in store. As soon as it became clear that she and her compatriots were to be removed, she fought back with a coordinated attack."

Nigel sucked in breath. "An attack?" he asked, suddenly afraid.

Hiroji shook his head sadly. "There was a gun battle. The men of the village, who were absent from the sit-in, ambushed the police as the officers moved deeper into the village. The men had erected a makeshift blockade and fired on the police using Chinese-made rifles, acquired on the black market. This all occurred without my knowledge," he said, sounding frustrated.

"What happened to the villagers?" asked Nigel in a quiet voice.

"Some of the men were shot by the police. The remainder, including the women, were arrested, though a few villagers fled into the countryside and were picked up and taken by our people to a secret location. The government launched a full-scale investigation into our organization and, as if out of spite, immediately went ahead with the flooding of Ryūiki, declining to give us the time to exhume the remains of our ancestors beforehand. The blackened bones of many former Champions are now at the murky bottom of a deep lake."

Nigel paused, trying to process the shocking information, a sudden thought occurring to him. "What became of the former Grand Master's family?" he asked anxiously, thinking of Aika.

Hiroji shrugged. "They left with a contingent of others before any of this happened, around the time Grand Master Yukada died."

That was some relief at least. "Where did they go?"

"To one of the other communes possibly or maybe they stayed in the area. I do not know."

So, it was over then. His village was gone, its inhabitants scattered, the whole area at the bottom of a lake, and he would probably never see Aika again.

Hiroji's unblinking black eyes regarded him, betraying no emotion. "Wouldn't you like to know what became of your parents?"

"Of course," said Nigel, though he assumed they had been captured and imprisoned along with everyone else. He was only half-right.

"Your mother was one of the first to be taken. She is in Nagano Prison now, awaiting trial." He cleared his throat roughly. "When your fath—" Hiroji's voice cracked with emotion. He shook his head, cleared his throat again and continued. "When your father saw your mother being beaten by the police, he rushed them, seriously injuring three of the officers before he was—" Again his voice caught. Nigel stared at him, wondering what could possibly move the hard-hearted man in such a way. "Nigel-san, your father is dead. He was gunned down by police."

A silence stretched. Hiroji seemed unable to meet Nigel's eyes, rubbing the top of his bald head with a *swish, swish* and staring at the floor. A car honked on the street. "I must go now," Hiroji said, gently brushing the crumbs of the meal from his pants onto the carpet, giving Nigel a pained look.

Nigel said nothing. Feeling numb, he sank back into the folds of the couch, his eyes unfocused, barely registering his former teacher's parting words. "I will shortly be travelling back to Japan, to meet with your mother's lawyers," he said, standing up, pulling on the teal windbreaker he had folded and left at the base of the lamp. "Remember, governments do not always serve their people and their leaders are often most guilty of this. Continue investigating the mayor. I think your friend is on to something."

## ✣ 22 ✣

# ELECTION DAY

Karissa awoke with a full-throated scream, sharp and loud, yet so brief that, upon gaining full wakefulness, she wondered if she had actually made the noise or if she had only dreamt it. She checked the bedside clock: 5:48 a.m. Sighing with frustration, she allowed her head to sink back onto the pillow. The alarm was set to ring in twenty-seven minutes; precious little time for her to make any significant dent in the debt of missed sleep she was carrying these days. Lately, her sleep had been extremely light and filled with disturbing dreams; not the kind with terrifying images or situations, but the other kind, the kind characterized only by sensation – falling, drowning, being buried alive.

Her next sigh became a growl as she hoisted herself out of bed and padded into the living room, irresistibly drawn to the television, though she knew nothing important would have happened yet; the polls were not even open. Nevertheless, she clicked on the 27" tube TV, blinking in the bright blue light issuing from its screen. She found Channel 6 and was greeted by a serious-looking blonde news anchor, wearing a red dress with expansive shoulder pads. She was discussing the mayoral candidates with some kind of municipal political expert, who was sitting with her at a round, elevated table. Adjusting the volume so it could be heard in every corner of her apartment, she began her morning routine, not wanting to miss a thing. It was election day.

At a quarter to eight, Karissa exited her building at 249 Church Street, the sun rising bloodless and shallow on the November horizon. She wore her tan overcoat, a navy pantsuit, and dark tortoiseshell wayfarers, serving to conceal the purplish circles of fatigue under her eyes, which she had been unable to hide with makeup alone. Her brown heels clicked on the dewy pavement as she made her way toward the franchise coffee shop where she intended to buy a steaming cup of black coffee, eagerly anticipating the jolt of caffeine as it combined with the nicotine in her gum to jumpstart her sluggish system and catapult her into the day.

She was met with a busy day of work at the INS. Word had come from Washington that they were to enact a comprehensive new protocol concerning the detaining of suspected illegal immigrants. The President had read an article in the New York Times featuring the remaining 276 *Golden Venture* passengers, still in prison after five months. The exposé had also contained, in list form, the names of another fifteen-hundred asylum seekers, who had come to America illegally and who were being held for up to five years, with no end in sight. The court system had been in no hurry to provide them with hearing dates and the people had been largely forgotten.

The President, reportedly moved by the article, had signed an executive order to have the detainees released from prison, and introduced a series of bills representing a new national stance on the treatment of certain categories of illegal immigrants. At its core, this legislation considered asylum-seeking refugees, even those who had come to the US by illegal means, innocent until proven guilty. Thus, INS protocol now included an elaborate strategy for keeping track of aliens who were released from prison but who were still awaiting a court date.

Dick Lamphere had dubbed this the 'Babysitting Protocol.' He had been in and out of meetings all morning, pink-faced and fuming, and had aimed a kick at a wayward trash can as he had passed by Karissa's office. Grinning to herself as she remembered the look on his face, she twiddled the dial of the portable radio, which she kept at low volume in a desk drawer, following the election results as they unfolded.

At noon, Karissa left the office to vote at the Mariners' Temple Baptist Church. It was just her luck that she picked the polling station where Rusty Kincaid was casting his ceremonial ballot. She waited impatiently as cameras flashed and the moon-faced mayor chatted loudly with reporters, taking his time, making a show of it.

On his way into the voting booth, she thought she heard him say, "Wow, this is a *tough* decision," sarcastically, to a chorus of guffaws from his entourage and from some of the press. He finally finished voting and swept out with his aides and hangers on. She bristled as he walked by her, badly wanting to cold-cock the bastard, knock him to the floor in front of everybody and demand he explain his involvement with the *Golden Venture*.

After she finally made it to the front of the line, Karissa hastily checked the box next to the name of the other guy and, taking less pleasure than she had anticipated in the act of voting against Kincaid, she stalked from the church in search of something to eat, still fuming.

Karissa returned to the INS several minutes late from lunch. Fortunately, Dick Lamphere was gone, probably outside smoking, as he was want to do when stressed. Frowning, she headed back into her office, her heels sounding on the thinly carpeted floor. Reaching her desk, she bent down and unlocked the bottom drawer, exhuming the white leather-bound ledger she had stolen from the mayor's shipping company. She flipped through the pages, finding the one that contained the coded information surrounding the *Golden Venture* HIN.

Marking the place with a post-it and tucking the book under her arm, Karissa made her way to the elevator, taking it three floors up to Visas, in search of her friend Charity. She wasn't quite sure why she felt the need to show Charity the ledger. Perhaps it was the fact that she hadn't shown it to many people and the reactions of those to whom she had shown the document (Nigel and two inept cryptographers recommended to her by Admiral Rat) had been less than satisfying. What she needed, today of all days, was someone else to believe that the mayor was mixed up with the *Golden Venture* and for that person to be outraged along with her.

She found Charity sitting in her cubicle, on a call with what sounded like a visa applicant. "No ma'am. Please don't take that tone with me ma'am. I understand, but you're going to have to lower your voice." Charity noticed Karissa standing off to the side and rolled her eyes ostentatiously. "No I can't check that for you. As I said, you'll have to wait for that information along with everybody else. No. Yes. You have yourself a good day." And with that, she hung up, swivelling in her chair and, leaning back, wiggled her eyebrows at Karissa.

"Heyyy," said Karissa and made an exaggerated arcing wave of her arm. "Are you as fucking slammed as I am today?"

"Probably," Charity replied, "how fucking slammed are you?"

"Slammed. But I thought I'd take a quick break to come say hi."

"Hi," said Charity, succinctly, an ironic smile playing on her lips. Then, she patted the seat cushion of the other chair in her cubicle and Karissa sat down. "What have you got there?" she asked, noticing the ledger tucked under Karissa's arm.

Karissa was pleased. "It's a key piece of evidence in the *Golden Venture* investigation. And it's been pissing me off royally."

"Oh, how so?" asked the other woman, curiously.

"We believe that Rusty Kincaid could be behind the *Golden Venture* disaster in June, that he might be a big-league human smuggler." The use of the word 'we,' was technically true, if only because it referred to her and Nigel, though Karissa realized that it might have the effect of misleading Charity as to the official stance of the INS on the matter.

Charity gaped at her. "Holy shit." She considered this, her eyes becoming round. "The bastard might be re-elected today for Chris-sake. I'd better get out there and vote!"

"Yes," Karissa exclaimed, "you should! And take a look at this," she said, cracking the ledger for Charity and showing her the marked page. "See this number here?" The other woman nodded. "It's the *Golden Venture* hull identification number. We pulled it from a safe in one of Kincaid's company warehouses. The rest of it is in code."

"No," breathed Charity.

"Yes," Karissa said meaningfully. "But I have no idea what any of the rest of it means and I need to figure it out so we can nail Kincaid."

"Mind if I take closer look? I love puzzles."

"Sure, but listen, I have to get back to work soon."

"Can you leave it with me for a few hours? I'll take it back down to you on my afternoon break." Karissa hesitated, wondering if it was a good idea to let the ledger out of her sight. "Come on, I'm really good with these things. Maybe I'll find something you haven't."

Karissa shrugged. "Okay, sure" she said, "have at it." And then, almost as an afterthought, "This is all very hush, hush, capisce?"

"Of course." Charity mimed a zipping motion across her lips.

"Thanks Charity, you're a pal," said Karissa, initiating their familiar parting ritual.

"You're a swell guy," her friend returned.

Karissa left the other woman at her desk, the matter slipping from her mind as she began thinking through the tasks she had to complete before she left at the end of the day.

At five minutes to four, Karissa was interrupted by the sound of her desk phone. She let it ring a couple of times as she finished the last sentence of the email she was typing. Answering the phone distractedly, she heard a small voice on the other end say, "I think I messed up." It was Charity, Karissa realized.

"Charity, what—"

Her friend interrupted, her next words coming in a rush, "Benny was just up here asking about visas for asylum seekers and we got chatting and I brought up Kincaid and I, I didn't know I was supposed keep it a secret from him too." Karissa closed her eyes, guessing what must have happened before Charity could finish her stammering account. "He took it. He took the ledger, Karissa. I am so sorry."

Karissa could hear shouting filtering down the hall from the direction of Dick Lamphere's office and she replaced the receiver without saying goodbye, an icy blade of dread slashing at her insides. She stayed where she was, frozen, as the shouting grew louder.

"LACEY!"

A moment later, Dick Lamphere rounded the corner, looking like an enraged bull. Benny was hot on his heels, an expression of consternation on his face. Karissa leapt to her feet.

"As if I don't have enough to deal with today!" Lamphere bellowed, violently slamming the ledger down on the corner of her desk, "This is the last straw. You disobeyed a direct order to leave Kincaid alone and not only that, but you seem to have decided to add breaking and entering to your list of offenses. I said I'd have your job Lacey, now hand them over."

"Hand what over sir?" asked Karissa, in a state of shock.

"Your badge and gun. You're done here Lacey. You're through. Pack your shit. I'll have you out of here by the end of the day."

Shakily, she handed over the articles to Lamphere, who snatched them away. She glanced at Benny who looked aghast.

"You're in on it, aren't you?" she screeched. "Both of you! And when I prove it, I—"

Lamphere's roar drowned her out. "You're lucky I don't have you fucking arrested! But mark my words," he said in a quieter, deadlier voice, "this isn't the last of it. Your ass will be subject to a full tribunal, after which you'll more than likely see the inside of a cell."

"You'll be sorry," she said to him in voice quivering with hurt and rage.

At this, Lamphere's expression darkened even further, if such a thing was possible. "You know what, I've changed my mind. The end of the day's too fucking long from now. Lin, help me locate two agents to throw *Ms.* Lacey out of the building. If I do it myself, I'll be up for my own tribunal." And with that, he plunged out of the room, looking both ways in search of more of Karissa's colleagues, before disappearing down the hall. Benny shot Karissa a tormented look before following his boss out of the room.

Whirling around, Karissa grabbed an empty packing box that happened to be in the corner and began to frantically dump the contents of her desk drawers into it. She left her files, instead filling the box with the knickknacks she had accumulated over the last three years, personal items that were probably worthless, but which she could not bear to leave behind in this place. When the last drawer had been emptied, she stood and surveyed the area through the tangled mess of her hair. In his hurry to find others to expel her, Lamphere had inadvertently left the ledger behind on the corner of the desk. Without thinking, she scooped it up, jamming it in the box with her other possessions. Then, she tugged on her overcoat, hefted the box and made for the exit, swiftly moving in the opposite direction from the way the two men had gone a few moments before.

THAT EVENING, KARISSA MADE SURE SHE WAS VERY, VERY DRUNK. She started with a small bottle of whisky from her own small liquor supply then, at a half past seven, she left in search of more alcohol, finding herself on the Bowery after twenty minutes of hazy, aimless wandering. She stopped into the first Bowery dive she saw, finding it unusually quiet, which suited her just fine. The television behind the bar was broadcasting the election, adding to Karissa's feelings of agitation, yet she found that she was glued to the screen, unable to look away. And so, as she drank one glass of whisky after another, she watched the final election results come in...

"Rusty Kincaid has won it," the announcer declared. "The final count is 930,237 votes to Stripling's 876,868 and Stripling has conceded defeat. We go live to the Bowery Hotel where the mayor will be delivering his acceptance speech within the hour." On screen was a shot of a raised platform inside the ballroom of the Bowery Hotel, around which several hundred well-dressed Kincaid supporters clustered, waiting for him to make his address.

"Waitaminute," Karissa slurred. "That's right around th'corner." The bartender stared at her without deigning to reply. Karissa clumsily paid the woman and made her way unsteadily toward the stairs leading up to the street, her hand trailing along the wall to help her balance.

Rain was falling outside when she finally managed to push open the heavy double doors to the street. Once she was clear of the building, she immediately vomited half on and half off the curb. She cackled, wiping her face with the back of her hand, managing to solicit a cigarette from a suited businessman who was smoking in an alcove and had seen the whole thing. He seemed concerned about her.

"Can I call you a cab?" he asked. And, when she shook her head no, he pressed. "Come on, you'll freeze to death out here without a coat." She looked down. Where had her overcoat gone? She must have left her apartment without it. Taking a deep drag of the cigarette, she staggered away down the glistening sidewalk without thanking the man, fixed on the route to the hotel.

She couldn't have said how she found her way there, or how she made it into the venue, visibly drunk, soaking wet and underdressed as she was, but eventually she found herself pushing though the press of the crowd, eagerly awaiting the arrival of the man they had elected to the ballroom.

The mood was high, with shouts and whistles splitting the air, and widespread laughter and chat. She felt like one of the ghosts that were supposed to haunt the Bowery Hotel, a relic of an older, simpler time, invisible to the people tightly packed around her. She giggled, drawing a suspicious look from the woman to her right.

A cheer went up, swelling as the mayor stepped onstage, rock and roll music erupting from several large speakers strategically placed around the room. His beady blue eyes, set in the middle of his enormous face, glittered with self-importance. Taking in the room with a childish, lopsided grin, he raised a meaty fist, the symbol of revolution and change, appropriated for his victory. Karissa was close enough to the front that she could make out the sheen of sweat covering Kincaid's cheeks and forehead, commingling with the gel he had liberally applied to hair and scalp. Her mood shifted dramatically the moment she saw him and she almost choked on her hatred and rage.

"Thank you," Kincaid began, finding the podium and leaning forward to speak into the microphone. "Thank you for your patience. There are *way* too many formalities on election night." Scattered laughter. "I want to be clear that this victory is about all of us, not just me. Well, it is about me, but you get the idea." More laughter. "But it's not only for us, and the others who voted for me in this election; my victory goes to all New Yorkers." Several shouts of approval. "Over the past four years I've gotten to know many of you well and I consider you my family." An exaggerated 'awww' issued forth. "Yes." Kincaid said fervently, "I do. And I'm protective of my family. As this city's father figure, I will not stand for the rampant crime we see on our streets. My first act in my second term as mayor will be to dramatically increase the size of the NYPD, which will stamp out everything from organized crime to panhandling, from drug dealing to squeegee boy shakedowns, and will continue to target the activities of the illegal aliens who are enjoying a free ride at the expense of hard working American New Yorkers." A zealous cheer went up at the last, causing the hairs on the back of Karissa's neck to stand on end. "It is my sincerest wish, as I carry out my many intentions for the betterment of our city, that you will be proud of your mayor, as I am so proud of all of you." And he touched a hand to his heart.

The root of Karissa's loathing for Kincaid was suddenly so clear that she wondered if she was experiencing a vision. She saw the mayor not as a person, but as a large mechanical puppet, worked from within by his wizened, grub-like ego. She hated that ego creature with every fibre of her being, for she could see that it was insatiable, that it would say anything, do anything to protect itself, even ruin a city, or smuggle in boatloads of people to keep itself going. Kincaid was a puppet without any external strings, strings that should lead back to the citizens of New York. Why couldn't these people see that?

Ever since she was young girl, Karissa had wanted to be a superhero so she could put a stop to men like this, having been aware of them even then. She had settled on law enforcement and had become a federal agent before she was thirty years old. Now, she was nothing, stripped of the power to protect the world from the likes of Kincaid. Yet, a part of her knew that even if she was a superhero, she couldn't have changed the outcome here tonight. It had been up to the voters, who had been duped by this shell of a man. And then there were those who hadn't even bothered to vote.

"I don't want to take up any more of your time. Let's party already!" Kincaid shouted, his voice coming distorted from the speakers. There was a deafening roar, as the mayor jumped from the stage and began to shake hands with everyone in sight, an exaggerated smile plastered on his face. *Sympathy For The Devil* by the Rolling Stones issued from the speakers, the sound of the bongo drums on the track adding a surreal quality to the moment. He was coming straight for her, Karissa realized, her hands closing into tight fists at her sides. He stopped in front of her, a look of confusion appearing on his broad face, perhaps thrown by her visible animosity toward him. They stared at each other for a moment, the room seeming to go quiet. Karissa raised her shaking fist, then he was gone, enveloped by the crowd.

She turned and stalked away. *Fuck it.* She still had the ledger, and with it, the power to bring Kincaid down. All she needed was to extract his confession and then she'd hand him over to the police. She would need Nigel's help, but that shouldn't be a problem. He was almost as unhappy with the way the world worked as she. That much was obvious.

# ❧ 23 ❧

## VETERAN'S DAY

**M**ayor Rusty Kincaid sighed. Rain fell heavily on the glass sunroof of the Lincoln as it carried him from his Veteran's Day address at the Brooklyn War Memorial back to City Hall. It was a long ride from Brooklyn, packed in with Mark Hendricks, his Chief of Staff, and his two staffers, whose names he had forgotten, moving sluggishly along with the heavy traffic. He irritably wondered why they hadn't thought to arrange for two vehicles, one for them and one for him, which might have afforded him some much needed peace and quiet.

Kincaid wasn't exactly sure why he'd run for mayor a second time. It had been a week since the election and the demands were still pouring in from supporters, eager to move forward with this or that initiative. But he was tired. Over the last few years, between this job and the one at his father's shipping company (it was his company now, he remembered), he had been spread thin. And, with his recent divorce, he had been indulging more and more the urge to go out on the town, carousing with faceless blue collar simpletons in the bars of Brooklyn, wiggling his sweaty body in the press of young ravers at secret drug-fueled parties, and taking cocaine and meth with drug dealers, immersing himself in their gritty world. All were attempts to distract himself from the fact that, although he knew he should be acting as caretaker and nursemaid to the city, he didn't give a shit. And, despite what his critics might say about him, he felt guilty about that.

After the news story broke, reporting that he had been in possession of an illicit substance, he had promised his Chief of Staff that he would seek rehab and, for a time he had secretly attended an addictions facility in Westchester, but he had soon withdrawn himself due to the repugnant collection of losers who had occupied the place. If there was one thing Kincaid had always known, it was that he was a winner.

Many of his friends had abandoned him since the meth scandal, and although the media storm had sputtered and died after he had been acquitted, the liberal press had been waiting around like jackals for him to slip up again. On his most lucid days he was aware that, given the amount he was partying, it would probably only be a matter of time before another scandal broke, which he dreaded, for bad press cut deep.

When he had first campaigned four years ago, all he had wanted was to stir the pot a bit, meet some new people and move up in the world. He'd thought that maybe he would stand out more as a shit-disturbing politician than as a boring shipping baron. And, as he campaigned, he had begun to covet the idea of becoming a household name. Unbeknownst to Kincaid however, or at least to the part of him that was aware of such things, running for mayor had been an attempt to address the empty, worthless feeling, which had gnawed at his guts every day as far back as he could remember, and which he had been having difficulty ignoring of late.

After the initial triumph had worn off, he was surprised to find that he was bitterly disappointed. In his new life as mayor, he felt even more hollow and afraid, even more bitter and angry than he had before. Thus, he had chosen to spend his time with people who were excited just to be near him, numbing himself to those nasty emotions, though on some level he maintained deep misgivings about the lasting positive effects of such a strategy.

The second, recent campaign had been nowhere near as exciting as the first one had been, though he had enjoyed the spotlight again for two solid months. But it had seemed to pass by in an eye blink, marred by the drug scandal and the temporary closure of his company after the police raided his event. It had been a party for fuck's sake and not even an illegal one and on private property no less. He hadn't known that the staff were Chinese illegals when he hired them, had he? Or that those women had been underage? Sure, he took drugs, but that was his business.

A point of pride for Kincaid, which he clung to like an amulet, was his moral code. Although he wasn't conceited or stupid enough to think that he had contributed anything meaningful to the city as mayor, the main thing was that he had been honest. He wasn't involved in any shady business dealings, didn't use taxpayers' money for unnecessary expenses and certainly didn't take any bribes. Even the permitting he had arranged for the Hip Sing Public Association was on the up and up. No, he had never done anything illegal, not anything of any real significance anyway, for he hated nothing more a corrupt politician.

The Lincoln turned off Park Row onto a path reserved for pedestrians and maintenance vehicles and the driver jumped out into the rain to open the metal gate. There was no particular reason why Kincaid wanted to use the back door, except that he had forgotten his umbrella and the walk up the front steps would have resulted in damp hair and the possibility of ruining his Italian wool suit. Hendricks perked up as the car rolled to a stop. "There are some things we should discuss before the afternoon," he began.

"Why didn't you bring them up in the car?" Kincaid asked, irritably.

"I thought you might want time to reflect after the address," Hendricks said. The mayor's father had stormed the beaches at Normandy and had lost several friends there, but Kincaid had given it barely a thought.

"You have 'till we're upstairs," Kincaid grunted, his two staffers following closely behind as they exited the vehicle. Hendricks talked rapidly as the rain fell on Kincaid's heavily gelled red hair.

. . .

AFTER INSTRUCTING THEM NOT TO DISTURB HIM, KINCAID CLOSED the heavy Georgian door on Hendricks and his staffers and, when he was sure they had gone, he strode over to his liquor cabinet. Removing a bottle of scotch, he pried out the cork with a *thwop* and had two long swallows of the whiskey straight from the bottle. He coughed, his shoulders shuddering as he peered through watery eyes at his magnificent office.

Even on his off-days the room brought a smile to his lips: the mahogany book cases lining the wall, the soft blue and white patterned carpet, the chestnut brown desk chair, the delicate material of the flags in their wooden stands, the brass of the lamps, which took on a golden cast in the soft light from the ample six foot windows, the two figures, one crouching in the window recess, the other leaning against the frame. Kincaid froze, emitting a noise somewhere between a snort and choke.

The two figures were not a part of the room, he realized. Kincaid's eye was drawn to the one squatting in the window: a man, covered in a bizarre material, which shifted in a dizzying and unimaginable way. The man stood up on the ledge and hopped down, adjusting his black mask, which covered only his eyes, exposing his mouth and nose, the only bare skin visible. He leaned against the wall, folding his arms with a certain weightiness and gazed fixedly at Kincaid.

The other was a woman, dressed in a tight-fitting suit made of what seemed to be a fine, midnight-blue mesh. There were brown leather straps wrapped around her elbows, wrists, and knees, with several wider bands cinched around her torso and chest. She was wearing a sky-blue ski-mask, which he registered only briefly, before his eyes slid to the retractable baton she held fully extended in one black-gloved hand. Kincaid's mouth opened and closed like a fish just landed, no air passing in or out. He gaped at the woman as she advanced on him.

"You bastard," she whispered, the utterly frigid tone of her voice chilling him to his marrow. She stepped closer still, almost crooning the frosty words, "Did you think you could just get away with it?"

"Get away with what?" he asked, his lips feeling like they were made of wood.

"You know what," the woman said tonelessly. Kincaid said nothing, glancing over at the man whose suit looked like molten metal. He remained motionless by the window, looking uneasy.

"Please," Kincaid said to him, but the man looked away.

"Hey," said the woman, snapping gloved fingers in his face. "You had to know someone would come sometime." Kincaid shook his head and she emitted a dry, mirthless chuckle. "Come on, it was going to come out eventually." She watched him closely, as though waiting for him to confirm something.

"What would come out?" he asked, perplexed.

"The *Golden Venture*," the woman said, as though the name held all the weight in the world. But she had succeeded in confusing him even more.

"The Golden... What?"

"The *Golden Venture!*" she shouted, suddenly raising the baton, the mesh on the arm of her suit whispering restlessly as she did so.

"Wait!" he cried, lifting his hands to protect his face. Then the name *Golden Venture* slid home, connecting with a memory of five months before. The *Golden Venture* was the vessel that had beached itself in Queens in June, with its cargo of three hundred Chinese aliens. He had used the incident politically at the time, to rally xenophobes to his banner as he had gone into his re-election campaign and, when the ploy had worked, he had allowed The *Golden Venture* to drift into the recesses of his memory, where it had lain, nearly forgotten, until now.

"What about it?" he asked "Are you accusing me of something?"

The question did more harm than good because, with a growl, the woman gave him a mighty shove and he sat down hard on the carpet, his lower back jarring painfully. As he fell, the man leaning on the wall jerked his arms out like he wanted to catch Kincaid, but he folded them together again, settling back into position, looking a little sick.

"I figured you'd play dumb," the woman sneered. "It's so *you*. Here's a little about me though: I'm not a very patient person, even on my better days. And today," she said, prodding his kneecap none too gently with the end of the baton, "today my patience is hanging by a fucking thread."

"Now," she said, suddenly business-like, "why were you meeting with the Hip Sing?" He was taken aback. How could she know about that? Seeming to detect his surprise, she said, with hint of amusement, "Mr. Johnny said it was about *permitting*."

Despite having the feeling that the truth wouldn't help him here, Kincaid's mouth moved as if by its own accord. "It was."

"Excuse me?" hissed the woman, her eyes narrowing to slits.

"I met with the president of the Hip Sing Public Association about municipal permitting. It was in the best interests of the city," he added, ready to explain more, but before he could, he heard a meaty *thud* and, a split-second later, came the pain. She had struck him with the baton on the upper outside of his leg where quadriceps met hamstring, a place rich with nerves and the sensation was all but unbearable.

Standing over him as he howled and cringed, she called out to her accomplice. "Block the door!" And after a moment's pause, the man headed in the direction of the only exit, hefting two huge filing cabinets, placing them carefully with inhuman strength, one by one, in front of the heavy Georgian door. He seemed to do this reluctantly, saying nothing. Kincaid could almost feel what would be a huge purple bruise spreading over his thigh.

"Let's try this again," said the woman, over Kincaid's whimpering. "Who else are you working with?"

"I don't know what you mean," he said through gritted teeth. *Thunk*. He cried out again. She'd hit him in the same place as before, his mouth forming a silent 'O' of agony. She crouched, leaning close to him, her face swimming into focus through the tears leaking from his eyes. She raised the baton again.

"That's enough!" he shouted, feeling a rush of sudden anger fueled by the brutal and unjust treatment. "Just tell me what this is about, goddamn it."

The woman paused, considering him and then, with venom in her voice, she laid out her twisted theory: "Either you were a human smuggler before you became mayor, or you thought you'd give it a try after you were elected. Your shipping company purchased the *Golden Venture* to smuggle a boatload of illegal immigrants overseas to the US. To cover up a botched job, you shifted the blame onto the aliens themselves using your platform as mayor and allowed law enforcement to believe the culprit was a middle-aged immigrant woman. And hmm, let's see," she said, tapping her thin, pale lips, which protruded from the front of her mask. "You used illegal immigrants as staff, who were probably still in debt to you from their trip here. You have access to hard drugs and you consort with known gangsters. And, oh yeah," she said as if just remembering, "you've been running this city into the ground for the last four years and you obviously don't give a shit about anyone but yourself."

Kincaid thought for a moment, his mind reeling. "You must think you have proof of all this. Unless you're a complete and utter," and he cringed as a spasm shot up his leg, tingling nastily somewhere near his spine, "nut."

She stared at him for a moment, twisting the metal rod in her hands, leather gloves squeaking, then she reached behind her, removing a notebook tucked into the leather strap encircling her waist. She tossed the notebook next to him on the floor and stood up.

"There's your proof."

Reaching a trembling hand toward the notebook, Kincaid saw that it was bound in a kind of faux white leather. It was a fair size and seemingly well used, the pages ruffled and creased. He cracked it open, flipped through and saw that most of the pages were covered with what appeared to be nonsense, scrawled in a cramped, angular hand. Then he recognized the script.

"Where did you find this?" he asked, scared.

"Turn to the marked page," she ordered. He did as he was told, his eye immediately going to a twelve-digit sequence of letters and numbers he recognized as a hull identification for a ship. The HIN had been circled in blue pen with such force that it had ripped through the page in two places. "Recognize the number?" she asked him sharply. He shook his head, looking up at her questioningly. "It's the hull ID for the *Golden Venture*. I found that in a safe at your company's dry dock."

He remembered hearing about the break-in; one of the security guards had been in the hospital afterward.

"It appears," she continued, "that your company acquired the *Golden Venture* at the end of May 1992, almost exactly a year before it ran aground off the Rockaway Peninsula. Care to explain that, Mr. Mayor?"

Kincaid allowed himself a small sigh of relief. He knew now that this was all a big misunderstanding. But would the truth be enough he wondered? "Listen to me carefully," he said, trying to ignore the pain in his leg. "This is a *sales* ledger. My company *sold* this ship on May 28th last year." He paused, waiting anxiously. She had become very still.

"Bullshit," she finally said.

"It's true," he said, "really."

"Then why the fuck is it in code?"

"It-it's not code exactly," he stammered. He could see her eyebrows climbing her forehead, even under her mask. "The foreman is a very creative dyslexic. His shorthand's based on a made-up language invented by some academic in the sixties," he explained, wondering why he'd bothered to pay attention when the man had explained it to him, though now he was glad he had. "It makes more sense than written English to him, apparently." He turned the notebook toward her. "See this?" he asked, pointing to a capital letter 'Y' next to the HIN. "It means sold." There was a deadly silence.

"Liar," she said in a barely audible whisper.

"I get it," he said with a grimace, trying and failing to pick himself up off the floor, "I'm not the best mayor in history. I haven't come up with any great ideas or snappy policies. I'm the last guy you'd want in charge if you care about poor people or social justice or whatnot. Plus, I'll admit, I don't have a lot of respect for women." He shrugged. "And politics aside, I truly believe we should either send illegals back to their shitty countries or lock them up and throw away the key. But believe me when I tell you: I'm no human smuggler." He knew he might be a self-absorbed bastard, harboring what probably amounted to some narrow-minded beliefs, but at least he was no monster.

Unfortunately, she didn't seem to share this opinion. "Liar!" she screamed again and began to lay about her with the baton, beating him indiscriminately. The solid metal rod rose and fell with terrible force on his legs, his arms and shoulders, his chest and stomach, then hammered him in the jaw and face. Through a sea of pain, he beheld her standing astride him, her chest heaving, her hands shaking violently. He could see tears shimmering in her eyes.

"It's true," the mayor said in a barely audible whisper. Then the baton came whistling down. There was a blinding flash of light and pain, and then, for Kincaid, all was blackness.

NIGEL SUCKED IN A BREATH IN THE SICKLY SILENCE AFTER KARISSA had finished beating the mayor senseless. *Why hadn't he stopped her? She had attacked a defenseless man and he had just stood there, staring.* Bewildered, he moved beside Karissa, who had removed her balaclava and was brushing sweaty, dirty-blond hair out of her face with a gloved, blood-specked hand. She turned to him then, oblivious to the thin red streaks she had smeared across her forehead.

"Come on," she said in a tight voice, "let's search the desk. There might be some correspondence or..." She trailed off, watching him as he peered down at the mayor's motionless body. Nigel said nothing, a profound weight settling on his shoulders, intensifying the longing to be rid of the crushing responsibility he carried with him everywhere he went. He had never wanted to become a superhero because somehow he had always known that such a thing couldn't exist. Not in a world filled with fallible people like him.

"What have we done?" he asked.

Her lip curled in an ugly sneer. "The bastard deserved it," she spat.

"I believe what he said. Kincaid's no criminal."

Karissa shook her head. "You're wrong," she said, her eyes flicking down at the figure on the floor. "But it doesn't matter."

"It doesn't matter?" cried Nigel, suddenly seizing her by the shoulders. "How can you say it doesn't matter?" He was shaking her now, flooded with a sudden, urgent fury, directed as much at himself as at her. "He's innocent!" He was interrupted by an insistent knocking at the door.

"Mr. Mayor! Police. Your staff heard screaming. Open the door!" The door shuddered as it was buffeted by something heavy.

"No one is fucking innocent," said Karissa.

He let go of her then and stalked over to the window, ripping it open. "Wait," she said behind him, her head swivelling nervously toward the sound of the sustained hammering on the door. "I need your help." He turned back and, without knowing why, he allowed her to climb onto his back. She clung to him with her arms and legs as he ran toward the window. Behind them the door splintered and Nigel heard one of the officers shout something at them as he dove into space.

As THE TWO FIGURES BOUNDED UP, UP AND AWAY, ONE HOLDING tight to the other, they failed to notice the small, shabbily dressed man sitting on a bench outside City Hall. As they hurtled out of sight, Admiral Rat turned his shrewd gaze to the many police cars arriving from every direction. Interested, he waited patiently to see what additional information he could collect, for he had recognized one of the people fleeing the scene, and he would be damned if it hadn't been Agent Karissa Lacey.

## ✣ 24 ✣

# EVERYONE MAKES MISTAKES

K arissa didn't know how they had identified her, but they had. When she reached her Tribeca apartment that day, there were several squad cars pulled up on the sidewalk and three uniformed police standing on the front stoop, deep in hurried conversation.

Still dressed in her distinctive midnight-blue bodysuit, she knew she ran a high risk of being caught, unless she found a change of clothes and a safe place to hide. The trouble was, she had no money, no phone and could think of no friends who could be trusted to conceal her from the police. She barely knew anyone outside the INS if she was being honest, besides Larry, her next-door neighbour, with whom she sometimes played squash.

Making her way toward the Bowery, Karissa kept mostly to alleyways, zigzagging as she went, stopping and pausing to skulk in graffiti-covered doorways, deftly scrambling over chain-link fences, whisking wraithlike and unseen through a light industrial complex, on the way to her childhood quarter of the city.

She borrowed some clothes from the back room of the Chinese laundry where she had gathered change from the machines in her youth. She didn't think the proprietor, an elderly Chinese immigrant, would mind it if she took some clothing from the enormous lost and found bin the woman carefully maintained for her more absentminded customers.

Now Karissa lurked behind a parked car, across the street from her father's house, a slim, three-story row house he now occupied on the edge of the Bowery. Karissa realized she hadn't thought about him in a long time; when considering possible refuges though, he had immediately come to mind. She was nervous at first, but it had occurred to her that her feelings toward the man, though still complicated, no longer presented a significant barrier to reconnecting with him; only stubbornness might get in the way, hers and his both.

She had heard through the grapevine that he was no longer with the NYPD, that he had quit ten years ago and now headed a boutique private security firm, one of the first of its kind in New York. He had done well for himself, but had not once reached out to her since the day he had ordered her to leave. Despite this fact, she knew that if there was anyone in the city who could understand her violent attempt to take down Kincaid, it was he.

Screwing up her confidence, Karissa took in a deep shuddering breath and crossed the street, looking surreptitiously around her for unfriendly eyes. Thankfully, the street was deserted. Dressed now in a baggy, grey knit sweater, faded, well-used jeans and a stained Yankees cap, pulled low over her eyes, she doubted she could easily be identified, though she knew it was still risky to be crossing East 1$^{st}$ street without full cover of darkness, not with what would certainly be a widespread search for her under way.

Shoulders hunched, she rang the bell, burying her hands deeply in her newly acquired pants, their pockets riddled with holes. After what seemed like an eternity, the door opened, revealing the outline of her father, who stood silently, cloaked in the half-light within.

"Dad?" she asked, hesitantly.

There was a pause. "Karissa," her father said quietly.

"Can I come in?"

Another pause. "Sure," he said, at last.

Her father led the way through the narrow, unadorned hall, turning abruptly left into the kitchen. It looked like he had been cutting chicken for dinner and all the fixings for kebabs: onion, peppers and mushrooms, sat waiting by the chopping block. The place was ordered and clean and a faint citrus scent hung in the air, from disinfectant or air freshener, she couldn't tell which. She smiled, unexpectedly comforted by the thought that her father seemed to be taking care of himself. She studied him as he resumed cutting.

He was dressed in a red and green checked shirt of good material and wore brown dress pants with pleats, their color accented by the bronze frames of his eyeglasses. He looked older than she remembered him, with deep furrows etched in his brow and a slackness in the skin on his cheeks, hinting at a habitually serious expression. There was silver at his temples and flecks of grey were scattered through his curly mop of short-cropped hair. His waxy complexion was still that of a man who lived with a bottle in his hand, though no alcohol was in sight.

She wondered if he had met anyone. Single, middle-aged people often seemed to find each other; though something in the way he moved, his slight hunch and shuffling feet and the silence of his home, all somehow led her to believe that this was unlikely.

"I didn't think I would say it right off, but I'm happy to see you Dad."

"Likewise," he said, smiling thinly, yet neglecting to look up from his cutting. He flicked a piece of bumpy chicken skin into a trash can, which was positioned next to him on the floor.

"I like your new place," she said, walking around the kitchen a little, admiring the crown moulding, poking her head into the living room, which adjoined the kitchen. Then she wandered over to the kitchen window and peered into the alley below. She noticed that, although the front door had been level with the street, there was a two-story drop to the ground in back. An old mattress leaned against the base of a rickety wooden staircase, which could be accessed by the kitchen door, presumably for purposes of fire escape.

"Thanks," he said, watching her carefully as she toured herself around. "Just finished the renos."

She eyed him, attempting to read his expression. "I heard you quit the force."

"That's right," he said, clearing the block of the excess pieces of poultry. Setting it in the sink, he replaced it with a fresh cutting board and began to skillfully chop the pepper into squares, the sharp knife moving fast. "Hated working for the man."

"Now you're the man," she said, pulling one of the bar stools from under the lip of the island countertop where he was working.

He frowned. "I'm a way better boss than any of the uptight pricks I worked for."

"Of course you are," she said, soothingly, though she knew that her father was, at least historically, both extremely inflexible and perfectionistic. She certainly wouldn't want to have him as a boss.

"Keeping busy with it anyway," he said, a little sullenly, as if he could read her thoughts. Karissa was familiar with his fluctuating moods, but something in his manner belied the absence of his characteristic fire. He seemed wrung out, sapped of that essential something that had made him seem larger than life when she was younger.

"Glad to hear you're keeping busy," she said, thinking how strange it was that a thirteen-year hiatus should end in such mundane conversation.

"You married yet?" he asked. She held up her left hand, wriggling her bare fingers in reply. He shrugged, moving on to quartering the mushrooms. She supposed she should count herself lucky that she had avoided a decade of having to field questions like that one, though hearing it still made her feel sad. Not because she was afraid she'd disappointed him, but because she thought she'd detected a note of real curiosity in his voice. He seemed to know that if she had been married, she probably would have neither invited him, nor told him about it. Seeing the lonely, harmless man he had become, made her question why she'd maintained her silence all these years. *Why had he?*

"Still beating up scumbags?" she asked.

He looked at her sharply, as though this was a sore subject, then he sighed, resuming chopping. "Gave that up too," he muttered after a few moments, "a long time ago."

Extracting a package of bamboo skewers from a drawer near his hip, he tore it open with his teeth and began to impale the meat and vegetables at intervals, placing the skewers one by one on the slatted surface of a broil pan after they were complete.

"Did you train anyone else after I left?" At one time, he had wanted her to become his replacement, to watch over the neighborhood after he grew physically unable to do it himself.

"Nope."

"Yeah? How come?" She was becoming slightly irritated by his cursory replies.

Placing a colorfully adorned skewer on the pan he said, "Because it's fucking psychotic, that's why."

"What is? Going around in a mask and hitting people with a metal pipe? Or training someone else to do it?"

"Both," said her father, scrubbing his hands vigorously in the sink before pushing the broil pan into the oven. For some reason, she began to wonder if there was something he wasn't telling her.

"I should tell you," he said, his back still to her, "that I contacted your mother last month."

Karissa sat very still. "Why did you do that?"

He turned and shrugged. "Thought I'd bury the hatchet," he said, filling a tall glass with tap water and taking several long swallows.

The shift in conversation to the topic of her mother had caught Karissa off guard. He set down a second glass of water next to Karissa's elbow without her having asked for it. She stared at the liquid in the glass.

"Where's she living now?"

"Greenwich Village. She's become quite the bohemian."

Karissa could feel her face becoming hot. Her father got to visit her mother but she hadn't seen the woman in thirteen years. How was that fair?

"Did you talk about me?"

He looked at her appraisingly, "What's there to talk about? She's never had any interest in you." It was a lie she knew, but she let it go for the moment. Maybe he hadn't changed as much as she thought.

"Maybe I should pay her a visit," she said, expecting him to put up a fuss, as he had done every time she had suggested seeing her mother before.

"Do what you like," he said, leaning on the counter, veins standing from the tendinous backs of his spidery hands.

"So you'd have no problem with giving me her address?" she asked, again anticipating his back to go up. Instead, he withdrew a retractable ballpoint pen from his shirt pocket, snatched up a pad of paper from near the microwave and began scribbling.

"Here you go," he said, tearing off the top sheet and handing it to her. Clicking the end of his pen, he returned it to his pocket. She stared at the page where he'd scrawled the words: *Irena (Irene) Ponomaryova – 131 West 3rd St. Suite 7, above Blue Note jazz club.*

The ease with which he had handed over the information triggered something in Karissa. When they had lived together, her father had fiercely dismissed any request for her to see her mother. The few times she had asked him, he was so angry that she had been forced to say that she hated her mother just to placate him. And, for a period of time, Karissa had even come to believe that she did hate her, though deep down she felt terribly guilty for betraying the woman.

"Where the fuck was this fifteen years ago?" she demanded, waving the paper at him.

Her father shrugged. "I've moved on since then," he said, and then, almost as an afterthought, "I hope you can too."

"Um, here's the thing," she said, struggling to keep her voice calm. "I would move on, but there are one or two things we need to address first."

"Such as?" he asked flatly.

Her anger was plain now, though it didn't seem to faze him. "Something you might not know about me;" she said, almost choking on the words, "I'm not big on unfinished business. But between you and Mom, I have a shitty pile of it to sort through." And then, taking a deep breath, she said, "Look, I know today's probably not the day, but we need to sit down sometime and sort out where we went wrong." She waited, hoping that he would at least meet her halfway. "Don't you want closure?" she asked him.

"I already have it." he said and she watched, dumbfounded, as he stepped over to switch on the small, obsolete television they'd had in their apartment throughout Karissa's childhood. Then he headed back over to the sink and began vigorously washing the chopping block. The news was on, but Karissa ignored it.

"Dad," she said, "I need your help." He said nothing in reply, only adding more soap to the steaming sink. "Please," she said, "it's important."

Wiping his soapy hands on a kitchen towel, her father turned around, then nodded over at the television, which was blaring a special news bulletin:

"The dragnet for disgraced INS agent, Karissa Lacey, and her masked male accomplice has been widened this evening, in the aftermath of this morning's brutal attack on Mayor Rusty Kincaid. Police blockades have been instituted at major transit points, including on all bridges leading out of Manhattan, bringing traffic to a standstill." On screen, a reporter stood on a causeway at the foot of the Brooklyn Bridge, the winking headlights of the stop and go traffic visible in the background.

"Oh," Karissa said. "Yeah. I was going to get to that." He stared at her impassively, his arms loosely folded across his chest. "The man's a fucking crook Dad."

"It doesn't matter," he said, giving his head a slight shake with what might have been disappointment, if he didn't also appear so infuriatingly indifferent to her. "What you did was monstrous."

"Oh please," she said with a snort of derision. "I once saw you melt a petty thief's sneakers to his feet with flaming kerosene."

"That was a long time ago. And I never did *that*," he said, pointing to an image of a bloodied and blanket-swaddled Kincaid being gently carried on a stretcher down the front steps of City Hall, toward a waiting ambulance on Chambers Street. It was clear, even from the brief video clip, that his injuries were severe.

"Yes you did!" she shouted indignantly. "Many times. You had no qualms about attacking out and out criminals, but him? Just because he's the fucking mayor, he deserves our patience and sympathy? Don't make me laugh." She snapped out a vibrating middle finger at the TV screen as the mayor was loaded into the ambulance, his enormous pale face reflecting camera flashes. Her father nodded his head, as though confirming something.

"I need your help," she said again. "I need to get out of town and I bet you know how I can do it." She wilted a little under his cold gaze. "I'm your daughter," she said, pleadingly.

"I can't help you," he said, making an odd beckoning gesture with one hand. "As I said before, I've been trying to move on, and today, with all of this," he said, gesturing in the direction of the TV, "I think I finally have."

As she stared at him, standing there, implacable before her, a cold dread spread through her insides. Just then, she caught a flicker of movement in her periphery. She sprang from the stool, taking a fighting stance, her hands instinctively balling themselves into tight fists. Out of the shadows of the living room emerged a small, unkempt man wearing faded, moth-eaten clothes. Admiral Rat.

"You," she snarled at him. "What the fuck are you doing here?"

Without a word, he sidled past her and proceeded to drag one of the stools around to the other side of the island, putting the counter between himself and Karissa. With disgust, she realized that he must have been skulking somewhere in the darkened house throughout. Sitting himself onto the chair, Rat remarked in his nasally falsetto, "Smells bloody good Lacey. Grub close to bein' done?"

"I'm sorry," snapped Karissa, "I didn't realize I was interrupting your date night."

Sighing, her father bent and switched on the oven light, checking the kebabs through the window in the door. "Ten more minutes," he said, straightening.

"Fast response time today," Rat commented, "The boys in blue must really care about the mayor of New York." Karissa's father said nothing but went on with the washing up. How could Rat know about the response time unless—

"You were there," she hissed, drawing Rat's dark, beady gaze. And then, with dawning comprehension, "you told them it was me." She didn't understand how he could have identified her, except that he must have seen her leaving the building, clinging like a camping backpack to Nigel as he'd leapt away. She cursed herself for having removed her balaclava. Growling, she stepped around the counter, her hands groping for Rat's lapels, but her father blocked her path.

"Actually," he said, "I told them it was you." His eyes smoldered under his heavy brows.

"You?" she asked, thunderstruck.

"Me."

"Why would you—"

"Admiral Rat," he said, talking over her, "came to me and told me what happened and I went straight to the police."

Tears sprang to her eyes. "Dad, I—"

There was a loud knock at the front door, causing Karissa to jump. "That'll be them now," her father said. "Told them you might come calling. Said they'd check up on me tonight, just in case." She looked between him and Rat; two stony expressions regarded her.

"Sergeant Lacey?" came a male voice through the wood of the door.

"Just a minute," shouted her father, and then to Karissa, softly, almost tenderly, "Sit tight honey. I have to get the door."

She goggled at him, numb, frozen to the spot. Then with a tremendous force of will, she managed to say, simply, "No thanks."

She sprang to the back door, which lead to the alley. Unfortunately, her father had nailed it shut with two short lengths of wood, one at the top and one at the bottom of the frame, which she had failed to notice before. She saw her father leave the room, and go down the hall toward the front door. Rat sat there, watching her impassively. With a great heave, Karissa managed to loosen the door's fastenings a fraction. She kicked out at the length of wood at the bottom with her booted foot. There was a splintering of wood as the block ripped from the door. She heaved again, the shriek of the nails dragging free from the door frame music to her frightened ears.

Then she was pounding down the rickety steps of the fire escape, her foot suddenly punching through one of the rotten, mossy boards. She wrenched at her trapped ankle, the splintered board digging painfully into the skin of her calf. Only when the boot came off, did she manage to tug herself free. She ran the rest of the way down the stairs and, leaving the boot behind her, she sprinted off into the darkness.

As she turned the corner, she heard a nearby police siren and suddenly found herself illuminated by the headlights of a car; she knew she was caught. The car pulled away from the curb with a chirping of tires and pulled alongside her, but it wasn't a police cruiser. The back door was flung wide, revealing a balding Japanese man sitting in the back seat.

"Get in," he called urgently, in accented English, and, without thinking, she heaved herself into the still-moving car.

## 25

# SEPARATION ANXIETY

Fear wasn't an emotion with which Amy Kang had much experience. Sometimes other people wondered if, while cleaning the artifacts, dusting the long-forgotten volumes, and changing the waste bins far beneath the city, she didn't feel afraid. Wasn't it creepy, working in those subterranean galleries, those darkened catacombs with only herself for company? To these questions, she had always responded in the negative, sometimes in the face of skepticism from her questioners, because, while most other people might feel afraid, alone in those settings, she did not.

Likewise, fear was absent as Amy Kang handled the heavy, high-voltage cables through the thick, insulated gloves she was using to protect her hands. She supposed that fear might have been useful in this instance, that a dose of adrenaline might sharpen her senses so that the risk (of massive electrocution followed by cardiac arrest in this case) would be reduced. She thought that, in the absence of fear, she would simply have to force herself to focus on the task at hand. The problem was that she kept feeling the presence of the other woman tugging at her attention, causing her to look over distractedly at the shadowy figure perched on the edge of the long table, clad in a midnight-blue body suit, impassively regarding Amy as she worked.

Karissa Lacey, formerly Agent Karissa Lacey, had surprised Amy Kang earlier that evening by making an unexpected appearance in the museum archives, that place with the silent, garishly-lit shelves and the identical black boxes, the long table, the tiny office cubicle and wash station, where Amy had been attempting to assemble an apparatus of her own exceptional design.

Seeming somehow to know that Amy was anticipating the appearance of Nigel Nakagawa, Karissa had indicated that she too would wait for the Japanese superhero to arrive. Amy deduced that the chamber was also a convenient place for Karissa to avoid the unwanted attentions of the police and residents of New York City, who would happily see Karissa face charges for the serious crimes that had been committed against their mayor. Amy had no opinion on that matter, yet the heightened anxiety she felt, which accompanied the former INS agent's presence here, had been affecting her work.

Two nights before, Amy Kang had called Nigel in his Chinatown apartment to deliver the news that she had new information regarding the parasite. She had found an even more obscure and deeply buried record by Juarez, detailing the Spanish sea captain's second encounter with the Maya of Mesoamerica, which had taken place shortly before the Spanish had invaded the region in earnest, laying waste to the cities of the Maya and slaughtering their men, women and children.

The core of Amy's discovery was that Juarez had claimed to have returned to the city that housed the former champion, whom he had previously met and seen sapped of his powers by a bolt of lightning on a mountain top, and that three years later, the former champion had been alive and well.

Nigel had said little over the phone, merely giving her the go-ahead to construct what she had succinctly described as "a bathtub filled with electricity," a tagline that wasn't strictly accurate, it had to be admitted, but *bathtub filled with electricity* had a nice ring to it.

Taking her time, Amy carefully unspooled the heavy cable from the bed of the wheelbarrow. She had broken into a high voltage substation used by the MTA to power the nearby subway line, which was conveniently located in a tunnel adjacent to the one leading to the archives, and had diverted a portion of its power. All she'd had to do was brush up on her lock-picking and industrial electrical skills, and recruit a pair of discrete fellow janitors to help her down with the equipment, and voila, now she had two live 10kV cables to play with. *No, not play*, she reminded herself, *what I'm doing here is incredibly dangerous. But my god is it exciting.*

Her spirits remained undampened even as she considered the possibility that, tonight, she might electrocute a man to death. Such an eventuality would certainly mean jail time, or juvenile detention perhaps, not to mention the killing of a friend, but knowing what Nigel was, she didn't think it would come to that. She hoped that it wouldn't, at least.

In the back of her mind she heard the steady *drip, drip* from the nearby faucet, which she had used in combination with a rubber garden hose to fill the bathtub with tepid, slightly cloudy water. The beige porcelain appeared grey in the yellowish light shining from above. Standing over the tub, Amy Kang contemplated the safest way to introduce the high voltage cables.

"Why don't you just hand him a hair dryer?" Karissa asked irreverently from behind her. Amy did not immediately turn or respond, Karissa's words slowly penetrating her thoughts. That wasn't such a bad idea. Maybe she would hand Nigel the cables once his body was submerged, instead of having him leap into an already electrified tub.

Amy turned to Karissa who was casually leaning on the table, her arms stretched behind her for support. The nonchalant air the older woman projected seemed incongruous to Amy, considering the week Karissa must have had. Perhaps she was one of those, like Amy herself, whose tumultuous inner world was concealed from others. This had its advantages, as Amy knew from first-hand experience, but it also often hindered making lasting personal connections with others. She and Karissa had known each other for two years, yet neither had ever managed more than small talk and one-way conversation; a common problem for Amy. It was both comforting and perplexing to be dealing with someone who had the same interpersonal issue as she.

"Think this is going to work?" asked Karissa, nodding at the tub and the cables.

Amy still didn't understand how Karissa had known to come here tonight or how she knew what Amy planned to do with the equipment. She supposed Nigel might have told her but she thought not. When Amy had suggested inviting Karissa to assist with the 'experiment' as she was now calling it, Nigel had changed the subject and she had not mentioned it again.

"It's an estimate," said Amy Kang, "but I think that 20,000 volts should be sufficient." At this, Karissa's brow furrowed, and it was difficult to tell with the shadows, but it looked to Amy that the other woman's face had lost color. Probably a normal reaction given the circumstances.

"Aren't you worried you'll fry him?" Karissa asked.

Amy Kang thought about this. "No," she said, "not exactly. It is a possibility but I believe the parasite will protect him initially and I will remove the cables as soon as the separation is complete. But the timing will be," and she paused, searching for the right word, "delicate."

"Okay," said Karissa, blinking rapidly, "so now all we need is the star of the show and we can—" She was interrupted by a voice from the rafters above.

"What are you doing here, Agent Lacey?"

Tilting her head up, Karissa called out, "Why don't you come down where we can discuss it?"

Suited and masked, Nigel hit the floor beside them with a resounding *BANG*, which seemed to shake the stone beneath Amy's feet. *Why didn't he use the strength of his legs to fully catch himself?* she wondered. This led to her think about the law of conservation of energy. Amy startled as she heard her name. "Pardon me?" she asked.

"I asked if you had invited her here." Nigel said.

"No," Amy said simply, "but she could be useful."

"That's why I'm here," said Karissa, "I owe you after your help with Kincaid."

Nigel snorted. "Why would you think I would want you here for this?"

"Look," Karissa said, standing up from the table and brushing off her hands, "I get it, you feel used. But we did what superheroes do. We hurt the guy who needed hurting." She reached out to touch his arm, covered with its sluggish, liquid, living metal, but he jerked it away.

"I keep telling you," he said roughly, "I'm no superhero."

"But you are" Karissa replied, "whether you like it or not." They stared at each other for a long moment before Amy Kang finally broke in.

"This discussion is academic," she said, with more force than she had intended. "After tonight the point will be moot."

"Maybe so," said Nigel heavily, "but I rather think that all this," and he gestured at the brimming bathtub, the thick cables and the rusty wheelbarrow, "is a waste of our time."

So, Nigel didn't think it would work then, even after hearing of Juarez' second account. He was here because he was desperate and maybe, she thought, aside from the slim hope that he could finally rid himself of the parasite, maybe he was here because he was ready to die.

Nobody said anything for a time, then Karissa asked, "But this is still what you want?"

Nigel sighed, looking between Karissa and Amy, then running his eyes over the ominous-looking equipment beyond. "Yes, it is," he replied quietly.

"Part of me wants to stop you," Karissa said, "because I still believe you could do some good with those powers of yours." She regarded him steadily. "But when it comes down to it," she said "it's your choice."

"I don't need your permission," he said, seemingly unmoved, but Karissa only grinned.

"Let us proceed then," declared Amy Kang and she turned back to her work. Only then did she feel an unfamiliar pang of fear needling at her stomach.

NIGEL HADN'T BEEN UNDER WATER SINCE THAT JUNE MORNING OFF Rockaway Beach, while frantically attempting to save the people who had thrown themselves from the deck of the *Golden Venture* into the sea. The water in the bathtub was cool he knew, but he felt no urge to shiver, nor did he actually feel wet. He had only the vague sense of there being something on the other side of his metallic exoskeleton, made of the parasite that had been a barrier to experiencing many things during the latter part his life.

Having agreed to help Amy Kang handle the electrical cables, Karissa stood to one side, clutching one thick chord with both hands, using a spare pair of insulated electrical gloves Amy had given her. On the other side of the tub, Amy tightly gripped the second cable, tightly he could see, a few feet from the exposed end, which she had indicated would deliver 10,000 volts of electricity to anything it touched.

His view of the two women was from the waist up, their legs hidden by the sides of the tub as he lay prone, as he had many years before, clad in his metallic diver's suit, on a granite slab, one fateful October day. He felt as he had then, terrified and smothered, once again finding it difficult to breathe.

An image of Aika smiling mischievously from behind the rutted trunk of one of the great trees in the grove near his village came to him, unwelcome for the insufficient comfort it brought with it. Then he saw her again the day of his transformation, arms flailing while she was dragged away by her mother, his ears straining to catch the sound of her stricken voice, her mouth framing the word: *Nigel*.

"Do it!" he cried, closing his eyes, reaching his hands, claw-like into the air. He felt the two cables slapped into his palms, one then the other and, without hesitation, he plunged their ends into the water with him.

The effect was immediate. The water in the tub was abruptly reduced by half, as the liquid instantly transformed into a great geyser of steam, billowing upward in a superheated cloud. Nigel screamed, the sound of his lung-shredding shriek lost in the loud crackling and fizzing of sparks and the hissing of steam. And though the pain was excruciating and the fear suffocating, he welcomed them as old friends.

He was wrestling with something, something black and viscous, something that seemed to want to choke the life from him, coiling around his body, his arms, his legs, his chest, squeezing every bit of the remaining air from his lungs. He fought it doggedly, attempting to free himself from the sticky, cloying substance as the blind, serpentine thing threatened to engulf him. He was filled with the urge to run, to escape, but the *Resident* held him fast.

After what felt like an eternity, though only seconds could have passed, Nigel sensed the thing's hold on him weakening as the throbbing electricity poured relentlessly through him. The parasite was losing its adhesive quality, sliding off him and running through his fingers as he swatted it away and, as the *Resident* weakened, he could feel his own pain building to crescendo. His body was weakening, dying, but he gritted his violently chattering teeth and held on, desperately willing the *Resident* clear of himself before he was forced to call for an end to the electricity.

Suddenly he was hit with a weight, again driving the air from his lungs and again, he was wrestling with something. This thing was more solid, with arms and legs, and she was screaming too. It was then he realized that Karissa had hurled herself into the tub with him.

At first, he thought she might be trying to save him, but then he saw her rolling around in the sludge of the *Resident*, taking great handfuls of the stuff and slathering it on her body, and he realized that she was trying to gather the parasite in an attempt to bond it to herself.

The effects of the electricity must have been too great, because her full-throated bellow suddenly ceased and she seemed to lapse into unconsciousness. Amy Kang dragged away the cables just a moment too late and, Nigel feared, maybe too soon for him.

He stood up and looked down at himself. His naked skin was clear of any trace of the parasite and he felt lighter, if a little unsteady. He saw Karissa, whose rigid form was curled around his legs and covered with ropey globs of weakly pulsing black goo. It clung to her, seeming to take on the midnight hue of her ceramic blue suit. She was still breathing he saw, and he wondered how she could have survived the effect of the high voltage electricity. The *Resident* must have protected her somehow.

"Help me carry her," he called out to Amy Kang.

"Do you need the help?" she asked curiously, giving him pause. Before the separation he could easily have lifted Karissa on his own and he had assumed he would need Amy's help to move her now, but suddenly he wasn't so sure.

As a test, he stooped down, sliding an arm under Karissa's legs, the other under her back, cringing as soggy dark material stuck to his skin, tackier than it had been a few moments earlier. Fighting the urge to let go and leap from the tub, Nigel heaved and, to his intense dismay, he hefted Karissa relatively easily, her body pulling free from the ooze in the tub with a sucking sound. Though he noticed she was heavier that she might otherwise have been, as if a significant quantity of his power had left him with the material now coating her body.

Stepping over the side, he walked to the long table and gently laid her down. The dark material that clung to her seemed be establishing itself, forming snaking ridges, which somehow blended seamlessly with the material of her bodysuit, so that it was impossible to tell where ceramic mesh ended and living parasite began.

Looking down again at his own skin, Nigel tried flexing the internal muscle that had allowed him to form his suit at will. To his horror, the metallic *Resident* began to form again in small patches on his skin. He howled in rage and frustration. *How dare she?* Karissa had tried to take the power for herself and now here he was, the parasite still seeping from him, the separation only partially complete.

"Again!" Nigel roared, and he launched himself in the direction of the tub. Amy, acting fast, dashed away, returning a few moments later dragging a running garden hose, discharging water over the spotless floor as she ran.

Nigel tried to calm himself as the water rose around him in the tub and Amy wrangled the cables. *This time*, he told himself, hoping against hope, *this time it would bloody-well work.*

Amy handed him the cables again, one at a time, and again he thrust them in the water with himself. However, instead of running off him when re-charged with electricity, the *Resident* formed involuntarily on the outside of his body. This time he felt next to nothing. Even when the blistering steam rose spectacularly around him, all he could feel was a slight tingling sensation. He sat up and gazed down. Electricity sparkled and danced over him, miniature lightning bolts traversing the iron-grey veins on his arms, chest and stomach, before fizzling out. Somehow, the *Resident* had learned to deal with electricity.

Nigel staggered to his feet, almost tripping over the lip of the tub in his haste, waving away the steam that obscured his vision, almost colliding with Amy Kang, whose usually expressionless face contained a mixture of horror and fascination. He stumbled away, beating and tearing at the *Resident* covering his body. Finally, he remembered how to release the suit and did so, the material dissolving and streaming from his skin onto the floor around him. He stood there blinking, suddenly cold in the chill air of the chamber.

His head swivelled to Amy, who stood rooted to the spot, silently regarding him, then his eyes swung to Karissa, who had begun to move. She sat up, rubbing her head, then she reverently ran her hands over her parasite-encircled arms and torso. She turned to look at him. Her smile was one of triumph, but her expression became a look of concern, for his skin had gone pale he realized, glancing down, and a sudden surge of vertigo took him. He saw Karissa leap up from the table, reaching for him with arms wrapped in thick metallic coils of shifting, midnight blue. Then he collapsed in a heap of exposed flesh, atop the oily, tar-black pool of the parasite he had hoped to shed for good.

❦ V ❦

## ✵ 26 ✵

# EXODUS

Sitting in her office cubicle at the INS, Charity Ng stared at the dark screen of her computer monitor. She was due for a vacation. If anything, the visa office had become busier after Benny Wu's capture of Sister Ping, the middle-aged business owner and snakehead who was behind the smuggling of huge numbers of illegal Fujianese to America, including those who had been aboard the *Golden Venture* the previous June.

The INS had been awash with pride after the arrest and subsequent trial of Sister Ping, which had been all over the news, restoring legitimacy to an organization that had been foundering due, at least in part, to the scandal around Karissa Lacey. The disgraced former agent was supposed to have broken into the mayor's company headquarters and attacked Kincaid in his office on Veteran's Day, beating him nearly to death. These actions had ignited widespread outrage, shared by Charity herself, who still couldn't believe she had been friends with the woman. But the INS had managed to distance itself from Karissa and had leveraged the recent positive press around the Sister Ping case. Now it seemed like the federal agency was here to stay, better funded and more legitimate than ever before.

Unfortunately for Charity and the others in her department, there had been a flood of asylum requests after the INS had seized Sister Ping's records and dozens of illegal Chinese immigrants had been identified. Suddenly brought into the light, these people, many of whom had been living in the US for more than ten years, were faced with certain deportation unless they could prove they would be in danger if they were forced to return to China. And, given China's stance on its citizens abandoning the People's Republic, they probably were.

Thinking about the people she and her team would be forced to deny, despite the probable legitimacy of their claims, made Charity feel more than a little bit sick. And though it would be incredibly inconsiderate for her to abandon her overworked colleagues, Charity thought she just might take that vacation she'd been planning.

Perhaps she'd travel and visit her parents and sister in Singapore, taking the time to relish the taste of home. Then maybe she'd make a detour to Japan and investigate the job offer she had received. A little thrill went up her spine when she thought of the mysterious letter she had been sent with the official looking seal at the bottom.

Apparently, she had been head-hunted by a non-governmental organization calling itself 'Hitsujikai,' which she had discovered meant 'Shepherd' in English. Although she hadn't been able to find out much about it, the NGO sounded like it was doing some good in the world, which aligned with Charity's own long-held desire to make a difference. Yes, the more she thought about it, the more she wanted to discover what this Hitsujikai was all about.

Beyond the plush dividing wall of her cubicle, Charity glimpsed a small rectangle of window from across the room. Through the glass, she spotted a jet in the far distance, catching the morning sun as it gained altitude in the tiny, blue strip of sky, passing by in moments. Soon that would be her, she thought and inclined her head to scan the letter again.

FROM BENEATH HEAVY EYELIDS, RUSTY KINCAID WATCHED THE plane fly past the massive window of his hospital room. He was still faintly drowsy from the latest dose of pain-killing opioids that he was permitted to administer to himself via the hand-held switch gripped loosely in one pale, freckled fist.

He grinned, despite the persistent pain in his jaw and his still-sore gums, which had been disturbed by the recent dental surgery. Mark Hendricks, his chief of staff, had just departed, having left him with this morning's newspaper, the headline reading, "Party Lines Obliterated by Widespread Sympathy for New York mayor." He sat up, gazing down at the newspaper on his stomach and cracked another aching grin. He hoped the bitch who had assaulted him would swallow her tongue after she realized her attack had united New York in support of him.

Thinking of the plane that had passed a moment before reminded him that he hoped to a trip. Once his injuries were healed, he would fly down to the Caribbean, Barbados maybe, for a nice long soak in the sun. As usual, he would make a stopover to the Cayman Islands to check on his offshore accounts. This always gave him great pleasure, for he knew that if he ever was audited and his assets were frozen, those bulging foreign accounts would be his lifeline. Not that he would be audited. Any risk of a press-driven investigation into his finances was minimal, especially now, after recent events had dramatically reduced the media's appetite for digging into his affairs.

As usual, when he thought of these things, Kincaid found he could easily live with himself for neglecting to report all his income. He had earned it, hadn't he? Likewise, he could sleep at night knowing that he hadn't declared his foreign bank accounts. How could such things be crimes? Settling back onto the plush cushions provided to him by the hospital, he pressed the button that called the nurse. The intervals at which the machine allowed him to access the opioids were much too lengthy for his taste. Surely the nurse would not begrudge him more control over the drug dispenser, not he, the so-called 'Survivor Mayor' of New York.

IRENA PONOMARYOVA HAD ONLY BEEN ON ONLY ONE AIRPLANE IN her entire life. But, she thought to herself, watching as the massive jet soared skyward, maybe it was time to change that. She had received a written letter from her daughter, requesting they meet. Her heart had leaped at the opportunity to see her again, but she had also felt uncertain and afraid.

Instead of meeting her, Irena had sent a note in return, in which she had finally shared Karissa's true name: *Ajla*, which meant 'moonlight' in Slavic. Yet, in the note, she had also declined her daughter's request.

Irena had always dreamed of reuniting with her daughter, but had never imagined that it should be under such circumstances, with the police looking high and low for Ajla all over the city. When she had first heard about what Karissa had done, attacking the mayor like that, and in his own office, she had struggled to contain feelings of disappointment, anger and revulsion. She'd had to search her heart thoroughly for the feelings of love that lay buried there and, upon uncovering them, sparkling like tiny jewels, she had known she was still open to meeting her daughter, but not here, not now, and not like this.

It was then that Irena had made up her mind to leave New York. For which destination, she had no idea. But she knew she was ready, ready to put herself in the hands of fate, for she believed that if she was truly meant to see her daughter again, it must be by chance. Watching the plane, Irena reminded herself that, regardless, the two of them would be together again, and if it was not meant to be in this life, then it would be in the next.


AMY KANG COULDN'T REMEMBER THE LAST TIME SHE HAD SAT IN THE noonday sun. She relished the feeling of the warmth on her face, though the day was cold and she had been forced to bundle up.

Early that morning, she had been gripped by what she called 'daytime insomnia,' which was the worst kind of insomnia because, once she lay awake for any stretch during the day, the sunlight sliding through the cracks in her blinds and the sounds of the bustling city became for her an irresistible draw toward the waking world.

Giving in, Amy had risen after only two hours of sleep and had paced around the empty apartment thinking of what she might do. She'd had an unexpected desire to see her family but had remembered that her mother was at work, supervising the daytime janitors at Bellevue Hospital and her little brother Roger was at Rocklund Elementary for the day. She had decided to take a walk instead, finding a bench along the outskirts of Foley Square where she and Nigel had seen *Rockapella*, filming its music video some weeks before.

In the days since her experiment had gone awry, Amy Kang had discovered that she too was infected by the parasite. The infection had spread, not through her body, as it had in the cases of Nigel and Karissa, but into her mind. She simply couldn't get the *Resident* out of her head. There were too many questions.

*Of what material was the parasite? Where had it come from? Was it of alien origin, as Nigel supposed, or did it have roots here, on earth? Were there more of them?* And the most important question of all: *What were the biological effects of the parasite on the human body?* She thought if she could answer the last question at least, then she might still be able to find a cure for Nigel, and for Karissa too she supposed, though she doubted the woman would want that. Amy remembered the look of jubilation on Karissa's face after she had gained her powers, and she shuddered.

Staring off into the far distance, Amy imagined what it would be like to eventually quit her job and travel to Yucatán as she intended. There, she would unravel the mysteries of the *Resident,* while embracing the adventure of navigating a place fraught with unknown dangers.

Picturing the map of Mesoamerica, she was reminded of her game show experience, two years earlier, which had literally driven her underground, filled with shame at her failings. Thinking of it still hurt, she was forced to admit, but nowhere near as much as it had before she had met Nigel and realized there were more important things than names, dates and dust. She was coming into the light and, as she watched a jet deposit a soft contrail behind itself as it flew away from the city, she had the sudden urge to go even nearer the sun.

ADMIRAL RAT HASTILY PACKED HIS MEAGER POSSESSIONS INTO THE heavily patched red leather suitcase. Something had happened. Like a phantom, a balding Japanese man, even littler than himself, had appeared in the seat next to him the previous night at McCain's. The man, whose soft, raspy voice had grated on him like an iron file, had known things about his past that nobody could know. 'Details' the man had called them. But the details the Japanese man had laid before Rat, as casually as revealing a high hand of cards, were the stuff of nightmares. They were the kind of details that Rat had been running from all his life, reflected in the way he scuttled from place to place, in the way he rushed and stammered through his speech and in the way he tried to know about everything and everybody.

Now, Admiral Rat was forced to run again, the thought of it scaring him like never before. Every time Rat had felt threatened in his life, he had retreated into the dark, fusty corners of the city he knew so well. But now, for the first time, he felt as though his hiding places were not safe enough, nor far enough, not after his encounter with the Japanese man.

Rat had grown up in New York. Nearly all his memories were from here. He knew the place like the back of his hand, especially his kingdom on the Bowery. But now he had to leave all of it behind him, had to run. *As far as wherever they're going*, he thought as he watched the airplane pass by the flophouse window, banking, then steadily becoming a dot in the noonday sky. And though he didn't have the money to pay for a plane ticket, nor could he fathom which destination he would choose if he had, he knew he would find a way to put a vast distance between himself and the city, no matter how it pained and terrified him to do so. Admiral Rat would survive. He was built for it.


HIROJI BIT DOWN HEAVILY ON THE APPLE, MINUTE PARTICLES OF flesh and juice spraying from his mouth, forming a momentary mist in the air, picked out by the sunlight shining through the chain-link fence that bordered JFK International Airport. Shading his eyes, he watched the plane taxi on the tarmac, the enormous aircraft at once lumbering and agile, gazing as it hurled itself into the air. It was carrying precious cargo, he knew, both to him and to the cult.

Usually, he would have accompanied Hitsujikai's Champion on the transatlantic flight, but the situation had dictated he remain behind, at least for now. All the customs details were arranged, he recalled, a convincing fake passport and legitimate Japanese visa, which gave him a sense of peace as he watched the Japan Airlines flight become smaller and smaller as it travelled swiftly away toward the Northwest. The Champion would be met by cult representatives on the other side and housed in a five-star Tokyo hotel until the current mess was sorted out.

It was a very uncertain time for the cult. In all his long years of service to the organization, Hiroji had never experienced such upheaval – the Grandmaster imprisoned, the sacred village of Ryūiki demolished and now fully submerged in a man-made lake, the abdication of the cult's most recent Champion, who had predictably been too weak. But, despite the deep unease such events had fostered in the leadership, Hiroji felt solid, like the boulder around which the river rushed. As always, he would be instrumental in helping the cult rebuild itself, brick by brick.

He wondered how the other leaders would react when Fuyuko Natsume was deposed. It had been a long time coming, in his opinion. Her recklessness had resulted in the deaths of cult members at the hands of police, casting much aspersion upon Hitsujikai and resulting in unwanted attention from the government and press. In addition, the choice to send their Champion to New York City had never made much sense to Hiroji. Besides, Fuyuko would, in all likelihood, be spending the rest of her days in prison, after she was convicted of murdering police. Hiroji would have to find a new Grandmaster. He smiled self-assuredly. Finding suitable leaders was his specialty. He had recently discovered the new Champion and, once he convinced the others of her credentials, they would forget that she was both American and a woman. Hiroji was good at convincing others to do things. It was all in the details.

KARISSA LACEY FROWNED AS THE PLANE SPRANG FROM THE RUNWAY, the force of the takeoff effecting an unpleasant pushing on her body. She was leaving New York and the US for good. There had been too much heat after the incident with the mayor and her work was else-where now.

She recalled that Nigel had made the same trip to Japan himself, two days before. Imagining him on the same intercontinental jet with its extra amenities, its battalion of flight attendants and the whopping inch of extra leg room, she wondered if perhaps he'd experienced the same aching in his chest as she felt now, but she doubted it.

Karissa ordered a beer, knowing full well that the *Resident* in her bloodstream would nullify the alcohol. That she could no longer enjoy liquor was one of the many unpleasant side-effects that came with being bonded to the parasite. She hadn't experienced the dizziness that had plagued Nigel (she hoped she wouldn't have those symptoms for another ten to fifteen years) but she had accidentally ruined several outfits and five, *five* sets of bed sheets, involuntarily pushing the *Resident* through her skin and releasing it as she slept.

Disconcerting was the sensation of the *Resident* languorously sliding through her internal passageways. She felt occupied, colonized from within, as though her body were no longer her own. But she had chosen this, she reminded herself. She had made her bed and now she had to sleep in it, no matter how many sheets she destroyed.

She knew how it might seem to an outsider, bonding with the *Resident* on purpose, knowing that it would probably, eventually kill her. Ostensibly it would, but Hiroji had convinced her to look past a possible early death to the limitless potential of the parasite. *Crazy*, she thought, *I'm crazy*.

Ever since she was a young girl, Karissa knew that she was meant to become a crime-fighting superhero. And now she had become *Moondog* and was prepared to devote herself to all that the new identity would entail. But, despite the realization of her childhood fantasy, which, she mused, was remarkably intact after all these years, Karissa felt deeply uneasy. She sensed somehow that there were certain facets of her situation that she had been purposely ignoring.

It didn't help that the chaos of her life, and it was chaos she was forced to admit, had been wrought by her own hand. She had forfeited her job through willful disobedience and insubordination, had possibly pushed her mother away, had finally lost her father and had given up her right to roam free in her home country by attacking the mayor. She had simultaneously alienated her friends and signed up for a suicide mission in service of a mysterious Japanese cult. Considering all of this, her single-minded focus on her powerful new abilities might have been the only thing standing between herself and a breakdown these past weeks.

Here on the plane though, sitting motionless for the first time in what felt like forever, her immobility and the steady thrum of the jet engine had the combined effect of directing her attention to the question she had been avoiding.

Why had she done it? She thought about this for a while, oblivious to the dampened sounds of others shifting around her. Although she had wanted to make her mother and father proud, had wanted to serve her community, and had wanted justice for the people of New York, there were other forces that had influenced her decision-making.

The fact was she was angry, and had been angry for a long time. Angry and afraid. And though it now seemed obvious that these two emotions had played large roles in shaping who she was and what she'd done, the specifics still eluded her. It occurred to her that there might be nothing more terrifying and infuriating than acting without knowing why one was acting. Maybe nobody truly knew why they did what they did.

With a furious shake of her head, she pushed the meaningless thoughts away. She had achieved what she wanted hadn't she? She had stood up to evil and so what if it had cost her? She had become the superhero she had always wanted to be. So why was it, she wondered, that she couldn't shake the nagging feeling that something was still missing? Brow furrowed, Karissa gazed out the window, watching the endless golden carpet of clouds, as the jet flew on, seeming to chase the sunset.

## ❧ 27 ❧

# AT THE END OF ALL THINGS

T he prison walls were white. There was no other hue with which to describe them but, unlike most walls that were pure white, they lacked something, a certain brightness. If hope was a phosphorescent shade, the walls were dull with the lack of it.

As the female prison guard led Nigel deeper into Nagano Prison, the surroundings became noticeably rustier. The bars covering the windows, the stucco-dressed sills, the exposed pipes travelling from ceiling to floor, all were tinged with ginger smears, as though in a state of perpetual clamminess.

Nigel wiped his palms on his pants as he rounded the corner, entering a small cloakroom reserved for visitors. The female guard politely but firmly asked Nigel to place his possessions in a locker and hang up his coat, then she directed him into a room with tatami mats and small, hard cushions scattered around several low tables. Seated at the tables were two brown-clad female inmates and their visitors, both male. Quiet hung low and heavy in the room like a dense fog. Nigel chose a table near the exit, crouched and knelt on a cushion, waiting for his mother to be brought in.

Nigel had learned that Japan's prisons were refuges for many lonely or penniless women, particularly for the elderly and for other women who felt invisible in society. He had recently read a sobering article on the topic, featuring the stories of a few such women. Some had stolen small items such as cartons of orange juice or paperback books, in pursuit of meaningful work in prison factories, three nutritious meals a day and the company of other inmates.

Nigel gulped as a small woman in brown prison garb strode purposely through the door at the opposite end of the room, an irritated-looking guard hustling in her wake.

His mother looked older than he remembered, though it had only been a year since he had last seen her. Her face was drawn, her cheekbones more pronounced, with deep, purplish grooves beneath the eyes, emphasized by the room's harsh overhead lighting. Her movements betrayed nothing of the strain her features signposted however, nor did her ramrod posture belie the hardship she had endured in recent months.

*Her husband, my father, is dead.* The thought of it still caused the muscles in Nigel's abdomen to clench involuntarily, as though exposed to electricity. As she approached, he wondered how his father's death was affecting her, knowing that she had killed him with her pointless act of resistance against the police.

Fuyuko knelt across from him, taking the time to arrange her legs carefully beneath her, in cross-legged fashion, before settling onto one of the unforgiving cushions. She brushed a loose strand of silver-tinged hair from her face and sat still, regarding him imperiously.

"So," she said, "you have returned to Japan."

"Yes," said he, "I have."

"And here you are."

He gave a short nod.

"I hope you have decided to stay home," she said, her eyes sliding away from his as she glanced at the prison guard, who was supervising them.

"That depends," he replied, choosing his words carefully, "on whether there still is a home for me here."

Her eyes swivelled back to his face. "Of course there is," she snapped, "why ask such a question?"

"My father is dead," he said, "and you're in here. How could I possibly come home now, given all that has happened?"

"My Golden Boy," she said soothingly, "you forget: Hitsujikai is still strong and I am still its leader. We will find a way out of this mess. Our lawyers will—"

"No," he said, "no." Then, closing his eyes, he breathed, "I have decided to leave the cult. There are several reasons for this decision," he said quickly, before she could interject. "The first is that I am, and perhaps have always been confused about the cult's purpose. Why do we battle with the police at home, while simultaneously helping them in New York? Why do we sequester ourselves in the mountains, while at the same time, pretending to care about the people in the outside world? Why do we meddle in foreign affairs? Do we care about wider society or just about our own? Our cause grows murkier by the day, and I am profoundly unsettled by it."

"You know the answers to these questions," Fuyuko said tiredly.

"No I don't," he countered, "otherwise why would I ask?"

"It all boils down to protection. And those in the outside world are spectacularly bad at providing it. Without us, humanity would have descended into chaos a long time ago. We save who we can, bringing some into our fold, and we help the others by sending them our Champion."

"How could the answer be so simple?" he asked incredulously. "And how can you be so sure that everyone agrees with you?"

"Unity is the beauty of a cult."

"Among followers perhaps, but Hitsujikai is a complex organization, run by individuals, each with his or her own agenda."

"Yet all still look to me for direction," she said, lifting her chin a fraction.

"That may have been true once," he said, watching her. "But times have changed. The cult's sacred village has been destroyed and there will be a new headquarters selected and a new Grandmaster. These decisions are being made as we speak, in a hotel conference room in Tokyo, without you."

This news seemed to take his mother by surprise, as he had suspected it might. "How do you know this?" she asked.

"The new Champion told me."

Fuyuko's eyes bulged. "You are our Champion," she snapped. "You still carry the *Resident*, do you not?"

"I carry the *Resident* mother, but I am no longer the Champion. Karissa Lacey, of whom you've heard, stole part of the parasite as I attempted to separate it from myself, and it has grown inside her. Hiroji instructed her to do this, and he has convinced the other leaders that she should take my place."

"That snake," she spat, smacking a fist into her open palm. Her eyes found his. "But with you by my side, we can fight. We can reclaim our destiny. We can—"

"Another reason, I am quitting," he said over top of her, "is that I am tired of being used."

She gasped. "How dare you? I have given you everything, I—"

"You betrayed me," he hissed. "You and father both. Even if I hadn't been a seven-year-old boy, and it hadn't been done to me against my will, even if I could have given consent; even then, it would have still been betrayal, because you knew I loved you too much to say no." Tears of rage and grief fell from his eyes. "I had to learn about my terminal illness from a letter in a museum archive. But you both knew about that too."

Fuyuko sat silently, making no effort to deny it.

"This is to say," managed Nigel, though his throat was very tight, "your decision to bond me with the *Resident* has cost me dearly. I needed you to know that."

Still as a statue, Fuyuko looked past him, staring at nothing. Then she spoke. "I've never seen it that way. Every parent wants her child to reach his full potential. I always thought your destiny was to rise and protect those who could not protect themselves. I assumed any reservations you had were the fears of a child. I never dreamed that becoming a hero could be counter to your nature." She paused, wiping an imperceptible drop of moisture from the corner of one eye with the tip of a long finger.

"There were some Champions who lived long, healthy lives. Did you know that?" she asked. "Some lived much longer than other people do. I always held out hope that you would be one of the lucky ones.

But I should never have put you through such an ordeal in the first place." She shook her head sadly and Nigel sat back, surprised that his mother should so readily concede her mistake.

"Do you regret it now?" he asked.

"Yes," she said, "I do." She looked at the floor, apparently ashamed. "I should have seen it."

"Seen what Mother?" Nigel asked gently.

"I should have seen that you were too weak, too fragile to bear this burden. It is my fault that I did not try for another child, and for that I am sorry." She looked at him then, with a mixture of pity and disappointment; a look that dealt him a far greater blow than if she had refused to apologize in the first place.

"I must ask one more thing of you before your responsibility ends." She said, reaching out and grasping his trembling hand. Her grip was like cold steel. "I need you to help me leave this place."

"What?" he said, "I can't—"

"I need you to help me to break free and we will travel together to Tokyo, and once I am restored to my place as Grandmaster, then you shall do as you please. Whether you choose to go or stay after that will be up to you." Releasing his hand, she watched him expectantly.

To his dismay, Nigel had the powerful urge to bow to his mother's demands. He might easily return to the prison after dark and break his mother out of her cell. And he supposed he could fight Karissa and Hiroji for his mother's position. But he stopped himself. If there was one thing he had learned from his time in New York, it was that he was prepared to give up everything to be able to choose his own path, even if it meant refusing his mother, even knowing that such a refusal would thwart her life's ambitions and shatter her imagined destiny. But then he would become a man who had abandoned his mother in her time of need. Could he live with that? The moment seemed to stretch, his thoughts evoking a swirl of fear and shame and hope.

"No," said Nigel. "I will not free you from prison." She gaped. "And I will not be fighting for your reinstatement with the cult. I came here to tell you what father and you have cost me and nothing more." And with that, he stood up.

"You must," she whispered, looking up at him from the floor. She seemed so small, so much more delicate than he remembered her.

"No," he said again firmly, and turning, he strode toward the exit. There was a commotion behind him as his mother, screaming, attempted to chase after him and was restrained by the prison guard. Failing to resist the urge to look around, Nigel stole a last glance at her as she was dragged away. The image, which would stay with him for the rest of his life, nearly broke his heart.

SITTING ON THE BOULDER, NIGEL COULD FEEL THE COLD OF THE snow and stone beneath him through the fabric of his winter pants. He felt frozen, colder than he could ever remember being in his life, the boulder seeming to sap what little heat remained in him. His perch overlooked the ice-covered lake, deep in the mountains of Nagano, which had swallowed his former village. The great trees, the thatched roof structures, the river bend, all had disappeared without a trace and, in their place, was a flat expanse of white.

It was the temporary nature of things he contemplated, staring out over that vastness. That such a place as Ryūiki, which had stood for centuries could be gone in the space of a few months was almost beyond his ability to comprehend. *There are no fish beneath that ice*, he thought, irrelevantly.

He wondered where everyone had gone. From Hiroji's account of the village's final days, Nigel had learned that its inhabitants had scattered, that many had been either arrested or smuggled out of the region by fellow cult members. He remembered that there were a few former residents who had left before the incident with the police, and were supposed to be dwelling in the surrounding area, though who they were or where they lived, he couldn't guess.

It was then that the enormity of his situation fell on him and he began to feel utterly and completely alone. He had returned to Japan to confront his mother and claim what was rightfully his – the freedom to choose his own path in life. But now that he had gained this freedom, he didn't know what to do with it. What little life he had possessed, he had lost in his single-minded pursuit of breaking free. It hadn't seemed like much before – distant neighbors and acquaintances, a place where he had felt apart, parents whose love had been conditional on his becoming Champion – but compared with what he had now, it seemed like a great trove, which he hadn't fully appreciated until it was gone.

A dismal question had been circling his mind, like a clump of hair around a drain: *How long do I have left?* And though he didn't know the answer to this question, the thought of it threatened to overwhelm him. He sat on the boulder, desperately grappling with the swirling vortex of his emotions, here at the end of all things.

Ten minutes went by and his distress began to subside. He breathed easier in the chill air and began to pack up his things: the compass, the map, the thermos of tea, now long cold; all went into his backpack. He stood up, noticing that the grey sky had broken of a sudden; the gloomy, low-hanging cumulus had parted in the west, and the last light of the day spilled through the crook of the valley like a river of molten gold, bathing the frozen lake in gilt. He shivered. The wind rose and gusted around him and, as suddenly as the clouds split, they drew together and the first flakes of new snow began to fall.

Clambering down from the boulder, he scanned the shore of the lake for the path he had taken there. It was a long hike back to the road and it would be difficult for him to make it there before dark. It was then that he saw a distant, solitary figure making its way toward the cleft in the trees from which he had entered the valley. Intending to ask for the time of day, Nigel made his way hurriedly toward the figure seeing, as he closed the distance between them, that it was a woman.

"Excuse me," he said, approaching her with crunching footsteps, "may I ask you, what is the time?" She looked up, her dark eyes going wide with the shock of recognition.

"Nigel-chan?" breathed Aika.

He stood still, hardly daring to believe what his eyes were telling him. Could she be real? "It is you, isn't it?" she asked hesitantly and he nodded slowly. "What are you doing here?" She gestured at the lonely, frozen lake.

"I had to see it for myself," he managed to say, gripping the straps of his backpack tightly, hardly daring to move or say much, lest the vision of his lost childhood friend disappear.

"Yes," she said. "It's so sad. The end of an era." She shook her head sorrowfully and regarded him, opening her mouth as though searching for the right words, the whispering snow falling around them. "Have you—" she paused, searching his face with her eyes, "have you a place to stay?"

He cleared his throat roughly. "No," he said, "not really."

She smiled and took three crunching steps toward him. "Come on then," she said, "my parents would be honored to host you overnight at least."

He smiled back at her uncertainly, then followed in her footprints as she began to trudge back up the slope, into the gathering twilight.

CPSIA information can be obtained
at www.ICGtesting.com
Printed in the USA
LVHW082026310120
645518LV00001B/2/J

9 781999 226923